No One Will Believe You

Liars and Vampires, Book 1

Robert J. Crane
With Lauren Harper

No One Will Believe You
Liars and Vampires, Book 1
Robert J. Crane
with Lauren Harper
Copyright © 2018 Ostiagard Press
All Rights Reserved.

1st Edition

This book is a work of fiction. Names, characters, places and incidents are products of the author's imagination or are used fictitiously. Any resemblance to actual events or locales or persons, living or dead, is entirely coincidental.

The scanning, uploading and distribution of this book via the internet or any other means without the permission of the publisher is illegal and punishable by law. Please purchase only authorized electronic editions, and do not participate in or encourage electronic piracy of copyrighted materials. Your support of the author's rights is appreciated.

No part of this publication may be reproduced in whole or in part without the written permission of the publisher. For information regarding permission, please email cyrusdavidon@gmail.com.

Chapter 1

Lying is bad. Believe me.

I'm a compulsive liar, which means I've lied about everything you can imagine. Sneaking out? Lied about it. Stealing stuff? Lied about that, too. Even stupid stuff, like where I got that shirt someone asked about. Totally lied.

Getting chased by a vampire?

Well, duh. Of course I lied about that. But probably not the way you'd think.

Here's the thing—I actually *did* get chased by a vampire.

And when I got asked about it ... I lied. Never happened, as far as I was concerned. Because that's the problem with telling little lies. Eventually, you need someone to believe you when something big comes along. That's why I'm giving it up. Going cold turkey. Walking the straight and narrow. Whatever cliché you want for this puppy ... I'm leaving the way of the liar.

Who is going to believe you about a vampire chasing you down a Tampa street at night when you've lied about everything else?

Lies. The holes we dig with them.

This was what I was thinking about in Math League—my new parent-inflicted after-school activity—when my name pulled me back to the equation-heavy decor of the room.

"Cassandra?"

I stifled a sigh and brushed a hair from my eyes, wishing *again*

I hadn't cut my hair to just above my shoulders. The curls weren't very forgiving. "It's Cassie."

The teacher, a heavyset woman with an obnoxious mustard yellow sweater on, pursed her lips in what might have been a smile and nodded her head. "Cassie. Did you do your work this week?"

Definitely not. "Oh, yeah, I totally did." I shrugged as if this next bit was sadness incarnate. "But I left it at home. Sorry."

The girls across from me snickered, drawing my attention. I couldn't help but roll my eyes at them and their Ugg boots.

The teacher clicked her tongue in frustration. "If you want to be a part of this group, Cassie, you need to participate."

Joke's on you, lady. I didn't even want to join this dumb Math League.

The teacher glanced at the clock in relief when I didn't respond. "I guess I'll let you leave on time today. "

The mad dash to the door started, and I'm not ashamed to say I was right there with them.

"Cassie?"

I froze as other students filed past me, not even sparing me a glance. Slowly, I shifted around to look at the teacher, trying not to lose the ground I had gained toward escape. "Yes?"

"I got an email from your mother. She said she'd pick you up today."

My mom … emailed my teacher?

My jaw clenched, but I shrugged and flashed my best cover-story smile. "Okay, thanks. Guess my phone is dead or something."

I spun and followed everyone else into the hall, flowing down to the main lobby of the school, and stepped out into the humid but comfortable evening air. The sun had set, the last little bit of blue light overhead making the edge of the school courtyard look black against the sky.

This was peak Mom, going straight to my teacher, in full passive-aggressive style. She wanted to bring someone else into our battle of wills without actually telling them what was up?

That's fine.

I'll just walk home on my own. Boom—the simple elegance of a middle finger without me actually have to flip my mom off.

Besides, it was a beautiful night. It would be a shame to waste it.

I caught a glance of myself in the mirrored glass of the school's windows and stopped to brush some of my brown hair behind my ears. I frowned. How long had I looked like such a mess?

I shook it off and kept walking.

It was easy to see the Tampa skyline, only a few miles ahead, shining against the coming darkness. The pink and blue and red lights reminded me of Christmas trees, all twinkling and shining. I recognized houses, street signs, and restaurants along the way.

Across the street, Alexandra, a girl I recognized from Math League, walked along the far sidewalk. She hadn't said two words to me since I had moved here. But neither had anyone else, really. Tough being the new kid, I guess.

I turned left down the next sidewalk, a street with some more glowing streetlights and general suburbia. It was … peaceful.

Also … boring. Really, really boring.

But who knew when I would get another chance to walk around like this, all alone, unsupervised?

I glanced behind me. Alexandra must live this way, because she was still following along the same path, now behind me, on the same side of the street. But she had her headphones on, large bright green ones, and her nose was buried in her phone.

"Hey."

I almost jumped out of my skin as a voice sounded right beside me. I snapped my head around as I looked for its source, and my skin tingled with surprise.

A boy, probably my age or maybe a year older than me, grinned casually as if he had been walking beside me the whole time. His hands were in the pockets of his designer jeans. He wore a white North Face jacket.

And he was *gorgeous*.

He was lean, like a runner, with a narrow jaw, shaggy, honey-colored hair that hung over his forehead like he had woken up that way, and large, sad dark eyes.

The sight of him had my heart racing for a different reason than the fear I'd felt a moment before. And he was talking to *me?*

"Hey," I said, and then felt like an idiot for how breathy it sounded. Either he didn't notice, or he didn't mind my total dweebitude bleeding through. "You just got done with Math League, right?"

Clearly I would have remembered someone as hot as he was, but I couldn't place him. My school was huge, though. It was definitely possible I just hadn't come across him yet.

"Yeah. You're just getting out of …" He looked like a jock. It was like a high school rule that all jocks were hot. "Lacrosse?" What the heck sport was going on right now?

He shook his head, his eyes still on me, making my knees feel like jelly. "No. Drama club. We're doing *Hamlet*."

I nodded. I had no idea about *Hamlet*, at least nothing more than the name.

"I'm sorry, have we met?" I asked, feeling guilty. "I've met so many people since I moved here … " I shrugged as if to say, *Who can keep them all straight?*

It was only half-true. I'd certainly been in classes with lots of people. But as far as actually meeting anyone … say, that I could have lunch with?

Yeah … I wasn't struggling to remember that extensive list of zero names.

He grinned mischievously at me, but for some reason, the grin put me on edge more than it put me at ease.

"Not yet, no," the boy replied, his eyes sad and tilted. "But I was hoping we could be friends."

A shiver ran down my spine, and suddenly, I wished this part of town was more familiar. Who was this guy, and where had he come from?

"Um, yeah …" I took a small step away from him, pulling my

backpack farther up my shoulder. "Sure, I guess."

"You guess?" he replied. "I've been very interested in you since I first saw you, Cassandra."

I bit down on the tip of my tongue. *Red flags!* "It's Cassie," I corrected, and I glanced over my shoulder. I was looking for an exit. I was all about cute guys, especially when I was presently the loneliest girl on Lonely Island—not the comedy guys—but this guy was creeping me out.

Alexandra was still back there and, even more surprisingly, she was staring at me. When we made eye contact, her eyes widened as if she was trying to ask me a question.

I glanced back to the boy beside me before turning down the street to my left, knowing I was only a few blocks from home at most. Uh, I thought. I didn't know the area well enough to be totally sure. Why did all these houses look the same? Tampa was now to my left, the bay was ahead of me. I didn't know how far, but I could smell the salt in the air.

But "close" only counts in horseshoes and hand grenades.

"Can I walk you home?" the boy asked.

I smiled a tight smile. "I'm sorry, I don't even know your name."

He looked affronted. His brow furrowed, and his eyes searched my face.

"My name is Byron Vesper. Now … may I walk you home?" He spoke so formally, so stilted, as if he were going to drop to a knee and ask me for the honor of my company at any moment. It was strangely at odds with the aura of menace I was starting to pick up.

"No," I answered, feeling my first shock of cold in this *winter* in the South.

He stopped walking. I chanced a glance over my shoulder and saw he was staring at me. But he didn't look angry. No, he had a sad smile on his face, as if he pitied me.

I heard footsteps on my other side as Alexandra came up beside me, the look of a solidarity sister on her face. I turned to keep walking, letting her fall in next to me.

"Sorry, but was that guy harassing you?"

This close, I could see her eyes were a bright, icy blue. Contacts, maybe?

"I ... I don't know," I replied honestly. "He was ... kind of pushy. "

"Some guys are creeps, you know?" Alexandra said, looking back toward where we'd left Byron. She stutter-stepped to a halt.

"What?" I asked, and followed her gaze back over my shoulder.

I frowned at empty sidewalk. "Where did he go?"

Chapter 2

"Okay, that was super weird," Alexandra said.

I watched as she brushed a strand of shimmering blue hair behind her ear. *Did she put glitter in her hair?*

"You're not kidding," I said, still watching the spot where he had been standing. "Maybe he got the picture."

"Hmm … " She turned her bright blue eyes on me. "Do you know him?"

I shook my head, a new sense of dread washing over me. "No, do you? He said he was part of the drama club. "

Alexandra looked over her shoulder again, maybe without even realizing it. "One of my friends is in drama club. They don't even meet tonight. Maybe he's new?"

"Yeah, maybe … but he seemed too familiar with me." I tried to suppress a shudder. "He knew my name, too."

"Cassie, right?"

"Yeah." I almost smiled, immediately warming to her for not calling me Cassandra.

She nodded in understanding. She gestured for the sidewalk, and I fell into step beside her again. "Totally get it. I go by Xandra, but almost everyone calls me Alex." I looked at her hair, her style, and her small, absolutely adorable kitten earrings. Unconventional nickname? Made total sense.

We had come to a nice wooded part of the development we were passing, when a rustling sound reached us. It wasn't the usual rustling that came from bushes; normally that came from lizards, or squirrels, or even the occasional armadillo. This sounded way bigger than any of those.

I nearly jumped on Xandra's toes as I hopped away from the bushes. We waited, breath held—then, shakily, I dragged my phone from my pocket and, after a few fumbled attempts, opened the flashlight app.

The bright light shone into the bushes, and all I could see was green and shadow. A bush or two swayed as if caught in a wind, or maybe as if something had just vacated the spot. I half-expected to see Byron standing there, staring at us. He was not.

I turned off the flashlight, but I didn't feel any better.

Xandra stood staring at the bushes, chewing her bottom lip. Then, before I realized what was happening, she put her hand on my shoulder and whipped me around, guiding me away.

"Wait. I live down near the bay," I said, pointing toward the street to my left. I still didn't recognize where I was, but I knew I could get home if I could just …

"What if he follows you home?" she said, dropping her hands. "We should make sure we lost him." Oh … right. Okay.

Ignoring the unease creeping back into my stomach, I said, as conversationally as could possibly be expected under the circumstances (you know, with a possible creeper following us), "Do you have experience with this or something? Stalkers, I mean?"

She looked up at me, a shadow of a smile on her face. "I know these streets like the back of my hand, and yeah, I've had my share of unwanted attention."

I swallowed hard. "Okay. "

We walked in silence for nearly a block, the sky growing darker by the second. I listened to every noise, wondering if Byron was going to reappear somewhere.

"There's this great ramen shop a few blocks from here," Xandra said. "I go like, all the time. Do you like Japanese food?"

"I haven't had much of it, honestly," I said, and to my surprise, I realized I'd just told her the truth. Shifting attention to analyzing every sound was taking me off guard, and apparently I felt no need to lie. At least to her.

At least not yet.

She turned us down a street into another extension of Tampa, with more industrial buildings, warehouses, and fewer streetlights.

I hesitated, and Xandra turned to look at me. "You coming?"

I nearly shrieked, because standing behind her, just out of the light of the lamp, was Byron.

"What?" she asked, seeing what must have been a horrified look on my face.

Byron stepped into the light, and Alexandra jumped, hurrying to stand beside me under the safety of another street light.

His face was split in an easy smile, his hands in his pocket, his hair tussled in an alluring way. He ran his hands through it, making it even messier—and somehow, in spite of the alarm bells he set ringing inside me, even more attractive.

My heart thudded against my rib cage. I could hear Alexandra breathing a little too hard beside me.

I felt trapped, utterly unable to move. A slight shiver threatened to quake its way through my spine.

I stammered, "What … what are you doing? Why are you following us?"

"What are you talking about, Cassie? I've been with you this whole time." And then he threw back his head and laughed like it was the biggest joke.

The shiver running through me turned to a hard, painful prickling sensation, and I took a step back down the street.

It was weird how quiet this street was. There were very few cars for just after rush hour. The sidewalks were empty, and a lot of windows in the surrounding buildings were dark.

Byron took a step toward us, his eyes heavy-lidded and his gaze sharp.

"Stay away," I said, and I felt Xandra latch onto my arm, and squeeze with a vice-like grip.

He chuckled, low and deep in this throat, and with a sneer on his face, he started to walk toward us.

I grabbed Xandra's hand. Without looking both ways, I ran across the four-lane street. I didn't look back over my shoulder until we had reached the other side.

"Where'd he go?" Xandra asked.

I squinted through the dark, realizing the many shadows along the street were working against us, but I quickly understood what she meant.

Byron was nowhere in sight. Again.

"What the hell is going on?" I said, my blood pulsing in my ears, making it hard to track anything else over the noise.

"I don't know, but we need to get off the street," Xandra said. She pulled her cell phone out of her pocket and tried to click on the screen. "Oh, you have *got* to be kidding me."

"What?" I glanced at the screen.

It stayed dark.

"Battery's dead."

I pulled my own phone out. The battery at the top right of the screen was almost empty, and a lonely "1%" beside it taunted me.

"If I try to make a call, my phone will survive about as long as a show about adults living in the suburbs would on the CW."

"Could you send a text?"

"I can try," I said.

I tensed. The closest people would obviously be my parents. And the grief I was going to get when they picked us up would be almost unbearable.

Almost.

I opened up the texts between me and my mom, and saw she'd texted me to tell me she was going to pick me up at the school.

I'll be at the school at seven to get you. You better be there when I get there. Leave it to the lawyer to actually spell the words in her text instead of going for the easier "U"s and whatnot.

Admittedly, I deserved that level of distrust. One afternoon last week I completely skipped Math League, deciding that going to the coffee shop around the corner was a way better use of my time. It really had been; the cold brew coffee I had with coconut milk had been the best thing to happen to me all day. Especially since when I got home, I got grounded until next month. The sacrifices we make for caffeine.

Hey Mom, I typed, *I got lost. I forgot u were going 2 pick me up, so I decided 2 walk home with a new friend. Could u come find me?*

I looked around trying to get my location and saw the street sign.

We r on

And it died.

"Did you send it?" Xandra asked, looking into my face anxiously.

My face burned with frustration. "No. It died before I could."

She groaned.

"Well, we can't stand here all night," I said.

"No duh." Xandra looked back and forth down the sidewalk. "Do you think he's gone?"

"I don't know," I replied. "What do you think we should do?"

Xandra did a visual sweep of the sidewalks again. "Come on."

"Where are we going?"

"Just come on," she hissed, and she started at a slow run down the street.

I followed, not caring that I hadn't run since gym class on Monday, and knowing I was terrible at it. I didn't care because the fear was pumping my veins full of adrenaline, and even though my knees were super shaky, I felt like I could run for miles.

Mostly because I felt like my life was in danger, and the deepening darkness didn't help.

A street light overhead flickered and went out as soon as we ran beneath it.

"Way to add to the moment, municipal lighting failure," Xandra muttered. Then she gasped, and I nearly collided with her when I looked up and saw Byron standing there, not even twenty paces away, on the sidewalk, grinning at us.

Xandra turned and disappeared between two buildings, and I didn't hesitate to follow her.

Just before I rounded the corner, I locked eyes with him, and a horrifying realization hit me. It made me almost stumble over my own feet as I ran.

He's toying with us.

I sped up, trying to catch up with Xandra. I could hear her gasping, broken up by what sounded like an occasional sob. She quickly darted around another corner, and I followed.

The absolute last thing I wanted was to be left behind right now.

I found her leaning against a brick wall, a streetlight at the end of the alley flooding the ground with light. She was clutching at her sweater like it might strangle her, and she looked at me as I came to a halt beside her, my hands on my knees, also sucking breath in like I never had in my life.

"Don't slow down yet, ladies, or I might catch up." Byron's voice bounced along the sun-faded brick wall, and though we couldn't see him, it made both of us choke off our gasps and dart down the alley back into the street.

His laughter followed us.

Xandra dashed across the street, the tall, gleaming towers of Tampa like faraway, unreachable hope glowing in the distance. She'd darted between another pair of buildings, these appearing to be government buildings made of old stone block that looked like they might have been here since before the state was founded.

I caught up and saw her trying to steady her hand enough to punch in a code on a large metal door along the back of one of the tall, cinder block walls.

"Where are we?" I managed to get out between wheezes.

She didn't answer. She swore under her breath and tried the code again.

I looked back down the alley into the street, but there was no sign of Byron. That didn't make me relax. He was turning out to be really good at pouncing on us when we weren't expecting him to.

"There!" Xandra exclaimed, and she pushed the door open and waved me inside hurriedly, and then threw her whole weight against it, closing it behind her. It seemed to be working against her, and so I threw my weight against it too.

Finally, the blessed click came, and we both collapsed against the cold metal, breathing heavily.

Chapter 3

The room was dark, but I could see it was full of tall shelves lined with dark boxes with white labels on the front, everything very orderly. The room smelled of dust and old paper. Normally I would have appreciated that smell. But it was hard to appreciate anything at the moment except not being dead thanks to a stalker in the alley.

There were windows at the top of the tall ceilings, barely large enough for a squirrel to fit through. Wrought iron grates were bolted to the inside. Small pools of light spattered the floor, but not nearly enough to make the entire room visible.

"Where are we?" I whispered.

"The city government's archive," Xandra answered. "They keep a lot of stuff stored down here." She looked at me over her shoulder, though her expression was hard to determine in the darkness. "My dad works here. I've been coming here since I was a little girl. Luckily, the code hasn't changed. "

"Can he get in here?" I asked. "There's something really weird about this guy. Like, James Franco weird."

"I know. I was thinking the same thing. Not about James Franco, but … yeah, this guy is strange." She crossed her arms and shook her head. "And no, he can't get in here. At least he shouldn't be able to, unless he can somehow turn into a ghost and float through the fifteen-inch-thick steel walls."

She laughed, but her heart definitely wasn't in it.

I looked up around the room. "Is there another way he can get in, aside from the door?" I pointed to the one behind us.

She shook her head again. "That's the only door. And as long as we have it locked …" She crossed over to the entrance again, and double checked the locks she'd already secured. "It should be fine."

I took a deep, shuddering breath and swallowed. My throat was painfully dry. My heart had slowed, but every time I thought about Byron's eyes, a flash of fear caused it to hammer against my ribcage again.

"Maybe he could hack the code, though. Or maybe he saw us punch it in."

Xandra made a disgusted sound in her throat, as if we hadn't just been running from our lives. "He wasn't anywhere near us. He was across the street, remember?"

"Well, you're awfully calm now," I replied, crossing my arms over my chest.

"Why wouldn't I be? We're safe."

"How can you be sure?" I asked. "There's no guarantee he can't—"

"This is the old fallout shelter for the municipal building, okay? If it can hold out a nuclear blast, some teenage boy isn't going to get in."

Something like anger flashed through me, and I glared at her, hoping she'd notice in the shadows of the unlit vault. "This Byron isn't an ordinary teenage boy. I mean, neither of us recognize him, and he was able to get in front of us without us even seeing him—"

"Are you even listening to yourself?" Xandra said, her arms held out in disbelief. "You're getting paranoid."

My voice rose to match hers. "Did you not see what I saw—?"

There was a loud crash against the outside wall, and I let out a cry of terror, freezing, my hand anchored on one of the nearby bookcases, knuckles pale from the grip.

"What was that?" Xandra whispered from the other side of the shelves.

The crash sounded again, and I saw movement in one of the small windows up near the ceiling. When I looked, a face peered in through the glass, the lights from the street casting him into shadow.

"Byron," I breathed, and I clutched the shelf tighter.

He could see me, his gaze settling on me like an albatross around my neck.

"Hey!"

His voice was muffled. The glass was most likely bullet proof, if everything Xandra said was true. But I could still hear him, though his face was obscured by a cross-hatching wire that ran through the glass.

"Let me in." His voice was a whispered command, and it made me shiver as though I'd just been hit with a blast of New York winter right off the lakes.

I had to force myself to keep breathing. Long, slow breaths.

There was a loud smack against the glass, and then the face disappeared.

"How … how did he get up there?" Xandra whispered from the other side of the boxes. "That's got to be a twenty-foot drop … he would have broken his legs!"

"God, let it be so," I said.

There was a loud thud against the door.

"He's trying to break the door down!" I said, retreating from it.

"He won't be able to," Xandra said, but her voice seemed more uneasy when she said it this time. "Not unless he has dynamite."

"Or is on steroids or PCP." I looked at Xandra. "Is PCP still a thing? My parents talk about it like it's still happening."

"Never heard of it," she murmured faintly.

I shuddered, remembering the feel of Byron's gaze on me. The distance and reinforced glass between us had done nothing to dull the creepy touch that came with the glance.

"Xandra, there is seriously something wrong with this guy …"

Her silence told me she agreed with me.

"I mean, he just … appeared when we were walking. Did you even see him come up to me?"

"I wasn't exactly paying attention to you," Xandra said. "But, yeah, it was weird he just sort of showed up."

When I realized the immediate threat was on the other side of a steel door, I collapsed onto the floor.

"And then, the look on his face … it was like he was …"

For some reason, I had a super hard time admitting what my brain was telling me out loud.

"It was like he was enjoying himself."

Xandra cleared her throat and appeared around the other side of the shelf.

She sat down beside me. We could still see the window and the door, but were nestled in the shadows—as if we could somehow hide our faces from whatever was out there, waiting for us to come out.

Xandra huffed.

"You know, if you hadn't been wandering around in a place you don't know, then maybe we wouldn't have gotten into this mess."

I shook my head. Did I hear her right?

"Wait, this is all *my* fault?" I laughed, but it was more of a short bark.

She snorted. "Yeah, this is your fault."

"Way to blame the victim." I couldn't believe this girl. Who did she think she was? "You think I wanted attention from that … creep?"

"I don't know what you'd want because I don't know you."

My jaw clenched.

"Nobody knows you," Xandra continued. "You've been at the school for what, like a month? How could you expect anyone to know you aren't some sort of weirdo? You certainly don't act normal."

I ground my teeth. Was this *really* the time for her to highlight my—

Dweebitude?

Xandra made another noise of disgust. A silhouette, she rose to her feet.

"Do you have a phone charger?"

Do you have a brain?

I rolled my eyes and sighed heavily. "No, I don't. My battery usually lasts all day – when I don't have Math League."

"Shoot. I don't have one either," she said.

There was another loud bang, and I braced my hands on the floor to keep from falling over sideways.

"Come on, girls, let me in. The mosquitoes are awful out here."

"Is he serious?" Xandra said, moving into the darkness somewhere to my right.

"The mosquitoes here do suck," I said. "Also … yeah, he's relentless."

There was a smack against the door again.

"How long do you think he's going to keep this up for?" I wondered.

"I mean, eventually he'll get bored," Xandra replied. Then, more distantly: "I hope."

I swallowed hard, literally and figuratively, putting my pride down. "Thanks for not leaving me out there on my own."

I didn't really think she really deserved my thanks right now, but given that there was a psycho outside, this was probably the time to make friends rather than enemies.

"I'm not heartless," Xandra said. "And you apparently have trouble carrying on a normal conversation with men. Or anyone, possibly."

"What is your damage?" I lashed out. "Why are you getting after me when we are literally pinned in here until what's-his-face decides to leave?"

"I …" she started, and then I heard her exhale. "I'm sorry. I guess I'm just …"

"Freaking out?" I finished for her.

"Yeah."

I rubbed my hands up and down my arms, even though the

air was stifling and sticky. "Whatever. Let's just try to figure out how to get past him."

Xandra came back over to me and sat down beside me again. "I just wish I knew more about this guy, you know? Is he, like, an escaped rapist or something? A serial killer?"

The ideas made my chest ache with fear, but I shook my head. "He looked too young to have escaped from jail. But what do I know?"

Xandra shifted uncomfortably beside me. "What I want to know is how he could almost read our minds, you know? Like, he knew exactly where we were going to go. Beat us there, too."

I glanced at my watch, the luminescent hands showing it was almost eight.

Only eight? How long were we going to be stuck in here? It felt like hours, or even days, had passed since we left the school. Even facing Mom's fury suddenly seemed preferable to this situation.

"He can drop from twenty feet with no apparent problems," I said. "And what's even weirder is I didn't see anything out in the alley that would help him get up that high—no trash cans or dumpsters or anything to stand on."

"I've never seen him before, and I'm definitely not convinced he goes to our school."

"I thought he was lying when he was talking to me. There was something … off about him."

"You think so?" Xandra's nose was wrinkled in skepticism. "I know a liar when I see one. "

"Nice gift to have," I replied. She didn't catch the sarcasm.

"I just don't see why he was so fixated on me, and how he knew my name," I murmured.

"Why is it the worst guys are always the most gorgeous ones?" Xandra collapsed, bemoaning an uneasy truth that I, too, was wrestling with.

"Like, unnaturally so, wouldn't you say? That kind of guy doesn't actually exist in real life. His skin? Flawless. Which, I mean … with guys our age …"

Xandra nodded, shifted herself toward me, and leaned in closer. "Okay, hear me out. I'm kind of an anime junkie—" *no kidding, with the kitten earrings and the hair* "—and this whole thing just screams 'out of the ordinary,' right?"

"Right …" I agreed reluctantly.

"There's one I've watched at least seven times, and the guy who the main character falls in love with is just like our unwelcome guest outside."

"Go on," I said, unsure about where she was going with all of this.

"He's super hot, has super speed, and super strength," she said, voice rising in—was that *excitement*? Now? "All of the girls fawn over him, but he's not around very much. Only comes out *at night*, you see."

I blinked, processing what she was saying. There was something … uncomfortably familiar about her train of thought. "What, you mean like a superhero?"

More like the villain, I was thinking.

Xandra shook her head.

"No. What if our friend outside … is a vampire?"

Chapter 4

"Ha ha, absolutely hilarious," I said, after a silence that seemed to last forever. "Great joke when we're trapped in a claustrophobic bunker and we've got a lunatic banging on the door outside."

I was starting to question Xandra's sanity. That was a thing, wasn't it? For people to lose their minds when forced into scary situations?

"No, hear me out," she said, and she leaned closer. "Have you ever seen a person act the way he has been? Appearing out of nowhere, being sort of sweet and sensual one second, and then frightening the next? I mean, it's just weird. Beyond normal flip-flopping or manipulation."

"He's a weird dude," I answered. "But he's a *dude*. Guys are scary sometimes, okay? That doesn't make him some sort of man-bat creature who wears a cape and lives in a castle."

She made another sound of disgust. Already I was getting tired of hearing them.

"Vampires aren't like they are in those old stories. Maybe they used to be more like Dracula, but in modern times, they do way more to try to blend in with our society." I widened my eyes, and she added, "You know—if they were for real, that's how they'd do it, wouldn't they?"

There was another loud crash against the door, and I realized it frightened me a little less this time. No sign of him breaking the door down.

Yet.

I scolded myself. Of course not yet. Not *ever*. He wasn't strong enough to break through two feet of steel. No human was.

"Oh really?" I challenged Xandra, trying to do anything to distract my mind from the noises from outside. "And just how do they manage to blend into society? Last I checked, eating other people tends to be the kind of thing that gets sensational amounts of news coverage."

I could hear the exasperation in her voice. "Vampires aren't cannibals, okay? They don't *eat* people. They drink their blood. And they often find people who they keep as pets, or servants. Not all of them actually want to kill people. Those are usually their fledglings – new converts, you know."

Xandra spoke as if she was discussing her favorite store at the mall. The fact that she was apparently an authority on this did not make me feel calmer on the whole, since I was locked in here with her, and she was gushing about vampires while psycho-boy was trying to scare the beejeezus out of us.

"They're irresistible to humans as a way to lure us in. They look young—"

"You are talking about this as if you actually believe in vampires."

"Are you telling me you don't believe in supernatural stuff?" Xandra replied. "Not even, like, ghosts?"

I wasn't sure how to answer that, so I countered, "Does that mean you believe in werewolves and faeries as well?"

"Why not?" Xandra answered. "This is a strange world. If vampires exist, why not these other things?"

"Okay," I said, and got to my feet. I brushed off the back of my legs and decided it was best for my sanity, and my safety, to move to the other side of the room, away from Miss Crazy Pants.

"What?" Xandra got up too, and followed me through some of the shelves, peering at me between the gaps. "You think I'm crazy, don't you?" Like staring at me through shelves was totes normal.

I whipped around to face her, raking my hand through my hair to get it out of my face. "Yeah. I do."

"Well, do you have a better explanation?"

I froze, running through everything, anything that might make more sense.

"Didn't think so," Xandra said defiantly, before turning to walk back through the shelves.

I sighed, the sound echoing in the old chamber like a rush of air, and followed after her. She might be crazy, but she wasn't the one trying to pound her way into the building we were hiding out in.

I sat down on the cold tile floor beside her again.

"So," Xandra said rather coolly in an obvious attempt to change the subject, "how did a Yankee like you end up in Tampa?"

She meant *Yankee* as an insult, but I couldn't care less.

"Mom and Dad relocated down here," I answered, just as coolly. Also, lying.

"Jobs?"

"Mom's a lawyer, Dad's a doctor."

"Florida is Heaven's waiting room." Xandra shrugged her shoulders.

"Yeah," I said. "Lots of need for doctors and wills." That was true, if breathtakingly lacking in details about the real reasons we'd left New York.

Yeah, "jobs" was a good enough answer. Better than telling the truth.

"I've lived here for my whole life," Xandra said, staring off into the shadows on the far side of the room. "Remember that ramen shop I was telling you about?"

"Yeah?"

"My mom owns it."

I felt a twinge of jealousy. If my mom ran a restaurant, that would be the very last place I would ever want to go. But

Xandra said it was the best in town.

She was proud of her parents.

I wondered what that was like.

I'd fallen into thinking about what kind of family Xandra belonged to when the sound of something slamming against the steel door rang through the air again, startling us both.

Hesitantly, we got to our feet and walked closer to the door. Everything in my brain told me to run the opposite direction, away from the ear-splitting crashing. But the sick human curiosity in me urged me forward. My heart thumped against my ribs as if it were trying to get out too.

The slamming got louder and louder as we could see the outline of the door frame from the dim light from the high windows.

Xandra's hand tugged on the elbow of my sweatshirt, trying to stop me from moving toward it.

There was a bright red light beside the keypad beside the door, indicating it was still locked, but it was a small relief when Byron was slamming who knew what against the door itself.

Just as I was three or four steps away, something in the thrashing changed to more of a crunch, and then fell silent. My knees started to buckle, but I couldn't move, so it didn't really matter.

"What … what happened?" Xandra whispered behind me, her voice choked.

I swallowed hard, and took another hesitant step to the door. I reached my hand out, and ran it over the icy, smooth steel.

At least, it used to be; the steel beneath my fingers was now bent, like a piece of paper folded with a sharp crease. It was imperfect, jagged, and terrifying. The dents all converged upon a single, rounded shape.

A shape the size of a fist.

"My God …"

"What?" Xandra whispered.

I took a few steps back.

The silence was eerie, and even scarier than when Byron had

been pounding on the door. Everything seemed frozen, but I heard every creak of the floor, every scrape of the gravel beneath my shoes.

"I think …"

I couldn't say it, I couldn't. It was crazy, all of it.

Xandra grabbed my arm, and shook it, her fingernails digging into the soft flesh of my underarm.

"It … he tried … to punch through the door."

She hurried back across the space to where I stood and looked into my face. The little light where we stood reflected in her eyes like small lamps.

"Do you believe me now?"

"About what?" Another lie, a stalling one. I knew exactly what she meant.

She focused in on me, eyes glittering in triumph in the dark. "What in the world aside from a creature with super strength could do *that*?"

I shook my head, over and over. It couldn't be—

"Come on, explain this. Please. Come up with something reasonable. Rational. Something that doesn't sound like the batshit-crazy ravings of a teenager trapped in a basement." Xandra stared me down, and I stood there in silence, unable to come up with anything. "Please. I *want* to be wrong. Especially since, if I'm right, he could tear us limb from limb like paper dolls."

I took a long, shuddering breath. "Would you quit it?"

She leaned in, not letting me look away as she fixed me with her stare. "Why are you so determined to ignore reality here?"

"I'm not ignoring reality," I whispered. "I'm very much in tune with what is going on right now."

"You are believing what your eyes and ears are telling you. What we are seeing here defies reasonable explanation. These myths and legends we've heard about all our lives … how do you know they aren't true?"

I don't know what surprised me more: that I was actually still listening to her talk about this nonsense, or that I had, for a fraction of a second, considered that what she'd said could actually be true.

We didn't talk very much after that. We lapsed into silence, a mutual, unspoken agreement that retreating into the back of the room, out of sight of the windows, was the best idea. We didn't look at each other, didn't speak, just moved, staying out of each other's way. I found myself picking through the shelves and boxes, combing through the space for something to defend ourselves with. I came up with nothing better than a stray hammer and a glass coffee pot. There was no phone line, no means of communication to the outside world. And we were trapped, like prisoners, with no way out except through the front door.

The sounds disappeared for an hour or so, and finally Xandra broke the long silence.

"If he's a vampire," she said, voice cracking, "then he'll be outside until the sun comes up."

I didn't have the strength, or the confidence, to argue.

Sleep felt like a luxury I wasn't ever sure I could trust myself to experience again. I wasn't tired, but my body ached from the constant surge of adrenaline. Everything felt like jelly, even my neck, and it was all I could do to lean against one of the shelves and focus on breathing.

It felt like days had passed when Xandra shoved my arm, maybe a little harder than she needed to, and then pointed up at the windows.

"It's morning," I said.

She and I both stood and crossed the room, nearer to the door. Our footsteps echoed crisply in the empty space, and for some reason they made the bile rise in the back of my throat. I was ravenous, my mouth parched with thirst, dry like I'd taken a big old gulp of salty seawater.

When we got closer to the door, we heard a strange, snarling sort of sound, like an out-of-control dog.

Xandra looked at me, pointed at the dented metal, and her eyebrows knitted together.

I nodded. We were thinking the same thing: *it's still him.*

The door looked even scarier in the daylight. With the sun shining in through the windows, the folded mark in the steel did indeed look like a fist. And it made my stomach clench even tighter.

Another blow rang out as Byron threw himself against the door again. "Come out!" he shouted, voice muffled but clear through the metal.

I took an involuntary step back at the sudden, jarring noise, and Xandra matched my movement. I looked at her face, stricken with worry and doubt. The sun was coming through, making me wonder if all that speculation about him being a vampire was just the two of us pinning an extraordinary explanation on something very ordinary—that my stalker outside was a crazy person, that he was on drugs, that he was doing ordinary things like standing on a post or something we'd missed to look in the windows. Or that he'd hit the door with something heavy and blunt, like a sledgehammer. Not a fist.

There had to be a simple explanation. Simple was always better, when it came to lies, and when it came to explaining who Byron was and how he was doing what he was doing.

"I will find you again!" Byron's voice rang out through the door, cool malice through the warped steel. "Both of you." He let out a guttural, inhuman screech. It faded into the distance, the source of the sound becoming more and more faint.

"Do … " Xandra shifted uneasily on her feet. "Do you think he's gone?"

My breath came out shakily. I wanted, more than I had wanted anything in my life, for that to be true.

"I don't know …" I said. "Why would he give up now, when he was trying to get in here literally all night?"

Xandra looked at me, a look of withering scorn on her face.

"Vampire," I said, before she could.

Maybe it was the sleep deprivation, or the lack of anything to eat since noon yesterday … but part of me was starting to see her point.

We waited … and waited, until the sun was peeking through and between the buildings. Had to be past six a.m. now, easy.

"We can't stay here forever," Xandra said. "People hardly ever come down here. Maybe once a month, tops."

Okay, I thought. In that case, I had some important questions. How long could you survive without water? Without food? I'd heard somewhere you could last a month without eating, but only if you had enough to drink.

Here we had neither.

"We won't starve for a while," I said, and even as the words left my mouth, I realized they were crazy.

"Come on, we have to look," Xandra said.

I protested, and even tried to pull her hand away from the keypad, but she slapped my arm away.

So I guess this was how I was going to die.

I let Xandra peer out first, since she was the crazy one who wanted to look to begin with.

She looked back and forth, and again, and then hesitantly took a step into the alleyway. She stood there, drenched in sunlight, for a long minute, and I waited for something horrific to happen to her. I imagined her screaming, trying to lunge back inside as I shut the door on her, locking myself in my own tomb.

"I don't hear anything," Xandra said, not sparing me a glance. Which was good, because I feared she could see what I was thinking.

"Then we need to hurry," I replied.

"Yeah. He could come back."

"Or he never left at all," I whispered.

She stared at me, and her face hardened.

"What?" I asked.

"I just … never mind." She looked around. "I'm leaving."

And without another word, she turned down the alley at a jog and dashed around the corner, out of sight.

Fine. Didn't want to hang with you anymore anyway. Not after all that you're-such-a-weirdo, you-don't-talk-to-anyone, like-seriously-who-even-does-that stuff.

Glancing over my shoulder at the door, I pulled it closed. From this side, I could see four individual dents in the point of the impact on the steel.

Knuckles.

I shuddered, and ran in the same direction as Xandra had, hurrying home before anything worse could happen.

Chapter 5

"Mom, it's not a big deal."

"Not a *big deal*?" I wasn't sure her eyebrows could get any closer to her hair line. And that was the least of it. "You're joking, right?"

I rolled my eyes, but I had to hold onto the barstool in front of me for support.

"I already told you. I went home with one of my new friends." Lie number one. "My phone died before I could even read your text—" another lie "—and we fell asleep on her floor working on math problems." Three in one breath. I was on a roll.

The old saying *if looks could kill* was not nearly strong enough for the expression on my mother's face. She would have much rather ripped every hair out of my head, tied my hands and feet together, and tossed me off of the Sunshine Skyway Bridge into Tampa Bay, where a shark would eat me.

"And you didn't even think to call me? Or your father?"

I shrugged, unable to meet her eye. I stared at a dark, smoky spot on the quartz countertop. "I left my phone charger in your car, remember? You asked me for it yesterday morning." The best lies were seasoned with a truth. Like flour to keep a soufflé from collapsing on itself.

Mom's jaw clenched, and she lay both her hands flat on the counter. "Don't you dare to try to blame any of your idiotic decisions on me."

I flinched. She'd never used the word "idiotic" on me before. She must have been angrier than I thought.

It wasn't like I was going to waltz through the door, sobbing and trembling, and tell them I'd been chased by a *vampire* through the city streets last night. Talk about a kid who'd cried wolf too many times.

No, instead I tried to sneak into the house and pretend like I had just woken up for school. My hair was even nicely messed up as if I had been sleeping on it.

Oh, sleep. What I wouldn't give to sleep.

Of course, there was no doubt it would have been filled with nightmares.

I'd been all ready, my book bag on the stool in the kitchen where it always was before school, a bowl of hastily poured cereal in my hands. The spoon was clamped tightly between my teeth when my mother found me.

I hadn't guessed she would stay up until three in the morning waiting for me to get home, counting the hours until they thought they should file a missing person's report. I guess Dad had twelve hours in the pool, but Mom was holding out for twenty-four, sure this was all just another Cassie-being-irresponsible scheme.

Way to go, Mom and Dad. Both kinda nailed it, in their own ways.

I was told, in great detail, every worry and every terrible thought that had gone through my mother and father's heads the night before. First, I'd been yelled at, then cried at, and then yelled at again. It was almost thirty minutes before I could even get a word in.

"You can forget about making any plans with this new friend of yours," Mom said, running a hand through her long, auburn hair. It wouldn't have surprised me to see it turn into flames, fed purely by her anger.

No skin off my back. Xandra wasn't the happiest crayon in the box. Not to mention I wasn't sure I wanted to think about what had happened the night before. Ever again. Ever.

"Fine." I had probably said it a dozen times. I deserved their wrath, and I took it with as much grace as I could. At least I was there to receive the punishment, not lying dead in a dark alley. I kept telling myself to be thankful for it, even if my parents would never know, or ever believe me, about why I had been out all night. Mom continued to glare at me. Dad had left twenty minutes prior, having to get to his first shift of the day at Tampa General Hospital, but even though he was so angry with me he could barely speak, he still gave me a kiss on the cheek on his way out.

"I still love you, even when you don't treat us like you love us," he had said.

That hurt more than he would probably ever know.

Mom sighed heavily, and I wondered if we were moving to round three of the tears for the morning. She closed her eyes and pinched the bridge of her nose. "Go upstairs and get ready."

I blinked. "Ready for what?"

She opened her eyes again, but her fingers remained in place. "School."

I looked over at the clock on the stove. I had to be at school in fifteen minutes if I didn't want to be late for homeroom.

"But I'm exhausted. Can't I just use one of my sick days?"

She laughed, but I could hear the condescension in her tone. "And why would we reward you with a day off?"

I guess I totally deserved that.

"I'll be watching the security camera feed from my office. And if I don't see you home when I know you should be after riding the bus—"

"Mom, not the bus—"

She held up her hand. "You *will* be here. And you can bet your ass that I will be watching for you."

Thankfully, Mom wasn't one to lie. It made her predictable.

She waved her hand toward the stairs. "Go. You better hurry."

There was no way she joking, so I dragged myself over to the stairs.

"And don't think that this is over!" Mom shouted after me as I climbed.

I closed myself in my room and collapsed against the back of the door.

The familiar smell of perfume, fabric softener, and my favorite lavender and vanilla candle greeted me, and I felt safer than I had since I'd left school the night before. My bed, unmade, was pressed against the far wall, the four pillows I slept with were scattered, two on the floor. A pile of unfolded clothes sat in my laundry basket beside my closet. The shirts I chose not to wear were hung over the door. The dresser was cluttered with makeup, perfume bottles, and my jewelry case.

My room was my sanctuary. It was home, and the only place where I could be myself. No one to answer to in here, no lies to tell.

I stripped off my clothes and swore I'd never wear them again, throwing them into the dirty hamper, almost knocking it over.

I grabbed a clean pair of jeans from my dresser and pulled a faded blue t-shirt from my old high school over my head, fully embracing my Yankee heritage—maybe to spite Xandra.

I checked my hair in the mirror and grimaced. I didn't have time to style it, so I grabbed some mousse and ran it through my curls. They looked a little wild and a little greasy—not to mention dusty from all those boxes in the bunker—but I didn't have much choice.

I felt queasy at the memories.

I ran to the bathroom, brushed my teeth and washed my face with water as cold as I could make it. It was still only marginally cold.

Stupid Florida. Is nothing ever cold here?

I slammed my hands against the sink as I stared into my eyes in the mirror.

Yes, something was cold here in the Sunshine State.

The heart of Byron Vesper.

The tears came before I could stop them, and then they kept coming. I grabbed a fluffy bath towel, pink, and pressed it to my eyes, stifling the sound of my sobs.

They racked my sore and spent body, and I had to sit down before I collapsed. Before I got too worked up, I forced myself to take long, deep breaths. Then, when my tears had stuttered to a halt, I washed my face again, and closed my eyes, breathing deeply and evenly, willing my heart to slow.

I'd have to face what had happened, but I couldn't do it now. Not so soon, not with a fiery tempered mother down in the kitchen, and not without any sleep.

At least I was still thinking rationally.

Or maybe I was just trying to survive.

I wondered how Xandra was doing, or how her parents had reacted. Would she have told them we'd been chased by a vampire?

Would they have believed her?

Eyeliner done—and not a bad job of it, although if I started crying again I was going to look a total emo dork—I grabbed a pair of sandals from the floor of my closet and sat on my bed, pulling them on.

I checked my clock on my side of the bed.

Two minutes until I had to jump back into a car with Mom and suffer the whole ten minutes to the school.

Xandra really believed what she was saying, didn't she?

And what was crazy, I thought as I gave myself one last mirror check, was that by the end of the night, I was starting to think she was making sense.

Even admitting it to myself felt crazy. How could I believe in a fictional creature out of a fairytale? It was absolutely insane.

But how else was I supposed to explain the speed, the height of Byron's jumps?

More importantly, how could I begin to explain the dent in the steel door?

Chapter 6

I had exactly a minute and a half to tear down the hallway to my homeroom class before I was officially late. The hallways, all fluorescent lights and kitschy colored tiles, were pretty much empty. There were brightly colored, encouraging signs all over the walls, reminding us to stay in school, stand up against bullying, and to love to read. There was even a couple making out on a bench in one of the study lounges with the vending machines.

I got a look from my teacher when I arrived, panting in the doorway.

"Sorry," was all I could say. I quickly took my seat. Near the door, as per usual. Allowed me to be the first one out and the last one in.

School was buzzing—typical, for a Friday. I heard snatches of conversation through the hall as I exchanged my books at my locker: talk of plans to go shopping at the International mall, or head to Plant City for the strawberry festival. I heard some of the wrestlers talking about going fishing and crabbing. One kid even said he was going to go sharking with his dad off the pier of the Sunshine Skyway Bridge. I wondered if that was to impress the pretty brunette he was talking to.

I was getting used to the taste of blood in my mouth, since I was relentlessly chewing on my bottom lip, unable to control myself.

Before third period, which was English class, I desperately scanned the halls for Xandra's brilliant blue hair. It should have been easy to pick out, but the three hundred other students roaming about complicated matters somewhat. Why wasn't she trying to seek me out? She'd had all these crazy ideas, after all—shouldn't she take some responsibility for them? Maybe she was skipping school. Therapy—advocated by her parents, possibly. If so, I wanted them as *my* parents instead of the unrelenting hardasses I'd gotten. The longer I couldn't find her, the more anxious I grew. She was the closest thing that I had to a friend right now—yep, the blue-haired anime-club girl who called *me* the weirdo was as close as it got—and definitely the only person that I could talk to about what had happened.

The bell sounded, obnoxious and like a fog horn—nothing like the firehouse sort of bell I missed from my old school in New York. My lack of sleep was quickly catching up with me as my wiry English teacher, Mr. Procter, prattled on about *Hamlet*. The thought of the play made me drowsy, and all I could see was Byron's smug face in my head. I started to wonder if he had somehow known that we were going to start our new unit today, and paranoid thoughts started to buzz in my head.

He'd known my name, hadn't he? Would it have been that much weirder for him to know my class schedule?

I stared at Mr. Procter's back with my chin propped in my hand, my elbow resting on my desk. If I didn't physically hold my head up, I knew it would slam against the plywood desk and my blank notebook page.

I glanced up at the clock. It was only 10:30 in the morning, and I felt both elated and disgusted about it—disgusted because that meant I still had almost five hours until I could go home and sleep the rest of this awful day away; elated because that meant I still had a long time until I had to deal with the impending backlash from my parents.

It was a confusing mix of emotions, but not any more confusing than how I felt about the last twenty-four hours in general.

How was I supposed to fathom it all? Vampires? A stalker?

Oh, and let's not forget all the lies I was telling to cover it up. So much for going cold turkey.

I was blissfully unaware of anything Mr. Procter said, except once when he called on me to answer … *something* about Hamlet. I made something up. Got it wrong, of course, but all it got me was the shake of his head and some looks from some of my classmates.

I couldn't care less about what any of them thought of me at this point. Come tomorrow, they would forget all about me—just like they all had ever since I arrived.

"Cassie?"

I blinked and looked back up at Mr. Procter. He was staring at me in a funny way.

"What?" I asked.

"You have a delivery." His bushy eyebrow was quirked up, somewhere between amusement and scorn. I didn't know him well enough to tell which.

I glanced at the door. The secretary from the office was standing in the doorway. She was a tall, lean woman, who probably woke up before dawn to go out running. Her hair, always perfectly straight, hung over her shoulders. She gave me a thoroughly inconvenienced look. But what drew my eye, as well as the eye of every one of my classmates, was a bouquet she held of the most exquisite roses I had ever seen. They were all open and full, bright ruby red, the peak of perfection.

"For … me?" I said dumbly.

"You are Cassandra Howell, aren't you?" the secretary asked. That irked me more than her tone—clipped, annoyed, as though I personally had strutted into her office and slapped her off Facebook. I had been in that office at least twice a week since I started school, changing classes and updating my schedule. How could she still not remember me?

"Cassie, yes," I said, and got to my feet when the secretary held out the bouquet, almost carelessly, obviously not intending to cross the few feet to bring them to me.

I forced a smile, but I wondered how much it looked like a grimace. I could feel all eyes in the room on me, and the walk from my desk to the door felt like I was walking the entire Great Wall of China.

"Thanks," I said, and she pushed the roses into my hands. I had no sooner taken hold of them when she turned and closed the door behind her.

I glanced over my shoulder at the rest of the room and realized that no one was talking. They all were gazing at me. Some were wide-eyed, mostly the people who sat nearest me. A few girls looked annoyed; maybe they were jealous? Mr. Procter, however, stood with his hands across his chest, his notes in one hand, looking expectantly at me.

"Sorry," I said lamely, and hurried back to my seat.

I was sure that my face was as red as the flowers.

Mr. Procter seemed satisfied once I was seated, and tried, in vain, to draw the class's attention back to the lesson. He turned back to the board and started to write down some key points for the first few scenes. I tried desperately to ignore the huge blossoms in front of me. The whole bouquet was so large that it didn't even fit on the top of my desk, and I wondered if I should just set them on the floor. Somehow, though, that felt wrong. I would most likely damage the fragile petals, and they were so pretty, I couldn't bear to do it.

I still saw faces stealing glances of my roses out of the corner of my eye. Mostly the girls, probably wondering who in the world was sending the new girl flowers like this.

Plus, I knew enough about the world to know that deliveries of roses to students was not common in any school, anywhere. The roses were wrapped in a pretty silver-flecked cellophane, and as I adjusted them, allowing the blossoms to hang just over the side of my desk, facing away from the rest of the room, I felt a small tag made of cardstock.

My heart jumped up into my throat, and I clasped the note in my fingers.

Dearest Cassandra, I enjoyed our night. Parting was such sweet sorrow. I can't stop thinking about you and cannot wait until we can be together again—forever.
  All my affections,
  Byron

My heart dropped like it had been thrown out of an airplane at thirty thousand feet. Cold chills ran down my arms, and I barely controlled a hard shudder.

I should have known it was him.

So he really enjoyed making me run for my life, did he? What a sick, twisted … there was no word powerful enough to finish the sentence. My heart thundered in my chest, rumbling in my ears. And for the third time, I wondered—had Xandra been right?

Idiot. There was no such thing as vampires.

But what about people with enough strength to nearly punch through a steel door?

I shuddered.

He couldn't stop thinking about me? What on earth did that mean?

I looked across the room, out of the windows, half expecting to see him leaning on the window sill like a monkey on a branch. Memories from the night before were pressing in on my thoughts, and it took excruciating effort for my tired brain to push them aside.

Even if he wasn't staring into the room, how did I know that he wasn't here, at the school? How did I know that he wouldn't somehow intercept me before I was able to get on the bus?

And how did I know that once I got home, and was all alone, he wouldn't break in?

I was more grateful to be in a room full of people than I had ever been before in my entire life.

The last line in his card almost confirmed my fears. He couldn't wait to be with me?

Was he freaking kidding?

Heavy dread settled over me like a dark cloud. My pulse raced, and I suddenly had a hard time not hyperventilating.

The blessed bell rang and I nearly dove out of my chair and dashed from the room. The bathroom was just down the hall. If I could just make it before the other students got out of their classes and noticed me …

I heard a gasp from an adjacent classroom, but I kept my head down and my pace quick.

I slammed the bathroom door open and made a girl fixing her eyeliner in front of the mirror jump.

She looked from me to the roses, and then tossed her pencil back into her bag and left the bathroom.

Thank you, random girl. Maybe I looked terrifying.

I leaned against the sink and forced myself to breathe evenly. I was safe at the school. He wouldn't be stupid enough to try to get to me here. There were too many people. And they would know I was missing way faster than if he waited for me to leave.

I turned the bouquet so I could see every flower, all in full bloom.

Why did he choose roses? If the handwritten tag hadn't hinted as much, the roses themselves—a lover's gift—were a morbidly possessive symbol. And it was so bizarre. They were so attractive, so enticing.

Much like Byron himself.

I stroked one of the silky petals. The stark overhead lighting caused the roses themselves to look almost washed out.

I felt a lump grow in my throat as I stared more intently at the bouquet.

That was just a shadow, right? I pushed aside a few of the roses in the middle of the bouquet. That little spot of darkness was not … Thick thorns pricked my fingers, but the fear washing over me was too strong for me to really notice.

Deep inside the cellophane, hidden beneath and between the impeccably chosen, full, perfectly lovely roses, was a single shriveled, small, dead rose—like a secret meant only for me.

Chapter 7

My thoughts were slow, gelatinous. Lack of sleep was catching up to me, and my every thought was suspect at this point. Isn't judgment the first thing to go when you're tired?

Xandra. She was the only one who would be able to help me make any sense of any of this.

Well, if she was here, then at least there'd be two of us with impaired judgment working on this … which probably wasn't any better.

But at least she'd be someone to talk to about this before I exploded from bottling all the fear, the tears—everything—up inside.

She was the only one that I could talk to who would believe me. Was Xandra at school? I had no idea. But I had to find her. I didn't care if I skipped the rest of my day. I honestly felt like my entire life was at stake. I could handle some discipline from my parents if I missed a few classes.

At least that was what I told myself.

I ducked my head out of the bathroom and gazed up and down the hall. This hallway was where all of the juniors had their lockers. I could stuff the roses in my locker and leave them there, and then try and find Xandra.

Since she was in Math League with me after school, I knew that she was a junior too. So she had to stop here eventually in order to exchange her books for classes.

I looked up and down the hall. Blue hair, blue hair, blue hair.

My heart leapt when I saw a blue messy bun, but then realized that it was just the underside of a blonde girl's head. Not Xandra.

"What are you doing?"

I turned so fast that I smacked my cheek against the edge of the door.

"Whoa, you all right?"

Hand pressed to what would surely be a bruise, mouth open in a silent groan of pain, I looked up and saw Xandra. A single, perfect eyebrow was arched at me. Her blue hair was in a pair of long, thick braids.

"Xandra, thank God. Get in here. "And before she could protest, I grabbed her by the wrist and yanked her into the bathroom.

"What the hell, psycho?" she said. "Did you get a Byron personality transplant?" She squirmed to pull herself free of my grip.

I let her go when the door closed behind us and brandished the bouquet. She leaned against the wall behind her and folded her arms across her chest.

Today she wore a pair of grey skinny jeans, a black Coldplay t-shirt, and a black and white plaid flannel shirt tied around her waist. I absently thought that a black beanie would complete the look. Maybe she had one in her locker.

"You bought me flowers?"

I nearly threw them at her in exasperation.

"Are you kidding me?" I ripped the card out and thrust it at her.

"Wait … these are from Byron?"

I nodded.

She took the card from my trembling fingers and quickly read the words. A faint scowl rolled across her face. "Passive aggressive much?"

"Who, me or him?" I asked.

"Him, obviously. Though I won't rule you out yet either," she replied, her eyes still on the card.

"And that's not all," I said, and I pulled back the fully bloomed roses to reveal the single dead one hidden among them.

She appeared to take it the same way I did. Her gaze met mine, and I could see fear plain as day in her pale blue eyes.

The door to the bathroom swung open and a pretty redhead no older than a freshman walked in, her nose in her phone.

"Get out," I said. Forget about making friends right now. I didn't have time to be nice.

The girl looked up, startled.

"But I need to use the—"

"I don't care. Use the one down the hall!"

The girl stared at me with wide eyes, her eyebrows high. "O … kay," she replied, and slowly turned to leave, texting feverishly as she did so. Probably reporting me to the administration for bullying.

I pinched the bridge of my nose and sighed as the door closed again. Then, turning, I dropped the bouquet of flowers into one of the sinks. A few stray petals fluttered down onto the dirty tile floor. I grimaced at them.

"So," Xandra said, breaking the silence. "What do you think it means?"

"The dead rose? Or the psycho-stalker Hallmark Valentine's Day card? I have no idea on either. That's why I was trying to find you. "

"Why do you think that I could help?" Xandra asked. "Do you think my experience runs to lunatic vampires?" She paused. "I wonder if there are non-lunatic vampires or if this is just sort of the way they are …?"

"You're the only one that I can talk to about this."

She turned her nose up. "You've got parents, haven't you?"

"My mom already blew up at me for staying out late. If I bring …" *Vampires*, I didn't say. No word for it though—I didn't dare say that aloud—so I threw my hands up. "*Byron* into this, she'd only freak even more." Xandra looked at me like I had four eyes. "You didn't tell your parents what happened last night?"

"*Of course not.*"

"So what did you say?"

"I told them that I went to your house to study and that we fell asleep."

Xandra's face flushed. Her eyes slitted under low eyebrows. "*You dragged me into your lie?*" She looked like a coiled snake, ready to strike. Apparently the idea of being used as cover really got her hackles up.

"Listen, you don't understand," I said, holding up my hands. "My parents don't believe a thing I say anymore."

It was harder to say out loud than I thought it would be. Lying had just been so easy, like second nature. But having to fess up to it, and not under the scrutinizing eye of my parents, was just … strange.

"I … I sort of developed a reputation for being a liar back where I'm from. When I was a kid, it didn't matter if I told the truth or not about things that happened to me. I'd usually get in trouble anyways. So I started telling my parents what they wanted to hear. It worked for a long time, but when I got to middle school and one of my teachers caught on to my lack of effort, she brought it up to my parents, and that was when they learned to not trust me. And this last year … it kind of caught up to me in a big way."

Xandra looked at me with a practiced skepticism. "So you told them that you were at my house."

"You're basically the only person that I know at this school," I answered. The reality of that statement was more depressing than I wanted to think about.

"You don't think that they would have taken it better if you told them, like, the truth?"

"The actual truth?" I echoed. "Are you serious? What would I have told them? *Hey, Mom, I got chased by a vampire last night.*"

I sighed, and leaned against the sinks. My fingers grazed the roses' cellophane, and I yanked my hand back, wincing as if it had burned me.

"Even if I told them that some creepy guy had been chasing me, they wouldn't have believed me. They'd just assume I was making stuff up. Like they always do." A different expression passed over Xandra's face chest at that. Pity? Sympathy?

"That's a shame," she said eventually, her tone surprisingly gentle. "I … I can't imagine not telling my parents what happened last night."

"You told them you were chased by a vampire?"

"Are you crazy? That stays between us. My parents may be eccentric, but they aren't quite on that level."

"So what did they say?" I asked. "You know, to … whatever you told them." A pause. "What *did* you tell them?"

"That some total creeper followed us a few blocks and wouldn't leave us alone, so we hid out in the bunker. After that …" Xandra sighed. "Well, my dad wanted to know Byron's name so he could call the police. So we did, and filed a report."

It made me wonder how in the world my parents would have reacted if they would have actually believed me. It was hard to imagine my father being so protective, my mother sitting on the couch with me, her arm around me, whispering reassuring words and encouragements.

"Anyway, the police called back about an hour before I left for school," Xandra said. "Apparently there is no record of a Byron Vesper in the US. Maybe he used a fake name, I dunno."

"Hm …" I said, taking it all in, pulse racing. Were teen heart attacks rare? It feels like they'd overindex in people who experienced the shock of waking up to the fact that vampires might be a for-real thing. And one could be stalking you.

Xandra shrugged her shoulders. "My parents drove me to school, walked me to the door, and explained the situation loosely to the principal, but he suggested that it was some drunk guy looking for anything with legs, if you catch my drift."

"So the school knows now?" I asked, feeling like this situation couldn't possibly get any worse. "Do they know about me too?"

She pursed her lips, and then exhaled through her nose.

"Yeah. I told them that you were there."

I blinked. "Well, I guess at least our stories line up that we were together," I said. When the bright side of the situation was no better than a smudge of grey, you took what you could get. "Why didn't anyone call me in to the office to talk about it?"

"I don't think they took it very seriously," Xandra said, scowling. "Big shock, right? Ignoring a woman's complaints."

"So what do we do?" I asked. It felt like it was the two of us against the world, like a bad 90s movie. "Because you and I both know that we are not crazy, and Byron Vesper does exist." I pointed at the card in her hand. "We have proof, after all."

"Maybe for us," Xandra replied. "But how would we prove we didn't write this ourselves?"

I swallowed hard. "What do we do?"

Xandra gave me a leveling look. "Do you believe me now that he's a vampire?"

"You're still stuck on that theory?"

"You've mentioned it a time or two since we've been in here," she said.

"I don't know." I looked at the flowers behind me, like they were going to leap to life and give me sterling advice to get us out of this mess. "Maybe we should just lay low. I keep telling myself he won't appear if other people are around, so at least we're safe at school."

"And I'll be going home to a house full of people," Xandra said.

I glanced at the time on my cell phone. "I'm going home to an empty house for two hours."

Xandra's face paled, and she reached into her own pocket for her own cell.

"What's your number?" she asked.

I hesitated, and she glanced up at me.

"Well? How else am I going to check in on you later?"

Despite her attitude—she was not exactly the *friendliest* soul I'd ever crossed paths with—I felt a rush of affection and gratitude for Xandra.

I gave her my number. She texted me a red rose emoji.

"Very funny," I said, cocking an eyebrow.

She laughed, and we left the bathroom together, the roses, both dying and dead, still lying in the sink.

Chapter 8

I waved up at the camera as I slid my key home in the lock. The street was bustling with screaming kids riding on scooters and playing basketball. Cars drove down the street, people on their way home from work or off to their night shift.

And it felt like a totally foreign world, one that I used to belong to.

"Yes, Mother, I know you see me," I said through my gritted-teeth smile, and pushed my way inside.

I had two hours before my dad got home, and in that time, I wanted to make sure I took every precaution to protect myself. I found a baseball bat in the garage that had belonged to my dad in his college days. Somehow it had found its way down to Florida with us, lucky for me. I made sure to stay in the kitchen while I worked on my homework so that I was near the knives, forks, and other pointy things. And for added precaution, I took a whole head of garlic and broke each and every clove off, scattering them around the room. It would probably stop anyone in their tracks, vampire or not.

Dad wasn't happy when he got home. He stayed on just this side of yelling. Which I had expected—Mom did the yelling, Dad did the quiet "I'm so disappointed in you" routine. Normally, that would have piled on the guilt, back when I was getting busted for legit lying.

But now I didn't care. Partly because I wasn't guilty in this case. But mostly because at least he was home.

I didn't want to be alone anymore.

I tried to take my banishment from the television, the mall, and any sort of social plans, as if I had any, with humility. The more I could be home and not out wandering the world where Byron could get to me, the happier I was.

Having said that … it wasn't like I was sure that he *couldn't* get me at home. Who knows, maybe he would just come in and kill my parents and me before I even knew what had happened.

For some reason, in spite of the Florida heat, I couldn't stop shivering.

Once my dad was finished laying on the guilt, I went upstairs to take a hot shower. I stood under the stream for so long that the windows and the mirror completely fogged up, and a cloud of steam swirled around the ceiling. Thankful that the mirror was misted over—I knew I must look awful, and I couldn't bear to look at myself—I brushed my hair out, threw some conditioning spray in it, and then padded to my room in my bare feet.

Slipping into pajamas, I collapsed onto the bed, staring up at the ceiling.

That was a bad idea, because as soon as I was lying down, my eyelids grew heavy. Terrified as I might be, now that I had a bit of downtime my body would force my brain to shut down for a bit in order to rest—even if it was to be a particularly restless sort.

I was glad I'd left the roses at the school, I realized as I lay there, staring at the ceiling as the cloudy feeling of tiredness crept in. The sight of them had almost made me ill, and the smell of them certainly would have.

And Xandra. She had texted me, just like she said she would, not long after I got home. I promised to let her know if anything went amiss. Thankfully, it hadn't so far.

Slipping into the fatigue produced by losing an entire night of sleep, I didn't even realize I'd nodded off.

I jerked awake, and realized that my room was now dark, lit

only by the street lamps' glow leaking in through the blinds. I clutched at my chest, feeling my heart hammer against my ribcage.

I sat up and wiped my hands over my face.

The clock on my bedside table read 12:34. I had been asleep for hours. And no nightmares. Yay for small miracles.

There was a clink like a spoon on a teacup, and I looked around. It came again, like something was hitting glass. Rain?

I stood and walked to the window, pulling back the blinds, and fell backward into a pile of clothes, a soundless scream filling my mouth.

Byron Vesper was standing in my backyard.

I scrambled backward until I was pressed flat against my door. I gasped for breath, which suddenly was unwilling to come. Tears wetted my cheeks. I clutched my hands to my mouth, trying to stifle the horror threatening to spill from between my lips. I couldn't tell if I wanted to bellow in fear at the top of my lungs or vomit, nausea creeping up and stirring my stomach silently.

Maybe he hadn't seen me yet. He had been winding up like he was about to throw something.

There was another clink, quiet, yet somehow it echoed through the room like a gunshot, and I realized that he was throwing pebbles.

What was I, some lovesick girl? He couldn't possibly think that I was going to fall for that trick.

Clink.

Clink.

Clink.

The sound was like the beating of the heart in that old Poe story. I kept thinking my parents were going to hear it, that between the rocks hitting my window, I'd hear their angry footsteps coming down my hall to rain more judgment and fury on me.

I forced myself to my feet, keeping silent, heart still screaming in my chest.

Well, he hadn't tried to rip my throat out yet. Maybe he had come to apologize?

Somehow, in spite of it all, I felt it—a magnetic pull. It dragged me toward the window, like the North Pole pulling relentlessly on a compass needle. Horror and fear overridden, I found myself stalking inexorably forward, breath held in my chest. At the window, I looked out. Byron was still standing in my yard, wearing a dark blue vest over a clean, crisp white button-up. He had dark jeans on, and his hair was tousled ever so perfectly.

He gestured for me to open the window.

I hesitated. He hadn't leapt up to the window to try and kill me. He was just standing down there, placid.

I bit down on my lip, but I threw back the lock and pulled the window open a crack. "What do you want?" I whispered.

"'But soft, what light through yonder window breaks?'" he asked, an air of drama permeating his words. "'It is the east, and *Cassandra* is the sun.'" He took a little too much pleasure in saying my name, and it made me feel a little sick hearing him say it that way.

"I'm not your Juliet—" I started to say, but gasped as he suddenly appeared at the sill, then somehow slid smoothly into the room through the crack I'd made. I fell backward again, scuttling on the floor. At almost the exact same second, he had crossed the space between us and clasped his hand over my mouth to prevent me from shrieking.

His eyes bored into mine, and his grip was as tight as iron.

"Don't make a sound, my little rose, or I'll be forced to take care of your parents."

That was all the persuasion I needed.

Chapter 9

"There now," Byron murmured, removing his hand from my mouth. "That wasn't very hard, was it?"

The scariest thing about the entire thing was not that he was in my room, accosting me, or even the fact that he had just threatened my parents like it was nothing.

No: it was that his skin wasn't warm, or even room temperature. His hand felt like a rubber glove packed with hardened snow wrapped around my mouth.

Cold skin. Super strength. Inability to stay out in daylight. Ability to evaporate and drift through the window like a cloud. Desperately attractive.

"What are you?" I managed to get out, my voice trembling. I felt my back bump into my dresser, a sharp corner finding its way into my kidney. I didn't even realize that I was backing away from him.

He was looking around my room. "Hmm?" His hands were in his pockets now.

"Oh, come now, you don't know?"

He picked up a small, porcelain unicorn from my bookcase that my grandmother had given me when I was six or seven. Turning it to gaze at it from all sides, he smirked. "Not one for myth, are you? Well, that's fine. You'll believe me soon enough."

Suddenly, and I really didn't understand how, he was standing directly in front of me, his hands wrapped around my waist, pulling me close to him.

I did what any sane person would do and tried to push him off, but his hold was unyielding.

"I thought that your new friend Xandra would have convinced you by now," he said casually, watching my face closely.

I did everything I could not to meet his eye.

I didn't want him to feel my fingers trembling, or hear my shuddering breaths.

He laughed softly.

"Did you like the flowers?"

That made me look at him.

His gaze was electric, a shock to my terrified system. He was so unbelievably handsome, even when I was scared to death of him. How was that even possible?

Is that how Stockholm syndrome starts?

"I guess you didn't like them enough to take them home with you," he said, his voice gaining a hard edge. "You left them in the bathroom, after all. "

My mouth went dry. How did he know?

He un-snaked his hold on me, and I jumped away from him, wrapping my arms around myself. His touch had seemingly sapped all of the heat from my body, and I shivered, my skin crawling from the chill.

"I'll make it easy on you, all right? I take you for an intelligent girl, *Cassandra*." He emphasized my name, then smiled mischievously. "Since that's the only way I've taken you thus far …"

I gritted my teeth, revulsion threatening to make me heave my guts up.

"But you have continued to surprise me with your lack of grip on reality."

"You're the one who lacks a grip on reality," I retorted. Childish maybe, but I was not enjoying having insults, suggestive comments and attacks hurled at me. Nor was I about to stand there and just take it.

He didn't seem phased. "Xandra is right about me, you know."

I snorted sarcastically. "What, about you being a stalker and psychopath? Figured as much."

"About being a vampire."

He said it so matter-of-factly, so calmly, that I wondered if I had heard him correctly.

"She gave me away. But don't worry," he said, holding his hands up. "I won't hurt her. She lives in a fantasy world already, and no one will take her seriously."

What was she going to think when I told her all about this little meeting tomorrow? Was she going to doubt it then?

"She was slightly *off* about some of the things that we can and cannot do," Byron continued, and paced back and forth in the small space. "But they are trivial. Good job with the garlic by the way, my little rose. But I wasn't going to come in and attack you this afternoon. I was at home, thinking of you."

My chest tightened.

I wondered if my heart was about to stop beating.

"And so here we are," Byron said, his voice almost jovial. He smiled at me like he was seeing an old friend for the first time. He crossed the distance between us and stared into my eyes.

"No, I won't hurt Xandra … because I love you, dear Cassie. Can you feel it? We should be together. Forever." He leaned closer to me and I jerked away. "I want to drink of you, to love you the way only I can … to give you the eternal embrace …"

His fingertips grazed my cheekbones, and I got the feeling he was trying to lean in to nuzzle my neck. "Just look at the color in your cheeks …" His fingers moved down to rest on my mouth. He was almost breathless. "Those lips, so red … so alive … I can hear your heart beating … fluttering for me …"

The intoxication in his voice made me sick, but I wouldn't let him have the satisfaction of looking away like a frightened kitten.

"I don't want you," I said, and realized I sounded a lot braver than I felt.

He smirked, and his shoulders shook with silent laughter. "Don't deny your true feelings. We are meant to be together, you and I."

I took a step closer to him, close enough that I could feel the lack of breath from his nostrils, but sure he could feel mine.

"Over my dead body."

He leaned in. "Absolutely," he whispered in my ear, just as coolly. "And then we can be together … forever."

He kissed my cheek, his lips like ice.

With a final touch that made me shudder, he stepped away, toward the window. His hands were in his pockets. He sat on the sill, swung his legs outside, wiggled his fingers at me sweetly, and then fell out of sight.

Chapter 10

I sank to my knees right there in the middle of my room.

I felt lost, confused, and violated. He had *kissed* me. My cheek felt frozen where his lips had brushed it, like it would fall off in little icy shards. How could he … why would he …?

I could only settle on one thought. A contradiction, really.

Either he was telling me the truth about being a vampire, or he and Xandra were in this together, and playing a really sick joke on the new girl.

If that was the case, then this was a twisted sort of hazing that would probably leave me scarred for the rest of my life.

Who was I kidding? This was going to leave me scarred for the rest of my life regardless.

If he was telling the truth …

I crawled across the floor to the window, pulled myself up on the sill, and stared out into the yard.

The yard itself wasn't very big, and it backed up to another house's backyard. Their little swing set was still, and the small citrus tree in our yard was not moving either. His smell lingered, the strong scent of his cologne turning my stomach all over again.

There was no wind, and only the sound of the occasional car driving by in the night.

And there was no sign of Byron.

I reached up and pulled the window shut, locking it at quickly as I could.

If he was telling the truth, then locking it would only delay him a second or two. It wouldn't matter.

How had he gotten in, though? Weren't vampires only allowed to enter a place if they were invited in?

If that was the case, had simply opening my window been enough?

And if I *had* permitted him entry unknowingly … did that mean he could just waltz right in again, at any time?

I eyed the lock with fearful, bulging eyes.

It might not be worth a damn.

I made my way to the bed, still on hands and knees, knowing my legs wouldn't be able to hold me up.

Shivering, I pulled the blankets up over my head, wrapping them around myself, and tried to force myself to warm up.

His touch had sapped nearly all of my body heat, leeching it out of me like a mosquito after my blood.

I didn't know whether to laugh or to cry; he practically *was* a mosquito, for crying out loud.

Could I believe him? How was it possible that anything that he had said was true?

But it was hard to miss the certainty in his voice, the determination, the resolution.

Regardless of whether or not I was going to allow myself to believe him, I knew one thing for sure.

He'd proven he was not going to give up.

I shuddered, and bit down on my blanket to keep myself from freaking out. I had had enough of that; all that mattered to me now was my own survival.

So that was it then, huh?

Did I believe him?

Yeah … I guess I did.

I mean, how else could I explain his crazy behavior? Everything that he did, everything he said, all of the creepy looks and caresses … My eyes welled with tears as I clenched the soft blanket tighter in my balled-up fists, wishing I could make it untrue—Byron Vesper was a vampire.

Was I absolutely crazy? Had I lost my mind? Was this some weird form of PTSD?

I rolled over and snatched my phone from the bedside table. It was quarter after one. A fresh flood of anger swept over me. Was he determined to make sure I never slept again?

I opened the internet, and typed in, *Are vampires real?*

I should have known. There was a split right down the middle. There were shady, poorly made sites claiming to be a part of a vampire cult, where they all wore capes, watched lame 80s movies, and ate food with decorations resembling blood. And then there were what looked like professional, university-level sites that discussed vampire bats, leeches, and other blood-sucking creatures from the animal kingdom. A few bloggers claimed to have encountered a vampire, and there were whole sites dedicated to chronicling weird circumstances, dealings with stalkers, and people who had skin that was inhumanly cold. But the comments sections of their posts were filled with ridicule, and a small handful of death threats.

A little extreme, sure, even if I could understand why people thought these bloggers were nuts.

Until Thursday afternoon, I would have thought the same thing. Over an hour of solid reading later, I still was not convinced. So I placed my phone on my bedside table, and stared up at the ceiling.

Lying there, I was acutely aware of my each and every heartbeat. They felt more pronounced than they ever had in my life.

If Byron was serious about what he said …

… and then we can be together … forever.

That meant …

Blood. Hot, wet, metallic blood. That was what he wanted from me.

I realized for the first time how fragile I was. If Byron could nearly punch through a metal door, then how easily would he be able to snap my bones? Would they break like twigs? Or like paper straws? If he could outrun me, there was no way that I could escape from him.

I rolled over and wondered if my parents were sleeping. The fact that I had so readily accepted Byron's word that he would hurt them, without question, frightened me. But then, why would I question it? I'd seen the impression his fist had made in the bunker door yesterday. I absolutely knew that he could hurt them.

So why didn't he? Why didn't he just get them out of the picture and take care of me right then and there? I could be dead by now, or a vampire, or whatever he was planning. The answer sickened me.

He was playing with me.

He had been watching me. He had known everything that Xandra had told me about vampires. He knew exactly what to say to me to freak me out.

That terrified me.

So why, when he spilled into my room in the blink of an eye, smothered my throat with his icy, immoveable grip, had my reaction *not* been to cower in terror? I should have quaked with tremors. Yet I had been obstinate, stood up to him—defied him, even.

He probably liked that.

I slapped the bed in aggravation. Of course he would. And that would explain why he was biding his time.

Well, if he wanted a fighter, he was going to see that I wasn't going to give in so easily. He'd better prepare himself for my iron will. I had never done anything that anyone else ever wanted me to do. That's why it was so easy to become a liar. I just didn't care what other people wanted or expected.

Rolling onto my back again, I resumed staring at the ceiling. My eyes followed the same crack that I had looked at every night since we moved in.

What I wouldn't give to go back to worrying about making friends or reflecting on the dumb and embarrassing things I said at school.

Now I was one of those teenagers that you hear about in movies.

How was this even happening?

Was there even a way out of this? Was my only choice to let him have his way?

No, that couldn't be. I wasn't ready to die. Seventeen is too young to die.

But what other choice did I have? It wasn't like I had super strength, or super speed, or anything like that. I could do nothing to defend myself. His vice grip was impossible for me to break free from.

There had to be a way.

He seemed to think the garlic was amusing, almost as if he thought I had been clever. Should I just start wearing a necklace of garlic around school?

Then there was the daytime issue. Byron couldn't walk around in daylight, no. But daytime always ended. In fact, the shortest day of the year had only been a few weeks ago.

There were months of long nights ahead.

I hesitated, and then rolled over and dug through the fluffy blanket again until I found my phone.

The battery was nearly drained, but I typed in one more thing. *How do you kill a vampire?*

Some of the results didn't seem plausible.

Sunlight—well, that would explain why Byron fled on the morning after he'd trapped us in the storage room. Religious objects … I didn't have any of those, my family being very lapsed Catholics from at least two generations ago. Then there were things like a wooden stake in the heart, decapitation, and even a suggestion about poisoning human blood and allowing the vampire to drink it.

I shut the screen off again and tried to suppress a shudder. I had a hard time imagining myself shoving a pointed piece of wood in someone's heart or cutting his head off. And as for poisoning myself before giving my body over to him … a murder/suicide felt more like an extreme final act of spite than a legitimate option.

It didn't look like I had many options to kill him.

Kill him. Just the thought of it drove a wedge of ice into my chest.

Well, it was kill him or let him kill me. And he wasn't human anymore, right?

In spite of how grim everything felt, a little ray of hope warmed me. Maybe I could kill him. Crafting a wooden stake would be simple enough. I'd grab a pocket knife from a corner shop, and whittle a few stakes to carry with me. The metal detectors at school wouldn't pick them up, and I could use the excuse that they were for a shop project if anyone found them. It was a start, at least until I could conduct more thorough research.

It was just a shame that it was almost dawn again by the time I came to that conclusion.

Two nights without sleep.

Maybe Byron wouldn't actually have to sink his teeth in me for me to die.

Chapter 11

Not long after the first pinks of sunrise started to filter into my room, I heard Mom and Dad get up. They both had to work today, I knew, and it wouldn't be long before one of them peeked in to say goodbye to me and let me know what my chore list for the day was.

With everything that had happened, I didn't want one of them to find me like this, lying in my bed with tear stains on my pillows. It might raise too many questions, and if they started asking, I wasn't sure if I would be able to hold it together.

I dragged myself to the shower, and stood in the hot water, washing the night away. I still felt cold all the way to my bones, as if Byron's touch had left some permanent mark on my skin, a kind of vampire frostbite. When I stepped out of the shower, my skin was bright red from the heat, and it still didn't feel like enough warmth.

I dressed in a pair of yoga pants and a loose-fitting tank. I couldn't stand the idea of wearing jeans or anything that might be considered cute. If Byron was watching, I didn't want him to think I was attractive at all. In any way. Just for good measure, I finished the ensemble with a bulky sweatshirt. Its high collar covered my neck.

There. Good luck sinking your teeth in now.

"Well, well, well, look who's awake before noon."

As I walked into the kitchen, I found my mom throwing a few dishes from dinner the night before into the dishwasher. The look she gave me could have melted glass.

"Didn't sleep well last night," I replied.

She made a clicking sound with her tongue, and I winced. It sounded too much like the small stones bouncing off of my window last night.

"It was probably the late-onset guilt from lying to your parents."

I closed my eyes. I couldn't react. She didn't know. She didn't understand.

What a cliché teenager thing to think, right? But she *really* didn't understand.

"Yeah," I replied quietly, and what she didn't know was that I was lying to her. Again. And that made me feel even more wretched.

Surprisingly, her face softened for a moment as she looked up at me, standing there lamely in the doorway.

"Are you feeling okay?" Mom said, pouring some coffee into a to-go coffee cup. She stirred in a spoonful of coconut oil. "You must be cold, wearing all those layers."

I shrugged, sliding into one of the barstools on the other side of the island. "Maybe I'm getting used to Florida already."

Dad walked in, briefcase in hand, adjusting his red tie. "Just wait until July. We'll all find we aren't used to any of this yet."

"At least it isn't snowing," Mom replied.

Dad looked over at me, also pouring some coffee into a mug that Mom had set out for him. "You're staying here today, right?"

No "good morning," no "how are you?" Just straight to the point.

Apparently he was still mad at me.

"Yeah," I replied, trying to scrub the tiredness out of my eyes.

"Promise?" he said.

Abso-frickin'-lutely.

"Yes," I said.

He frowned at me like I'd spoken with an attitude—when, right now, housebound was my greatest desire. Or second greatest—after Byron Vesper's head struck from his shoulders, or a stake through his chest, or a mouthful of poison, or …

Whatever my dad thought he'd heard in my voice, he didn't comment on it.

I had forgotten everything from before Byron Vesper appeared in my life. He was like when my grandmother got cancer, and everything else in the world went on hold for a few months—jobs, school, social life. It was an all-consuming blight that took over our lives. Byron Vesper was like that, blotting out my memory of life before him.

He was like cancer. Except instead of killing my grandmother, he was going to kill me.

Dad walked over and kissed me on the cheek.

"Are you going to drop the car off for the oil change?" Mom asked. She reached into the fridge for a Tupperware box full of leftovers.

"Yes. We still meeting for dinner at six?"

"Yes. I'll see you there."

They both walked around the island, Mom throwing some files in her bag, Dad pulling a coat on.

They made it almost to the garage door before Mom turned around and looked at me.

"There's a list on the fridge. Make sure to keep my dress pants out of the dryer when you throw the laundry in. And your father's shirts need to be ironed. There are leftovers for dinner in the fridge."

She had almost closed the door when I heard her say, "Love you, sweetie." Like an afterthought.

She didn't even wait long enough for me to say it back. This was how it was. Under normal circumstances, I wouldn't have even cared that they were cold-shouldering me. Their indifference would have been welcome, knowing I was going to have the house all to myself for the day.

But now, with Byron and all of his insanity, the last thing that

I wanted to do was stay at home all by myself.

Because I knew that I wouldn't actually be alone. And although I was perfectly happy to be stuck indoors, with Byron stalking me, I also knew that he would be out there, somewhere, waiting. Maybe not until after dark … or maybe before, if he had some way of avoiding sunlight. Like, say, by hiding in the bushes, or under an awning, where he could watch me through the windows—could be watching me right this instant, perhaps, eyes raking over my skin …

I shuddered.

I had promised my dad that I wouldn't leave today, but could I keep that promise if push came to shove? How did I know that they weren't going to get home today and find my drained corpse spread out on the couch? Just because he didn't kill me last night didn't mean that he wouldn't kill me today.

The only advantage that I was almost sure I had was that it was daylight.

I froze.

Daylight.

I ran back to up my room, tore off the sweatshirt and replaced it with a swimsuit, and then threw a t-shirt over it. I dug through my closet until I found a scarf, and tossed that around my neck instead—I didn't want to give Byron any temptation. But would the scarf draw attention to my neck?

I tossed it back into the closet.

Maybe I could play it off to him like I didn't care. I doubted he would believe it, but if I could somehow make him second guess his certainty that I was terrified, then I would have a leg up on him.

I found a sunhat that Mom had purchased when we had first gotten here, but since she didn't like it, she had given it to me. I grabbed my phone charger, found my favorite pair of sunglasses, grabbed the sunscreen from the linen closet, and ran outside.

The backyard was mostly occupied by the large screened in porch; "lanai," the Floridians called it. Inside the lanai was where we kept the grill, and, my favorite part of the entire house, the pool. After putting my stuff down, I dashed back inside, tossing food and sodas into a small cooler before returning to the pool lounger. Now I had everything I needed to make sure that he couldn't get to me.

I sighed as I stepped out into warm sunlight, let in through the screen even as the bugs were held at bay by it.

I pulled one of the lounge chairs beside the pool in direct sunlight, making sure not a single inch of it—or me—was in the shade. I'd have to keep moving it throughout the day, of course … but that was fine by me. The warmth of the sun heated my skin, melting the icy feeling that lingered on my flesh since Byron's nighttime visit. I could almost feel the cold evaporating from my bones.

I felt safe, at least for the moment.

I set an alarm for almost noon and promised myself that I would do all of the chores that Mom had given me while the sun was at its peak. There wouldn't be very many shadows. Hopefully I'd be safe.

For the first time since last night, I felt like I had a little bit of control back. I knew that I was probably too proud of myself, and that it was unwarranted, but it was better than cowering under my blankets in my room, waiting to see if he showed up.

I stacked the books beside the lounge chair and slathered sunscreen over my skin. With my complexion, I'd need to re-slather myself every half hour to keep from ending up red as a lobster, even with the relatively short hours of daylight.

Sunburned was better than dead, however.

I leaned back, basking in the sun, and finally started to relax …

Then I woke with a jolt. My legs were warm, and my stomach, on one side … but half of me was cold. The sun! It had crept across the sky, rising toward midday. What came through the screen now had long passed me by.

In a panic, I shuffled the chair into the new patch of sunlight. Then I settled back in, and checked my clock.

Two hours had gone by.

I kicked myself. Stupid. Yes, I'd missed two full nights of

sleep, but that was no excuse when there was a vampire obsessed with me.

I scowled. Wherever he was, he probably relished how tortured I was right now.

How much had my life changed in the last forty-eight hours? Definitely more than it ever had in such a short time. Even leaving New York to move to Florida seemed perfectly normal compared to being stalked by a vampire.

Seriously, what about me was so special? I knew girls who were way prettier than me, more athletic than me, smarter than me. Why in all the world had he decided to hunt me? I began a sweep of the backyard—the sweep I *should've* been doing for hours.

Nothing. Either Byron wasn't out there … or he'd found a place to hide where he was perfectly camouflaged.

I couldn't live the rest of my life like this, especially since I had no idea how long that might be. I didn't want to feel like a bunny trapped in a cage.

The same thought that had haunted me last night passed through my mind: there had to be something that I could do.

If I knew some weaknesses, had some real facts, then maybe I would have a chance.

Who was I kidding? I lay back on the lounger and pressed my hands to either side of my head.

I couldn't give up, not yet. Not until I had exhausted every option. I honestly had no idea what those options were, but I had to try and find a way to protect myself. Whittling wooden stakes and hoping they'd kill him was just a starting point, and not even a particularly good one. After my parents had left, a cursory look around the house showed that it wasn't exactly brimming with potential stakes—unless I wanted to chop a leg off the sofa in the living room, which probably wouldn't improve my parents' mood. Leaving was right out: Mom would get the alert that the front door opened and see me on the camera. Same with opening the lanai door—hell, she'd almost certainly already seen me come out here. Checking my phone more or less confirmed it: two text messages from her "reminding" me about the list of chores I needed to get done today.

I wondered if taking a martial arts class would prove helpful. Maybe learn how to shoot a gun? I came from a town where most families I knew hunted. I could probably call one of them for help.

But I hadn't talked to anyone from back in New York since I'd gotten here. Leaving hadn't exactly been my first choice, but I couldn't deny my parents' timing worked for me. I'd burned just about all my bridges on the way out of town. No one back there was any more likely to listen to me than my parents were.

I didn't think any of those things could really help, because as soon as he got close enough to me, I would be completely helpless. He was so fast, and so strong. I doubted trying to shoot him would do much good.

Not to mention the fact that I'd never held a gun in my life.

So this was what hitting the bottom felt like—utter desperation for an answer that I wasn't sure would ever come; terror so strong that I had gone nights without sleep.

Was this what my life had been reduced to?

I heard my phone buzz—a text from Xandra. *Hey, you doing okay?* it read.

It was like a lifeline, sent out to help keep me from drowning. I hastily started to text her back, wondering how in the world I could fit everything that had happened the night before into a text message.

But a text was a bad idea. No, I needed to actually speak with her. I pressed the call button without hesitating even a second. No way I was keeping this in anymore.

And more to the point … I couldn't do this alone.

Chapter 12

The phone rang and rang—and each time the tone played, my anxiety spiked.

"Hey, you reached Xandra—"

Beep. Cold disappointment settled in my stomach like someone had poured pool water down my throat.

I sighed and glared at the screen. She had *literally* just texted me. What was so important that she'd more or less instantly abandoned her phone?

I did a quick look around the yard. Still empty. Quickly, I tapped in a reply.

Hey, can you call me? We really need to talk. That was good. Urgent. No way she could misunderstand what I was trying to tell her.

My stomach growled angrily, and I put a hand over it.

"All right, fine, I'll feed you."

I pulled a granola bar, a Coke and an apple from the cooler. Everything was slick with condensation, but they were cold, and something as simple as food I liked was comforting.

I nearly inhaled the granola bar. The apple, I forced myself to eat more slowly. The Coke tasted good, and my body thanked me profusely for the caffeine. I checked my phone continually.

After ten minutes without a reply, I texted Xandra again.

Xandra, I'm serious. I really need to talk to you. My desperation level was mounting. I wished I could escape my own head, just for a few minutes.

Maybe there was something on Netflix that would distract me …

My phone buzzed, and I nearly dropped it in my haste to read it as fast as I could.

Can't talk now. Call you later.

I groaned. What in the world could Xandra be doing right now that was more important than this?

He showed up at my house last night. Surely that message would change her tune.

But:

Can't talk now. Call you later.

It must be one of those automated response texts. I felt my anger surge—and then a wave of fear swept in to replace it.

No Xandra to help; neither of my parents to keep me company.

All I could do was keep my butt parked, following the sunlight, and hope to distract myself from the way the world had gone terribly, terribly wrong. Eyes closed, I forced myself to focus on nothing but breathing.

In and out.

In and out.

In and …

It was dark. Totally dark. I blinked, hoping that it would go away—but still the darkness did not leave me. The scent of the pool's chlorine had vanished, as had all the faint noises filtering to me moments ago: the distant hum of a passing engine; twittering birds, tunefully singing, their worlds the same as they always had been. Even my own body seemed to have vanished. All I was aware of was the darkness pressing in all around me.

Then there was a loud bang, a sound of a heavy, industrial-sized switch being pulled, and a bright, narrow light shone to life.

It was almost blinding and standing bathed in it was a silhouette.

Byron's head was down, his eyes fixated on an old, yellowing tome he held in both hands like a man singing in a choir. He wore a sharp black suit, a crisp white shirt, and a dark red tie.

"These violent delights have violent ends

And in their triumph die, like fire and powder

Which, as they kiss, consume."

And then it was suddenly dark once more.

I stared in what I assumed was the direction of where the light had just been.

Another light switched on, to my left.

There he stood again, still holding the same old tome, still not looking up at me.

"My bounty is as boundless as the sea,

My love as deep; the more I give to thee,

The more I have, for both are infinite."

And once more, I was plunged into darkness.

The light reappeared, this time from behind me. I whirled around, and saw Byron standing there once more, drenched in light. There was something red smeared on his cheek.

"What's in a name? That which we call a rose

By any other name would smell as sweet."

I recognized those words. They played in my mind again as the light went out again like an old forgotten melody.

As if I was ready, I turned to face the light once more as it blared to life.

"For never was a story of more woe than this of Juliet and her Romeo."

And then he slammed the book shut as he looked up at me, a wide, taunting smile on his face, a trickle of blood dripping from the corner of his lips.

I sat bolt upright on my lounger, the infinite darkness replaced with the sunny day, the sight of the pool. I spilled my can of Coke as I sat up, the hiss of carbonation on the concrete like an animal in my ear.

My heart was beating so fast it hurt, and I clutched my hand over my chest.

I looked all around, getting to my feet, wrapping my towel around myself.

Where was he? Where did he go?

I could have sworn that he was right there, standing right in front of me.

And then I realized that I was in my backyard, in a swimsuit, in the bright sunshine.

I looked all over the lanai, and then out farther in the yard, just to make sure that he wasn't anywhere near.

There was nothing there.

Or, more accurately … no one.

I was still shaking as I went back to the Coke can to clean up the spill. I grabbed some of the napkins I had brought out with me and started to mop it up. The white paper turned brown, soaking up the sugary liquid, and something about the way it spread brought to mind the image of blood soaking into gauze.

I turned away, not wanting to look at the cleanup. Somehow, my phone had fallen underneath the lounger, and I saw it in the corner of my eye. I immediately abandoned the Coke. The inevitable ant problem would have to just chill for a second.

Xandra had not texted or called me back while I was asleep, but my mom sure had.

Cassie, please don't forget to take care of those clothes in the washer. I don't want them to get full of mildew.

Ten minutes later, she had sent another one.

And if you can, can you please pull out a bag of chicken from the freezer for tomorrow?

At least she had said "please" Another text had come through a half hour after that.

You remembered to keep those pants out of the dryer, right? Without a reply, she'd sent another message just a few minutes later.

Cassandra, are you getting these texts?

And again:

If you don't answer me, I am coming home to make sure that you are there! And if I do, you better have all of the things on the list done!

Well, that was just wonderful.

It was almost noon, and I chewed my bottom lip. She would be taking her lunch break soon. I needed to call her.

I absently looked around, trying to find inspiration for how I was going to explain why I hadn't answered her texts. And also how I was going to convince her that she didn't have to come home so I could actually do the chores she wanted me to do.

I considered telling her I had been in the pool, which wasn't a complete lie. I was definitely at least by it.

I sighed and shifted my gaze to the backyard, to the palm trees, to the fresh air, and when I did, I saw—something moved.

I looked in the direction of the movement.

The thick, horizontal blinds in the window of the house beside ours were rattling together as if stirred by the wind …

Or as if someone had just been watching me.

Chapter 13

I slammed the door shut behind me and pulled the blinds over the door. Normally I would have hated to shut that beautiful daylight out, but I went around to every single one of the drapes and shades until the entire first floor was darkened.

If Byron was using the windows to see inside, he definitely wouldn't be able to now.

At least that was what I kept telling myself. It had to be him, didn't it? It explained everything if he or one of his thralls, or lackeys or whatever you called humans in service of a vampire— if one of them lived behind me and was watching constantly. The Byron issue temporarily sidelined, I now had to deal with my mother before she decided to fly off of the handle and come home.

I called her as I ran to the washing machine, and when she answered, I hurriedly explained to her that of course I had remembered to take her pants out of the washer and I had already taken the chicken out for her before she had even texted me.

As she grumbled about how she was surprised I had actually been working, I pulled those pants from the dryer and hung them up, trying not to roll my eyes.

"So how's work?" I asked, trying to sound casual. Talking to her, though potentially stressful, was at least distracting me from Byron's spying. And if something happened to me while I was on the phone with her, she would hear it and be able to call the cops … for whatever good that'd do.

"Fine," she replied. "You know, I was thinking about coming home for lunch anyways—"

"No!" I said, probably too quickly. I berated myself for it in my mind. "No," I said, more gently. "Seriously, I have everything under control. Why don't you go out for lunch? Get some Starbucks, maybe go down to the Bay and enjoy the sunshine."

Her silence told me that she was actually considering it.

"You know," she said finally, "that's not a bad idea. Are you sure that you're okay, being home all alone?"

I hesitated, but then laughed. It was hollow, but I hoped that she didn't hear that over the phone. "Yeah, definitely. I have tons of homework to do anyways. I wouldn't be very good company." That was true. Who could focus on whatever silly little conversation she wanted to have when I had a vampire declaring his true love and intent to drink my blood?

I heard her laugh, just a little. "Well, all right. Hey, how about you and I do some shopping tomorrow? Get out of the house for a little while?"

I was so shocked by her proposition that I froze, my hands halfway into the freezer to grab the chicken I had promised I had taken out already.

"I know that all of this has been hard on you," she continued. "It's been hard for all of us. But let's try to have a fresh start, okay? No more lies, Cass. Not many people have the chance to remake themselves like this."

Where was all of this coming from?

"Sure, Mom," I replied, and I probably sounded pretty heartless. I just … didn't know what to say. "I'll try," I added, and I hoped I sounded more sincere.

"Good," she said, but I recognized the hurt tone in her voice. How could I communicate with her that I did want to try and stop lying? How would I ever get her to believe me, especially over the phone like this?

"Shopping would be fun," I added. And I was definitely telling the truth a little; shopping would put me out in public, and outside in the sunlight, especially if we went to the outlets where Mom loved to go. There would be tons of people around.

I'd be safe from Byron.

"Let's plan on it," Mom replied, though it sounded like I had taken the wind out of her sails. "If you need anything, just shoot me a text, okay?"

"All right."

"I love you," she said, and it sounded like she meant it this time.

"Love you too," I said, and we both hung up.

I exhaled, leaning against the door frame of the kitchen.

I glanced around the living room, the sunlight trying to peek in around the edges of all of the blinds. I needed the sunlight to keep the vampire at bay. But if I left the blinds open, he'd have someone watching—if he wasn't doing it himself.

My head spun. I felt like I'd gone for a swim in the deep end of the pool and suddenly found myself unable to paddle.

I wasn't sure that there was anything I could do to keep Byron out anymore. I wondered if it was just totally useless to even try.

I dragged myself to a bar stool at the kitchen island and slumped into it.

Setting the phone down, I rapped my fingers on the granite.

Xandra still hadn't called me, I hadn't finished my chores, and I was so tired that I could barely see straight.

And then the nightmare ... It had been so strange—Byron spouting weird lines of poetry.

No, not weird poetry. I knew it.

It definitely helped that he'd said that line about Romeo and Juliet.

First *Hamlet*, now *Romeo and Juliet*.

Could vampires influence dreams? No. That was crazy, right?

I couldn't waste my energy trying to deduce what powers Byron had. I didn't need to make him more invincible in my mind than he already was.

It must have been because of his amateur performance the night before outside of my window. It just brought back memories from when I took part in my old school's production of *Romeo and Juliet*. That had only been a year before; of course I would still remember the lines. I had been working backstage and had heard the actors recite their lines until I could practically say the entire thing in my sleep.

I needed some real sleep, longer than an hour or two at a time.

It made me second guess whether or not I had actually fallen asleep at all, and if I had actually seen those blinds move in the house next door.

I pressed my palms to my temples and tried to push all of the difficult thoughts out. Not like it would actually help, letting my brain run around in circles.

So he was so obsessed with me that he was resorting to breaking into other people's houses in order to spy on me from their windows? I had heard the horror stories about stalkers, but this was unlike anything I could have imagined. It didn't help that he had supernatural powers.

He'd chased me, he knew things about me, had declared his love, declared his … bizarre desires. Drinking my blood? When did that get fun?

Was there anything I could do? Or was I totally trapped now?

He was so confident last night, almost like he thought my struggling was totally irrelevant. I just … didn't understand. I couldn't understand.

I shivered, and not because the air conditioning was on too high.

I didn't even know what to think about the fact that he might actually be attracted to me. Should I be flattered? Terrified? Because I was definitely leaning toward terrified.

He was good-looking, but what did that matter when he seemed to be playing a game of cat-and-mouse with me, and I was the mouse? When I looked at his face, I didn't see handsome.

I saw cruel, vicious, a predator on the hunt.

I gingerly touched the spot on my cheek where he had kissed me the night before. Somehow it still felt cold.

My phone buzzed on the counter, and I flinched. It was like a death rattle, a siren going off in my head.

I was so strung out that any and every sound terrified me.

I picked it up, and pressed the screen on.

My heart sank when I realized that it wasn't Xandra—just some random number that wasn't in my contacts.

I sighed and clicked the screen off, then put it back down.

Was she ever going to get back to me? Maybe I should just try texting her again, her "Can't talk now" messages be damned. Anyway, that was hours ago now—surely she must be free by now.

I could hope it was as simple as that, at least. My anxieties were starting to really run away with me, my sleep-addled mind the only brake on coming up with crazy theories about how she was secretly in league with Byron or something.

I shuddered again. If Xandra was in on this … I was really doomed. Because there wasn't a soul in the world I could talk to about it if she was secretly on Byron's side.

I clicked the screen back on with the intent to bother Xandra again and glanced at the mysterious text. The number was one I didn't know, but it was local to the Tampa area. I debated ignoring it, but knew I'd have to look at it eventually. I touched the tiny little envelope on the screen, and the message opened.

I can help you.

I stared. Just four simple words—and yet I could not fathom them.

I can help you.

Help me with what?

Who the hell would text me that?

The first, most obvious answer, was that it was Byron—and that this "offer of help" was just another of his games, trying to get under my skin … or lure me out.

But what if it was a genuine message? What if someone out there knew what was going on—had maybe endured the same at

Byron's hands—and was reaching out to me so that I might evade him?

If I were less exhausted, I probably would've shot down that explanation a lot faster. In my sleep-addled state, though, the allure of real help was electrifying.

I can help you. What if it was a trick?

What if … it *wasn't*? My breathing was fast, but steady. I tried to slow it down, to think.

It was just a text message. And yet it felt … strangely enough … like someone was throwing me a life preserver while I was drowning. Maybe they were going to yank it back just to mess with me, but … what if they didn't?

What if they were actually sincere? What if it was someone who could help me? I was so far out on a limb, all by myself, Xandra not answering text messages. Byron could break my door down at any moment, and the thought petrified me.

What did I have to lose?

Drawing another deep breath, trying to get my shaking hands under control, I picked up my phone and considered my reply.

Chapter 14

Who is this?

I had never been so anxious to receive an answering text message—not even awaiting Xandra's replies this morning.

I scrolled through Twitter to satiate my intense need to fidget, glancing up at the notification bar every few seconds. A minute passed—and then the reply came.

I am your best chance at beating him.

My anxiety spiked. A second person had entered my life, in as many days, who knew more about me than I did about them. It was exhausting—strangers who'd been watching quietly from the shadows suddenly making their presence known.

And yet this one could, maybe, be salvation.

It was impossible for my breath not to hitch in my chest, to not be drawn in by their promise.

How did you get this number? I sent back.

It doesn't matter, came the reply.

If this was Byron—and it could well be; I was pretty sure he had my number already, seeing as he knew where I lived—I didn't think he would hesitate to tell me. His flair for the dramatic would shine through.

Even so, I had to check.

Is this Byron? I texted back.

Antsy, I awaited the reply, mind wandering its permutations. *Why, yes, it's me, darling. Why don't we get together tonight so I can drink your blood and remove that pesky desire to sunbathe where I can't easily get to you with my gross, cold stalker hands and lips.* But the reply came quickly, just one word.

No.

Who are you?

It took a few seconds longer for this one to come through.

My back was so sore from all of the stress that I relocated to the couch in the living room. If I was going to be tense, I might as well be so in the most comfortable place. I sank into the sofa and lay back, putting my feet up as the soft, velvety covering caressed my cheek. It smelled like home, like our house in New York, and burying my face in it made me feel better for a moment … and then so much worse, because I wasn't in New York.

I was in Tampa—alone, with nothing but burning bridges and severed connections behind me, leaving me no one to turn to …

And a vampire was stalking me.

A reply: *Like I said, I can help you beat him.*

I hesitated, fingers hovering over the touchscreen, weighing up whether I could trust them.

I had little choice. I had few people available to me who I *could* trust. Xandra formed one of the three, and she was indisposed. My parents, on the other hand, thought—no, *knew*—me to be a serial liar. And anyway—Byron had threatened them with death if I stuck a toe out of line—a threat I most certainly believed.

I had no one else.

Stomach twisting nauseatingly, sickness spiked through my throat. So I *had* to trust the person on the other end of the phone.

I replied:

But I don't know who you are. How can I trust you?

I know who and what Byron is. I also know what he's planning for you.

How?

The answer came seconds later. *Byron is predictable. He always makes the same mistakes. I know what they are. I can help you.*

I groaned. This was too cryptic. Why couldn't this person just … I dunno, save me? Just tell me what I was dealing with, maybe even use small words, because I was tired—physically, and mentally, thinking and overthinking everything I was seeing and feeling right now.

Although … I wasn't too tired to see the irony in a serial liar struggling with who she could trust.

Another message came in:

Are you safe?

I made to respond, but another text arrived.

Is Byron there?

No, I answered quickly. *Though I think he's next door, watching.*

Admitting that felt strangely liberating. I didn't have much to go on, but this person seemed to be on the opposing side of Byron, and that was the side I wanted to be on.

He will always have eyes on you. You don't have to be alone in this.

I typed back quickly, realizing I was typing the same thing over and over—but I didn't care. I needed the answers.

Who are you exactly? How do I know I can trust you?

Again, they sidestepped it.

If you want out of this, you don't have a choice.

Why did it feel like my entire life was full of non-choices now? Everyone else seemed to be governing it rather than me—and that was nothing if not infuriating.

But however I felt about it, this person, whoever they were, knew who Byron was, and said they were willing to help me. It was the first glimmer of hope I had seen since Byron had crashed into my life, chasing me and Xandra down and trapping us overnight in the bunker.

Since then, I had been penned in, like an animal—even more so, after Byron's little visit last night.

Now, though, I had … *something*. Maybe not options per se,

but there was an offer now of help, the chance to do something other than wait around for Byron to sink his teeth in my neck—or wherever he wanted to bite me.

That thought—Byron's teeth sinking into my skin—sent another shudder up my spine, another wave of gooseflesh rolling over my skin.

Of course, it was entirely possible that I was stepping into an even bigger trap by choosing to trust this person … but they knew about him, which was something.

And I got the vaguest hint that this person had an axe to grind.

Ok. Tell me what I have to do.

Tonight there is going to be a sort of get-together. You should be there.

Tonight? But of course. I was already way deep in trouble with my parents—so trust my one shot at evading Byron's clutches to be on a night when I had expressly promised I would stay in.

What sort of get-together? I replied.

You'll meet a lot of likeminded people there—people who don't like Byron. Think of it as an introduction to your escape plan.

People who didn't like Byron, huh? Sounded like my sort of place. Though, how many people knew about him exactly?

You'll have to play it cool when you do come, came another text.

Not *if*. It was *when*.

Why? I asked.

No answer.

Well, how very nice. I didn't entirely trust that they wouldn't get me eaten by my crazed vampire stalker, and they didn't feel the need to answer me honestly. This was going to be a great relationship, I could tell.

If you want to beat Byron, you need to understand the world he comes from, finally came through.

My fingers froze, poised over the keyboard. His world? But that meant …

Is this a vampire party?!

It was probably a measure of how worked up I was that I a)

texted the word "vampire" and b) added the ?! at the end in order to make known to this person that I was not feeling calm about going into a room filled with vampires when I was already having enough trouble with just one of them. There was a long silence. At first, I chalked that up to the texter issuing a long reply. But the more seconds went by, the harder it was not to twitch as thoughts spiraled and fears seeded, took root. Had I stumbled upon the truth? Had I blown the texter's cover, shown them up to be working with Byron after all, luring me in to use me like a bloodbank? Or had I maybe blown the cover of someone altruistic to me by being overt about the vampire threat, when they'd been so veiled all this time?

Every thought spun in a sickening lurch. Finally, an answer came. One word—and it caught my breath in my chest, made my heart skip a beat.

Yes.

So there were more of them.

It shouldn't have surprised me. Why would I ever have thought he was the only one like that?

But the idea of an entire subculture or society, hidden right under my nose, was a little mind-boggling. How big was it? Where did it exist?

In the night, obviously. When the rest of the world slept.

Be at the construction site beside Amalie Arena at midnight. The one on the north corner across the street.

Amalie Arena? That was down near the bay. There was no way I could walk there.

How will I recognize you? I replied quickly.

I won't be there.

Then why—

The reply came before I had a chance to fully form my thought. *I'll be in touch soon. Watch your back.* The conversation was terminated—and whatever reply I might've had died on my fingertips. Not that any would particularly suffice right now. My world had been shaken once again—and I was seriously losing track of how many times it had happened. Wearily, I sank into the couch, pressing my head into the stuffing as I closed my eyes and pushed a sweaty hand over them.

I was going to a vampire party tonight.

I clicked my teeth together, trying not to bite my fingernails down to the nib.

More vampires out there. More like Byron.

These ones did not like him, though.

That should've alleviated my anxiety some. But it did not. Not liking him was not the same as not *being* like him.

That promise dangled before my nose again: deliverance from Byron. All I had to do to accept it was go to this vampire party.

Two problems with that:

One, I had promised my parents not to leave the house. And there was *no way* they would let me leave at night, let alone for a party at midnight in downtown Tampa.

Second, and really what should have been my primary concern if only I had my priorities straight: *I would be a human walking into a party full of vampires.* Restlessness building yet again, I stood up and padded across the carpet, back and forth, back and forth, mind whirling.

This was all just crazy. Why in the world would I even consider going to a vampire party that some person I don't even know told me about?

I sighed heavily and knotted my fingers in my hair.

It was the only lead I had. What were my other options? Sit around my house as night fell and hope that the stalker who barged into my room uninvited last night didn't come back again tonight and help himself to a refreshing bite from my neck? Hell, he was strong enough he could have bitten me just about anywhere he wanted. Picturing his teeth sinking slowly into my skin, the hard points driving into my flesh made me gasp and flinch, twisted my stomach with nausea. There was no other direction I could turn—and this party, and whoever was attending, was my only real option.

They don't like Byron, I kept reasoning to myself—trying to talk myself into snatching at the carrot on a stick swinging in front of my nose.

On the other hand, the attendees were vampires too. I had no idea what kind of control they might have … and the one person who could possibly answer, Xandra, was … well, *not answering*.

However long I thought, whatever avenues my mind went down, I always circled back to the same thing: Byron had penned me in, and this get-together offered me a route to freedom.

Which meant I needed to go.

Numbly, I walked upstairs, the air conditioner running in a dull hum like the fog that enfolded my senses in this exhausted state. Into my bedroom—then the wardrobe.

Distantly, as though my body was very far away, I dug through clothes, like a teenager trying to find her best party clothes—like the teenager *I should be*.

I finally decided on a pair of black skinny jeans with a white and blue sequined top. Then I rummaged through my jewelry, and decided on some knuckle rings, a long silver chain with a clear crystal charm, and some diamond stud earrings.

I had no idea if this is what someone wore to a party, but at least I knew I'd be able to run if I had to. They were deceptively stretchy pants. Thank goodness for the yoga pants revolution, wherein we discovered that more stretch was better.

I found my black Converse at the back of my closet, still in a box, and I set them down next to the clothes I had laid across the chair at my desk.

Then I hurried downstairs, trying to clean up and finish my chores as fast as I could. I wanted there to be no issue from my parents when they got home after their dinner out—path of least resistance, and all that. Scrubbing pans in the sink, I wondered how I was going to get all the way across Tampa in the middle of the night.

If only Xandra had texted me back, maybe we could have made a plan together.

Dishwashing was more protracted than it needed to be. I kept pausing to dry my hands on the rough dish towel so I could check my phone—just in case somehow I'd missed the buzz of an incoming text. Nothing, of course, and I knew that—but I couldn't help hoping.

I sent Xandra another text. She didn't reply.

I was going to have to take an Uber into the city. It would easily drain half of my measly bank account, but what good was money when you were dead? Or undead, depending on how things went with Byron.

I kept asking myself why in the world I was doing this, why I was so determined to go to this party.

The only reasonable explanation that I could come up with is that I had no place else to turn. It was either stay in my own room that night and wait for Byron to appear and find myself at his mercy … or head to this mysterious party to try and find out a way to get him off my back.

It was no choice at all. He'd already proven that I was no match for him in strength.

I sighed and sank my hands in the hot dishwater again, feeling that this choice to go was no more of a choice than doing my chores—I had to do this, just like I had to do everything else in my life. I resigned myself to it with even less enthusiasm than I had for my mother's list, wishing that I could find any other way but the one I saw.

Chapter 15

The Uber I ordered was waiting on the street corner like I had requested just after dark. Mom had texted me just before she and Dad had left their respective workplaces for dinner, and I'd lied (big surprise) and told her I was feeling poorly and was going to bed early. Just to throw them off the scent, I'd made the bed before I left, creating a lumpy pillow Cassie in my place—sufficient if they stuck their head into my darkened room, although if they did much more than that, the game would be up. Sneaking back in late tonight presented another hurdle, but if I was careful I could dodge the consequences of the serious rule-breaking I was undertaking.

The drive was quick, since there was hardly any traffic going into the city. The driver, an eccentric woman in her sixties, told me stories about the way the world was thirty years ago.

I just tried to look like I cared, or that I was even listening, while I tuned her out and thought about the state of my world right now.

She dropped me off, giving me a strange look as I thanked her.

As I gazed out into the dark, vacant construction site, I grimaced and contemplated asking the Uber driver to just take me home. I didn't have to go to this thing. I was literally handing myself over to Byron's potential associates.

But I got out of the car, feeling like the biggest fool on the planet. Bad enough I was being stalked by a vampire; now I was walking right into their den.

The car's brake lights flared, like the tip of a cigarette as a pull was taken, and the Uber disappeared into the night. I was alone.

The city of Tampa looked a lot scarier in the middle of the night. The lights of the skyscrapers, though not far away, were almost engulfed by the surrounding night. Even the arena across the street did not produce enough light to carry across to the corner where I was standing. Anything, or anyone, could be lurking in the pitch black shadows of the construction site behind me. Relative to Byron, and what he could do to me, murderers and rapists didn't seem quite as terrifying. My heart spun at that morbid realization. Not for the first time, I thought about how much my life and my priorities had changed in mere days. Now I longed for the times when my biggest worry was the consequences of lying to Mom and Dad.

What was I even looking for? The texter didn't give me much to go on, other than to be here. Was someone going to appear out of the shadows? Was a car coming to pick me up?

Was the party somewhere deep in that construction site?

I groaned. This was too much, and I almost lost the little dinner I had eaten on the sidewalk with fear. Every sound was heightened—the soft flutter of a loose strip of tape in the construction site; breeze wending past plastic sheeting, pulling it this way and that.

No footsteps that I could detect.

That did not mean, though, that someone was not standing in the dark—that someone was not watching me.

What would someone think of me if they were to drive by? A teenage girl, dressed like she was going to a club, standing on the street corner in the middle of the night. I looked like a hooker. Mom would be so proud.

I shivered, not entirely due to the cool breeze whispering through, and drew the thin sweater I wore more tightly around my shoulders. It didn't help.

A pair of headlights appeared around a corner down the street, and I debated jumping behind the fence of the construction site.

The last thing I wanted was to be propositioned by some strung-out crackhead looking for a good time.

But as the car turned down the street toward me, I realized that it was a long, sleek, black limo—not entirely out of place in Tampa, wealthy as it was and all, but still ... a *limo*. Here. It came to rest at the stop sign where I was standing. The engine was quiet, the outside impeccably clean, like it had been waxed just today. My reflection looked back at me from the windows. The limo did not move. Still, its engine purred.

No door was opened, no window rolled down.

Then it hit me. Was this my ride?

I hesitated—then took a step forward.

The limo still didn't move.

I put my hand on the handle and was surprised to find the door unlocked.

I half expected an occupant inside to start shrieking at me, but the posh interior was entirely empty, leather seats waiting invitingly, soft jazz music playing in the background.

The window up at the front that separated the driver from the passengers suddenly rolled down, and I saw a pair of piercing green eyes staring at me from the rear view mirror.

"Miss Cassandra?"

I stared at him blankly.

His eyebrows crawled up his forehead. "Miss Cassandra?"

"Yes?" I finally replied.

"Please get in. We don't want you to be late."

Obeying in spite of myself, I nodded, slipped in, and pulled the door shut.

The man with the green eyes tipped his hat to me before the window between us rolled up again, leaving me alone again.

The limo pulled smoothly away from the curb and headed east down the street, following along the bay. The engine noise was muffled by the jazz, and I could smell the rich leather that permeated the passenger compartment. Where were we headed? I was still unfamiliar enough with Tampa that I easily got turned around in its grid like-layout, so once the driver had taken a few turns left and right, I lost my sense of direction—which was worrisome, since after my Uber ride I was nearly out of money.

I looked all around the spacious interior. It had blue neon lights inlaid into the ceiling, along with a sparkling mirror. Staring at myself, I wished that I had brought some concealer to hide the dark circles under my eyes. Could've done with spending a bit longer on the (messy) bun I'd pulled my hair into, too. All that effort on nice clothes and I'd thrown together my makeup and hair at the last minute. I consoled myself with the knowledge that I was heading into a party of vampires, and attracting their attention was probably the wrong move.

The seats were black leather, smooth to the touch as I brushed my fingers along the seams next to me, feeling the little bumps in the stitching. Along one wall was a mirrored front cabinet. Curiosity got the better of me and I pulled one of the doors open. Inside was a fully stocked bar, complete with frosted glasses and crystal champagne flutes.

Who was going to these lengths for me?

More than ever, I wanted to know who had been texting me.

I swallowed and closed the cabinet. The temptation to have a shot of something strong to help steel my nerves gave way to common sense. I needed my full wits about me if I was heading into the heart of the snake's nest. I was tired enough without compromising my judgment any further.

I did find water bottles and gratefully opened one up, drinking half of it in three gulps. I tried to imagine it cooling and calming my agitated nerves, but it didn't really help. The steady bump of the wheels against the road did though, lulling me just a little.

I sat back against the seat and took a deep breath. We drove past a brightly lit theater, and the light that pierced the windows fell upon a small, red box on the seat below the black, impenetrable divider. It looked so out of place that it immediately stirred my curiosity. Moving to the opposite seat carefully—to stop myself face-planting, and also to avoid attracting the attention of the driver—I examined the box more closely. It was wrapped in a shiny, reflective wrapping paper, like a way out-of-season Christmas gift, no bigger than the size of my forearm. I moved the package a little. The lights flickering by outside glinted off of its surface. Little reflective dots showed through in the paper as I lifted it. A small white tag hung beneath it, "*Cassie*" written on it in a swooping script.

This wasn't anything like the penmanship on the card that I had received with the flowers, so it wasn't from Byron. This script was much more elegant—and softer, as if the writer had not pressed pen to paper as hard as Byron did.

I pulled the top off, realizing that the box was not wrapped together, and found a black velvet insert.

Lying nestled among the soft, shimmering velvet was a slender piece of wood.

I picked it up and examined it more closely. It was about the length of my hand, from the tip of my longest finger to the bottom of my palm, and smooth to the touch. All of the imperfections had been buffed away. It was wider at one end and sharpened down to a point at the other. I touched it with the tip of my finger; it didn't pierce the skin, but with the right force, it could definitely hurt someone. It was cool to my touch, and there was something comforting about the feel of it against my fingers.

I glanced back down at the box and saw that there was another small piece of paper, folded neatly in the velvet. The wooden stick had hidden it.

I picked it up and unrolled it.

For your protection.

I rolled the stake between my fingers. It was such a thin, small, innocent-looking thing, like a chopstick. The implications of this gift caused my nerves to buzz. A wooden stake could kill a vampire, according to every vampire myth I'd ever seen or heard.

The idea of hurting another person, living or not, made my stomach clench tightly, and I had to hold the seat underneath me to ground myself. I had ankle-high boots on. I couldn't stow the stake by my heel—but at about the same length as my foot, and thin, I figured it could lie alongside my foot easily enough.

I slid the stake carefully into my boot so the pointed end rode along my calf. The fit was a little tight, but some jostling was enough to convince me I could walk with it. The stake offered safety, but also a reminder: my life was in danger—and most likely would be every second from now on.

And whoever had sent the limo for me, whoever had invited me to go to this party that night, had known all about that danger. If they were willing to provide a means of protection for me, then that surely meant that I could trust them.

At least that was what I kept telling myself. It was a pretty flimsy rationale, and it rang hollow enough that I had to repeat it a few times to try and settle myself down. I could be playing right into their hands, and I wouldn't know. My palms were sweating all over the leather seats, slippery and damp, the worry eating at me like—well, not a vampire, thankfully. But I had to trust someone at some point, I knew. Might as well be now.

The limo came to a stop, and I listened intently. I could hear a deep, throbbing bass somewhere in the distance, faint but constant. I heard the front door of the limo open, and then, only a moment later, the back door of the limo opened, and the man with the green eyes peered inside.

"Lady Cassandra, we've arrived."

Lady? Really?

I swallowed but nodded my head.

I had one instant to make a decision. I would either walk into this party looking like the lamb led to slaughter that I was, or I could pretend to be something I was not: someone who belonged there.

The green-eyed chauffeur helped me out of the limo and closed the door behind me. Its slamming sounded so very definite, like an audible reminder that my retreat had just been cut off and there was only one way to go—forward.

I looked up at a large condominium complex, right on the

edge of the bay. It was easily thirty stories tall, and I could tell by the flashing colored lights up near the top that the music was coming from there. Beautiful people were making their way into the building, like this was some sort of Hollywood red carpet party and I was the unannounced date of some key grip or makeup artist.

Actually, the makeup artist's date probably wouldn't have needed concealer the way I did.

These beautiful, glamorous people streamed in through the front door, greeting each other like old friends with wide smiles, handshakes, hugs. It was strange to watch, like it was intended to drive home that I was an outsider in this place, someone who did not belong here.

Were they vampires? Or were they humans, like me? I couldn't tell from this distance.

The green-eyed man's voice startled me out of my reverie. "I was asked to tell you that you will find what you are looking for on floor thirty-five."

I thanked him, catching that piercing gaze once more, then he tipped his hat at me, got back into the driver's seat of the limo, and drove off. Looking back up at the building, I swallowed the lump in my throat.

What had I gotten myself into?

Chapter 16

The lobby of the condominium was relatively ordinary, not totally unlike some where I'd stayed in on vacations with my parents. The crowd of beautiful people that had entered ahead of me had already cleared, disappearing into the clean, brightly lit elevators as I walked in. I was left to ride one by myself, fidgeting restlessly with my necklace and rings the whole way.

Floor thirty-five was right at the very top—the penthouse suite—not what I'd have expected from vampires, if I'd believed in them before the past few days. Glamorous, sure, but glass windows everywhere in the heart of the sunshine state?

Arrogant much, vampires?

My heart was in my throat by the time the elevator rose, not pausing even once, to the top of the tower.

A black wave of sickness pulsed through my body when finally it halted.

The doors opened—

Goosebumps sprang up on my exposed skin, as though the chill of New York winter had swept over me. Shrinking inward and folding my arms reflexively, I wished that I had worn a thicker sweater. Something faint and pleasant met my nose—the lingering scent of roses and lemongrass, I thought. Not what I'd been expecting—although, in fairness, I wasn't sure what that had been. The pervasive, metallic smell of blood? Did I expect to see the vampires standing around a body like wolves, their teeth sunk into it, like some Discovery Channel documentary?

I held my breath and peered out. The suite was dark, moody, lit only by candles.

And it positively *heaved* with people.

The room was round with tall ceilings, easily the height of a large theater. There were dark wooden pillars positioned around the floor, holding up what appeared to be a round balcony overhead. Right in the middle of the room, beneath the balcony, was what I assumed was the dance floor, for there were a few dozen people moving gracefully through pools of light.

The suite was a fascinating combination of old and new. The walls and windows were large, tall, and modern, all glass and metal and sleek lines, providing a view of the city out of one side, the open and expansive bay on the other. The floors were dark wood, inlaid in a herringbone pattern, clean and sleek. But the small collections of furniture spread around the room were chaise longues and high-backed chairs and sprawling settees, all in plush red velvet and blue silks that looked like they'd came straight out of a Victorian novel. People—or vampires probably—lounged comfortably, some with drinks in hand, some with arms thrown around others.

At the edges of the expansive windows were massive old-fashioned curtains, the heavy kind you'd see on a theater stage—for blocking out sunlight, I assumed. Now that the sun was down, they'd been thrown back for these partygoers to admire Tampa's impressive views.

For all my wild imaginings, in the short period I'd been able to ponder it, these vampires were downright *ordinary*. Most were a little older than me, at least in looks—but then, what was the myth about vampires? Once bitten, they were locked into the same age, even centuries on. The twenty-something whispering into the ear of a beautiful woman on the couch? He could've been a thousand years old, for all I knew.

A chill ran through me again, different from the cold in from the room. How old could Byron be? He might have watched

Shakespeare performed in the original Globe Theater.

I hesitantly took a step inside, trying to rearrange my face into the picture of calm. A few eyes flicked my way—another shiver caressed my spine. Vampires.

At least none of them moved toward me. Maybe I was blending in?

Or maybe they just didn't care.

I wondered if everyone in the room was a vampire, or if any of them were humans. Did humans and vampires hang out? Was that a thing? That didn't seem possible. What human would be insane enough to hang out with a vampire? Unless they didn't know …

There was a bar ahead of me. Curved, made of one entire log, and carved intricately, it stood in front of the windows and the sprawling view of Tampa Bay. An epoxy-like veneer reflected the glimmering lights from the bay like water. Beyond, a balcony opened to Florida's night air. There were quite a few people moving around on it, and I saw a dark surface along one side—an infinity-edge pool.

A sleek staircase curved along one side of the room up to the balcony, which seemed to made entirely of glass and had no railing on one side. I would definitely be able to look out over the room better if I were up there, I realized. So, carefully meandering through the throng, I made my way toward it, acutely aware of every pair of eyes on me.

Still, I forced my face to reflect calm.

I wasn't going to let them see me sweat.

It wasn't easy, though. One vampire, in the form of Byron, had been bad enough. Now I was in a room full of them—and penetrating deeper, my every step bringing me farther into the crowd—and farther away from the exit.

My heart thumped frantically in my chest.

With every thud, I willed it to be silent—for surely these creatures could hear, could identify me as not one of their kin—for their hearts surely no longer beat, no longer pumped thick, hot blood—

Stop it, I thought, grinding my teeth. *You haven't been bitten yet. It's a good sign, isn't it?*

I hadn't been immediately bitten by Byron either, though.

Sweat slicked my palms, icy in the chill.

Up the stairs, between two couches. New eyes on me. Taking in my expression? Or eyeing my neck?

I made my way to the edge of the balcony. A railing wrapped it, overlooking the dance floor.

As casually as I could—which was not very casual at all—I lounged against it.

Trying to blot out a thousand thoughts all vying to be loudest—fear of detection; my fight-or-flight response, which was firing off madly; the vampires' many advantages over me, including numbers, strength, *fangs*—I tried both to blend in and to take stock of the suite's lower floor.

Cliques, I suddenly realized. I hadn't spotted it down below—but up here, looking down, the segregation was more readily apparent.

The vampires on the dance floor, fluid and elegant, all wore what I would consider modern clothes. Most of them didn't look any older than I was—maybe a year, two at most. The girls wore graphic tees and jeans, rompers or short, cute dresses. The guys wore button-up shirts and shorts, or V-neck shirts and jeans. Many of them had sunglasses nestled in their hair as well—purely aesthetic, since none of them could actually be out in the sun.

Then there was the group on the balcony, many of whom wore long elegant dresses, or dark suits with long coat tails. I could even see one wearing a top hat. Another group down by the bar looked a little wilder than some of the others. Some had torn shirts or dirty, ripped pants. They didn't appear to be interested in the others around them. I watched some knock back a line of shot glasses.

My stomach turned over. I made a note to give them a wide berth. They looked like a rough crowd.

It was like the weird social circles in high school. The closer I looked, the more obvious the division between them all was. It didn't look like there was much intermingling happening. Well, that was one similarity between us—my species, and theirs.

It didn't ease my stomach much.

"Well, good evening," said a voice through the din, as soft as the velvet settees. To my left, two gentlemen stood beside me at the railing.

The man closest to me, leaning casually on the rail, looked to be about nineteen or twenty. He was quite good-looking and smiled effortlessly at me. He reminded me of those actors in old movies, sophisticated and handsome. His dark hair was short and styled in messy spikes, short along the sides. He had broad shoulders and was taller than Byron. His green eyes gazed at me with great intensity.

The other man was even taller, but much broader. He had a wide jaw, a large nose, and sandy hair that hung over his dark, aggressive eyes. His brow was furrowed as if annoyed by everything around him. He reminded me of a movie villain's sidekick: kind of dumb, more brawn than brains. His eyes were intense in a distasteful sort of way, prodding at me. I didn't dare look away for fear it'd make me seem like frightened prey, so I just stared back at him. His look and bearing reminded me of the Cro-Magnons we'd studied in school.

I swallowed, keeping tight rein on my panic; two vampires were talking to me. "Hello."

"I don't believe I've seen you around here before," the first, handsome man said, his smile widening. "And I know pretty much everyone at these parties."

I brushed a stray curl from my eyes and lifted a fake smile. Somehow, it was easier than I had thought it would be. "Yeah, I don't know you either. It's a lot busier tonight than I would have expected."

The handsome one arched an eyebrow, and then he and the man beside him laughed a little. "Really? I guess the last few times that Lord Draven has called a clan meeting like this, more of the sects have shown up."

I looked down into the dance floor and gestured to the trendy group out there. "Well, I knew that they would come."

The handsome one nodded, and the not-handsome man beside him followed suit. "You always know that they will come. Now, the Blackrose clan," he said, pointing to some of the elegantly dressed individuals up on the balcony with them. "Them I'm surprised to see." He had an accent—one I couldn't quite place, owing to its faintness. Scandinavian?

"Me too," I lied.

"Of course," the not-handsome one murmured, eyeing them warily, "after last time …" The handsome one nodded. "Thought for sure we were going to have another war on our hands." His voice had dropped too.

Another war? I filed that one away for later. It didn't bear pressing on right now.

"What about them?" I asked, pointing down at the vampires down by the bar. "Do you recognize them?"

"Apparently someone owes them a favor," said Handsome. "And you know how vampires can be about ensuring they get what they are owed." He leaned closer. "I think they're Irish, originally. Clan name is Conall."

I tried to hide my jaw clenching. I didn't care about the clan name, but that bit of character insight to vampires was interesting. Byron certainly thought I owed him something.

"So, mystery lady," the man said. He really was attractive, but I was more afraid than I was attracted. He, however, seemed pleased with what he was looking at. "What's your name? We may as well be properly introduced."

There was a choice that I had to make. It probably wouldn't do for me to admit that I was a human—especially after lying just now to blend in.

The text messages I had received flooded back into my mind: there were people here that I could trust.

I shuffled my ankle around in my boot—and I felt the presence of the stake up against my calf.

At least I had that. I wasn't completely without the ability to defend myself. And so I smiled, a toothy grin this time, and prepared to once again do the thing I was best at:

Lie.

Chapter 17

There's a secret to lying, and it's this: if you're going to tell a series of lies, you need to keep them small and as close to your experience as best you can. Because if you go out there and tell a series of big lies, you're a lot more likely to get caught.

Trying my best to look seductive—lips pouted, a finger in my hair, movie seductress style—and hoping vampires would fall for it (not unreasonable, with the likes of Byron and the way Mr. Handsome was looking at me at the moment), I introduced myself:

"I'm Elizabeth." Middle name—little lie, easy to remember.

"You new to the area, Elizabeth?" the taller, handsome vamp asked, turning his body toward me.

I laughed as heartily as I could without sounding fake and winked at him. *Winked.* What? Who did I think I was? "Is it that obvious?"

The music down below changed to a deeper, darker beat, and the vampires' moods changed too. Many of them moved to partner up with someone, their bodies entwining until they looked like one person. For little old me, used to high school dances, this was ... way more intense. There was a level of intimacy on display here that made me uneasy, but I put away that discomfort and smiled at the handsome man who wasn't actually a man.

The music was making my head swim. I shook it ever so

slightly to clear it.

The vampire across from me grinned, showing all of his teeth. "Maybe a little," he said, leaning a little closer. He studied my face a little too closely, and I wondered if the jig was up already. "So where are you from?"

"New York," I answered. "And no, before you ask, I'm not from the city. I'm from a little ho-dunk town outside of Syracuse. You wouldn't have heard of it."

Not a lie—though I probably sounded like a vampire hipster, answering that way. Did vampires have hipsters? Maybe they drank artisanal, small-batch blood. Whatever the case, I didn't really want them to know exactly where I was from. Someone could find out my history, or about my parents, and that was just too much.

The handsome vamp just smiled at me, waiting for me to go on.

I tried my best to appease him without nailing myself down. "Let's just say it snows a ton, the sun goes down very early in winter, and the closest Starbucks is at least thirty minutes away."

The vampire grinned, and then he laughed. His friend the unhandsome remained stoic, his stern face even uglier by virtue of its stubborn refusal to relax. "Must have made the hunt a little more difficult, huh?" He shook his head. "I hate those small towns. It's so much harder to make someone disappear quietly, without attracting attention."

I nodded pointedly. "You aren't kidding." Even so, a new shiver ran its way down my spine, settling into the small of my back and refusing to leave. A reminder—a real one—of what, who, I was dealing with—and what they could do to me.

"So what's your sect? You didn't mention them," he prodded, and looked curiously at me again. "Or are you more of the loner type?"

Sect. They mentioned clans earlier, and I did a quick sweep of the room. He had mentioned the Blackrose clan, and I knew immediately that he must have meant family of sorts. Obviously not all people were turned into vampires with their real families, though I was sure that must happen sometimes. But a sect must be like their version of a family. It made me wonder how they were chosen or formed—though asking was off limits here. "It's a small group that I met a couple of years back," I said, vague, airy, but hopefully with enough confidence that he was satisfied by the answer. "They were wonderful to me, but I didn't really want to stay in the same place for my whole life, you know? I like to travel."

The handsome guy me arched an eyebrow, and he and the silent one beside him exchanged glances. The quiet one even frowned.

"Just visiting," I added hastily. "A vacation, really. To see the place where one of my friends is from."

They both nodded, as if in understanding. I held back my sigh of relief.

I mentally filed away what I'd learned. Apparently vampires held their sects in some regard. That suggested to me that they were tight-knit groups. So me pretending to be here without mine was almost seen as a no-no. Apparently it wasn't that weird for vampires to take vacations, though, so I had dodged that bullet.

Maybe.

Still, despite their nods, neither spoke for the next few moments. The good-looking one's brow was furrowed, like he was trying to process my answer, even though he had already responded to it. Worry started to creep up again into my stomach, tightening my chest.

"What about you?" I asked, looking back over at them, hoping the question would derail whatever thought process was currently unfolding behind those intense green eyes. "I pretty much just told you my entire after-life story. You owe me." Another exchange of looks—silent communication. It set off alarm bells in my head, but I had to do my best to save this before it totally unspooled. So I asked, "What about your sects?"

The handsome one did a short, sweeping bow, which sort of surprised me. Very graceful. I made a mental note to myself to not fall down the stairs lest I give myself away immediately.

"My name is Theodore, and this is Mill." Mr. Handsome gestured over his shoulder. "But I go by Theo nowadays."

Nowadays? Just how old was this guy?

The one named Mill inclined his head but didn't move his eyes from my face. There was something about the intensity of his gaze that bothered me, and I couldn't tell whether it was because he was viewing me as food or a curiosity. Either way, it was deeply discomforting.

Mill was an interesting name, but I definitely didn't want to inquire about its origin. And Theodore sounded as old-fashioned as Byron.

Their names was the full extent of their answer though. Vampires held their cards close to their chests, apparently. I guess I didn't blame them. They didn't know me, I didn't know them.

Problem was, how could I get them to spill their guts?

As long as I didn't look like a threat to them, then I guess that was what mattered. I needed them to trust me, even if it was only marginally. If they didn't then it was likely I would end up as dinner.

Or breakfast, depending on the time.

"Well, it was nice to meet you both," I replied. I subtly turned my body away, as if to close the conversation.

"Likewise," Theo answered, and his easy smile made me feel a little more relaxed again. I kept my body angled away, though, continuing my watch over the suite's lower floor.

Again the music changed, this time to something more upbeat. A few others from around the room streamed toward the dance floor, clans finally starting to mingle in the middle of the room below.

"Do you dance, Elizabeth?" Theo asked.

"Only a little," I replied. I fumbled around for eras and dates in my mind. "I learned waltz in my younger years, but it's been a long time."

Yeah, I never learned how to waltz. I was lucky that I hadn't fallen off the stage doing ballet when I was five.

"I do enjoy dancing," Theo replied. "Though it has been a long time since I have found a worthy partner. "

He gave me a sly look and I felt my cheeks flush. Good thing the room was dark; it probably hid my face better. The last thing I needed was for a vampire to see pools of blood beneath my skin. Talk about temptation. The music faded, and all of the vampires on the dance floor moved back underneath the pillars and the balcony, gracefully, and almost as one. No command was given, which made it look all the more odd to an outsider like me. I glanced at Theo, but he evinced no sign of surprise, so I kept my own interest contained, just watching, placidly, as the sea of vampires below parted. A gong crashed, loud, and the last few stragglers on the dance floor moved away.

"About time," Theo mumbled under his breath. "Late, as usual."

I wasn't sure where the sound had come from, but it definitely shut everyone up. The other vampires up along the balcony had moved to the railing to peer down into the dance floor, just as Theo, Mill, and I were. A tall, dark-haired woman with black eyes came to stand beside me, apparently entirely unaware of my presence. I tried not to look at her, but I could feel her beside me, like a gaping black hole of cold standing next to me. Her dark eyes were focused over the balcony, not a thought spared for anything else. Around the rail, I saw the same, dozens of vampires totally focused on what was going on below.

Something was happening, and my heart begin to speed up. Whatever it was, I guessed that this was what I had been brought here for.

Chapter 18

"That's the governor for this territory."

I glanced over and realized a second late that it was Mill who had spoken. His voice was deeper than Theo's, almost raspy, like he didn't speak often. His eyes were on me, watching me carefully.

I raised my eyebrows in surprise but hoped that it came off more like irritation. "I knew that already but thank you."

Mill grunted and turned his attention back to the dance floor.

"Don't mind him," Theo whispered, his hand over his mouth. "He idolizes Lord Draven like no one else."

There was that name again.

Murmurs filtered through the crowd, and I looked down to see an eerily tall man—almost seven feet—standing in the middle of the dance floor, gazing around and up at all of the gathered vampires. He had long legs, long arms, and long fingers. His fingertips were pressed together in front of him.

He was wearing a dark suit, absolutely pristine. It looked expensive and was cut to fit him perfectly. His ivory shirt beneath the suit coat was only a shade paler than his skin. His flesh almost glowed, like the pale light from the moon on a clear night. His hair, slicked back and thick, had streaks of grey near the temples.

His mouth split open in a smile, and I almost recoiled. Long, sharp, thin teeth protruded out of his mouth, past his bottom lip—and then, just as quickly, they retracted. My heart did not just flutter, it practically pitched a spazz. I hoped like hell my poker face was as good as I thought it was. Whatever age he might have been when he was turned, I got the distinct impression Lord Draven was old. *Really old.* Maybe as old as the city itself. Theo, Mill, or even Byron didn't look anything like him. This man standing below me almost looked feral, like the sort of vampires in stories and movies. The others could easily pass as humans, and many of them did, Byron included.

But this man, this vampire, definitely couldn't mingle with us.

He held out his hands in a sweeping gesture, still beaming with that fanged smile at all of the faces that were turned to look at him. There was genuine pleasure in his look, but it was tempered with a coldness that made me want to shiver. I forced myself to keep looking at him, and to put a smile of my own up, matching the vamps clustered along the balcony rail.

"Friends, family, comrades." His voice was deep, like a rumbling river, carrying the entire span of the suite, booming off the windows. And then he paused—and in that silence, not one person spoke, even a murmur. No one dared. It was like the most intimidating teacher in high school times a thousand, silencing every soul in his class with lethal precision.

If there *were* any souls in the room, apart from me.

"Thank you all for coming this evening. It is a glorious occasion when we can all get together like this and behave like civilized beings."

Low laughter spread around the room. Lord Draven held up his hands again.

"It is important for us to get together, and to share stories and news from the other corners of the world, but at the end of the day, we are still the sects in control of this little corner of the Sunshine State."

Theo and Mill shared a snicker, and I realized the irony in the joke as well. It did seem strange that vampires would choose Florida as a place to live, being that there was so much, well, sunshine.

"I am glad to see that we can put aside our differences in order to better our own way of living. It is hard enough without conflict among ourselves." His gaze was cool as it swept over the room. From the little that Theo had said, he must be referring to the Blackrose clan and whatever dispute they had had.

His fingertips came back together, his hands looking like white, glowing spiders.

"We have done very well here in Tampa over the years, better than some sects have done in other parts of the state, I say with certitude."

He began pacing in a circle. Every eye followed him. "We have seen much success, and our sects have flourished, all without the knowledge of the humans."

I swallowed.

He stopped, and he grinned as he looked up into the balcony. Fear stabbed through me—was he looking at *me*?—but then his gaze moved back to the lower floor.

"But the days behind us will pale in comparison to the days ahead, this I promise. Be prepared, my flock, to take full advantage of the bounty that is to come."

Servants, or butlers, dressed like the sort who'd wait on a lord or lady in an English manor, had been meandering through the party. I'd snatched glimpses of them, although like any good butler, they mostly kept themselves out of sight, appearing only as a sliver between shadows.

Lord Draven beckoned one forward now.

The servant approached, bowed, and offered a tray. Upon it stood a single crystal flute. Its contents were dark—almost black.

Lord Draven took the glass, and the server excused himself, bowing again.

With a wide smile on his face, fangs bared once more, Lord Draven lifted his glass high into the air as a toast. Glasses seemed to appear from nowhere, were raised all across the room as the vampire gathering followed suit. Theo and Mill lifted their own, and I wondered how I had missed them before.

My knees turned to jelly.

Blood. They were holding champagne flutes of *blood*. I had to hold onto the railing to keep from falling over.

"To the naive, ignorant cattle," Lord Draven toasted. "May they ever be unconcerned about the threat to their necks."

Laughter came from the crowd—and even as my stomach roiled, as I felt myself teetering on a knife edge above an abyss, I forced myself to join in.

"Here, here!" many others cried—and the glasses were upended—drained.

I didn't have one, I noted with a spike of panic. But then, not everyone did—but then again, Theo and Mill were nearby—and Mill was watching me.

Why did he keep staring at me like that?

Lord Draven said no more. He seemed to vanish, in fact; the brief glance from the drinkers, lifting high their flutes of—blood—to Theo and Mill, and back again was enough for him to dematerialize. The party returned, as though it had not been interrupted at all: the music restarted, and the dancers returned to their dim pools of blue and purple and green light.

"He may not be prompt, but he does give engaging speeches," Theo said, still looking down at the dance floor.

"And brief," I said, eyeing their drained glasses with what I hoped was a hungering eye rather than disgust.

A stocky vampire appeared and, without a word to them, placed a hand on Mill's shoulder and whispered something in his ear.

Mill glanced at me again and nodded his head. Then he and the stocky man turned and left without a word, disappearing into the crowd.

Theo was nodding his head to the beat, the glass still in his hands. When the lights below strobed, I could see the bright red streaks inside the glass, all that was left of the … the drink.

I rubbed my hands over my arms. Goosebumps again, and because of the temperature.

Why had I even come here? My mysterious texter had lured

me here, baited me with answers, like a worm dangled before a fish—and for what? There were no answers that I could see, nothing that would help me stop Byron. Had I been supposed to meet someone?

Whatever the case, it hadn't happened.

And I wasn't stupid enough to believe that these vampires would believe my lie for very long. More than ever I felt exposed standing here, especially now that Mill had gone. And the way his gaze had fallen upon me time and again …

Did he know? I needed to get out of here. Even if he didn't—even if none of them had any clue. Because despite the fact that Byron might have enemies in this place, Lord Draven's speech had been perfectly clear: vampires did not think of humans as anything more than food. What an idiot I was, to think this would be a good idea.

Best to leave—to get home, and to text my mystery "helper" from the comfort of my room, where I was *not* surrounded by hordes of vampires.

"How about you and I take a little walk?" Theo suggested. His eyes looked darker, somehow, as I glanced to him, jolted out of my thoughts. A smile tugged at one corner of his mouth.

"I was actually just thinking that I probably should be going—"

There was suddenly a cold gust of wind, and Theo was standing close to me, his lips pressed to my ear.

It was incredible how quickly he had gotten so close to me. I hadn't even noticed it until it happened. Byron had done the same thing, and the fear made my breath catch in my throat.

"Nonsense," he said, his voice as smooth as silk, and he turned me around gently. He wasn't aggressive, but his hand was resting on my lower back—barely a touch, but I didn't think it would be wise to refuse him—and so I allowed him to guide me to double glass doors behind us.

The night air was cool on my face, but I felt hot with fear. My skin burned where his hand hovered over my back.

He steered me along between the glass-topped tables with ease. Then he opened the door for me, the panes frosted and dark.

My heart was in my throat, choking me. It took everything I had not to puke it up—not to bolt.

Surely he knew. And surely the other vampires around us did too—it would be written all over me, in the way my body moved, rigid and stilted and mechanical. Yet except for the usual passing glances, we were paid no heed at all. Theo guided me to the edge of the balcony. Distantly, I could just appreciate that the view was breathtaking. Tampa Bay stretched out before us, the lights from the surrounding buildings glittering like fireflies on its still, dark surface.

The wind was strong up this high, and it whipped across my cheeks. It felt like standing on the beach. Stray curls flicked toward my face and I caught the scent of my shampoo, strong and floral.

Could Theo smell it on me? Could he smell my flesh?

Had I given myself away via simply what I was?

I kept back the shiver, fought off the chill. Whether Theo was by my side or not, him or any of a hundred other vampires in this place—up here I was completely, utterly alone in the world.

Theo had acquired another champagne flute on our way. He leaned casually on the glass railing.

He swirled the glass. Blood lolled about, thick and crimson and metallic.

"This view is just spectacular, isn't it?" He sounded so calm, so conversational, no hint of the menace his voice had carried a moment before.

Something was off about him. He had been so cordial to me the entire time we were inside. But as soon as Mill left, his demeanor changed. He hadn't lost his poise or his charm, but he seemed … hungrier, somehow. Like his drink was laced with testosterone.

"Don't you agree, Elizabeth?"

"What?" I said. *Idiot. That was the name you gave him, remember?* "Oh, of course. Very nice."

He snickered, and then stood up taller. He really was very

handsome, but in a very different way than Byron was. More...animalistic in his magnetism. He moved to stand in front of me again and traced a finger down the side of my cheek.

Almost exactly like how Byron had.

My skin felt like it had been seared where his finger touched.

"So tell me, *Elizabeth* …" He smiled wryly. "Why did you really come out here tonight?"

My mind whirled, trying desperately to come up with any sort of reason that would make sense. It was a vampire meeting, of course; shouldn't that be reason enough? What other reason would a vampire have for coming to this sort of event?

"I—" I started to say, but he shook his head.

"Never mind. It doesn't actually matter." His mouth parted in a wide grin—and a long, thin pair of fangs extended where his canines should have been.

Chapter 19

If I was honest with myself, since first meeting Byron, since finding out what he truly was, this was how I thought my life would end. It all led to this moment, now, fangs meeting my flesh, blood spilling out of me, filling my captor's mouth—and I would die, slowly, in pain, unable to stop the blood being pulled from my fingers, my toes, and then my limbs, and finally from my heart, swallow by vampiric swallow. How long would I be conscious? For how long would I scream, feeling it?

And what next?

Would the police find my body? How long would it take for my parents to realize I was actually missing? Probably some time tomorrow. They would spend most of the day furious at me for sneaking out, not actually knowing that I was already dead. Then they would start to worry, and eventually call the police. They would look and look, probably track my text messages that led me here … and who knows?

Maybe they would find my lifeless husk with this stunning view over the balcony.

In that moment, Theo's fangs bared, I realized that all of the fights I had had with my parents had been stupid. Really stupid. And that I had not, in my seventeen years, left anything behind that was worth talking about.

Nothing good, at least.

That, in combination with simple survival instinct, cemented it in me: my time to go was not yet, could not be, *would not be*.

All of these thoughts flew through my mind inside of just a fraction of a second—and then I was glad that my dad had forced me to take those dumb defense lessons as an elective in my junior year. Ducking my head out of Theo's reach, I threw my arm up. I saw his eyes widen, another fraction of a second—then my elbow slammed the bridge of his nose.

It hurt more than anything I had ever felt before, but it was enough to throw him off for a half of a second—and I turned to run, not checking to see how much damage I had done, if any. Theo unleashed a deep, predatory snarl that seemed to sound in my ears like an air horn.

My chest went cold—and then Theo grabbed the back of my neck and yanked me backward.

I fell into him. It was like slamming into a wall. The wind shot out of me. Stars erupted against my eyelids, pain radiating from the back of my skull.

He grabbed for my shoulders, but I pulled one free. He snatched up my wrist instead, locking it in place.

He was really strong, and I could tell that he was not going to hold back anymore. He'd underestimated me the first time, and he was not going to make that mistake again.

Worse: this close, I could see that my elbow hadn't hurt him in the slightest. If I had hit a human that hard, it would have broken their nose. But Theo might as well have been made of solid marble; it had only made him angry.

He laughed, his face a sneer, his fangs still visible.

He thought this was funny. He knew he had won.

Not yet, pal. He pulled me closer—

One chance, Cassie.

—and I slammed the heel of my right palm into his eye.

Apparently vampires' eyes were still somewhat vulnerable, because he cried out in pain. Doubled over, he clutched for his eye with his free hand.

I tried to reach down to my boot, but he was still holding onto my wrist, and yanked me closer to him again.

He sure recovered quickly. And now he was just even more pissed.

He grabbed me by the shoulders and pulled me back into his body, pressing my chest to his.

I held up my arms as high as I could to protect my neck and face.

He was too strong, and I couldn't do anything. Try as I might, every fiber of my body screaming, I could—not—move!

Panic flared—fear unlike any that had flooded my veins with icy terror before. This was it—this was actually it. I was going to die.

Theo looked down at me almost lustfully. His fangs bared. His eyes were aglow with madness, an animal desire for my blood.

NO!

Fear-fueled adrenaline pulsed through me, granting me a last-ditch, desperate burst of strength—and I thrust out, fingers hooked into claws—and sunk them into his eyes.

Theo screamed.

He released me in an instant. Already scrambling backward, I stared as he gripped his eyes with both hands—and from beneath them, shining black liquid ran down his cheeks.

I stared at my fingers—also black.

I wouldn't eat with my hands ever again.

My brain caught up to me. *You're free! Go!*

Right. Twisting on my heel, I leaned into a run—

Theo lunged at me from behind. My feet went out from under me—and both of us toppled, spinning, a tangle of limbs—I pushed myself up onto hands and knees and skittered across the stained wooden deck as fast as I could.

The back of my head slammed against a cement wall, and the throbbing pain and spots returned. I collapsed on the floor, my back to the wall.

I was trapped. The doors were somehow farther away than when we had walked outside.

Theo was getting to his feet—and laughing, a maniacal cackle that carried out over the bay. Every last semblance of humanity seemed to have departed him.

Black ooze smeared his cheeks like tar.

He lumbered closer. My heart beat madly. My eyes darted, seeking salvation. But I had no way out. He was between me and my only exit. And I knew that all of those other vampires inside would not help me, even if by some miracle I managed to make it past him. In fact, they might decide that they wanted me for their prey instead.

Maybe it was better to just get it over with. I didn't think that my heart could take any more, anyways.

But wait—

The stake. Theo sneered. "Why the long face, *Elizabeth*? What? You didn't think that I knew?" His face hardened. "You must have taken me for stupid."

I inched my fingers toward the edge of my boot. I kept my eyes on him, showing him the depth of my fear. I didn't have to lie at all about how terrified I was. If I was slower than he was, then I was dead.

Even if I was able to get the stake, I could still be dead.

My fingertips touched the smooth wood, and I felt a thrill of hope, like a breath in my lungs when I was desperate for air. I pulled it closer, wrapping a finger around it.

Theo licked one of his fangs. "You were the stupid one to come here."

Then he lunged—

I was ready. Ripping the stake free of my boot—and scraping the tip along my leg on the way—I drew it up—

His face hurtled toward mine—reached me—

And I slammed the wooden point in between two of his ribs, right where I hoped his heart was. He gasped, almost frozen in air for a moment. Then his full weight slumped against me. I shrieked—he wasn't dead; the stake hadn't done it!—but then I shoved, and he rolled limply off.

His face was unmoving, a last glimpse of fear captured on it. Dark blood was oozing out of the corner of his mouth, and also from the wound in his chest.

It coated my hands, thick and black. Tear welled. Revulsion was like a kick in the stomach, at all this darkness everywhere, staining me—and guilt, guilt that I'd killed, even though my own life had been on the line ...

As I watched, his body started to almost sink into the floor beneath him. There was a pool forming beneath him of the same dark substance that was leaking from his lips. It was disgusting, and smelled putrid, like an animal carcass in the heat. The skin on his face started to pull and ripple, like it was turning to liquid. The bones on his hands were prominent for a few seconds, as well as the bones in his knees, his elbows, and even his cheekbones. And then—they all started to soften and decompose, so quickly I could not even make out the features of his face anymore—the features of the creature who'd tried to kill me. In the aftermath, the night was quiet. No horns honked below, and the breeze off the bay was still, like death—like Theo, or what was left of him.

I was alive. There were no bites on me.

The stake had *worked*.

So my mysterious texter *had* been looking out for me.

Each heartbeat felt like a relief. I clutched my hands over my heart, my back pressed against the railing. My hands, legs, and shoulders trembled, and I didn't think that I would be able to stand if I tried.

I wondered, somewhere in the back of my mind, if I was going into shock. That was what happened to people, right?

I had to find a way out. I had to figure out how to get out of here.

But how was I going to cover up the blood all over my arms?

The best answer I could muster was my jeans. Not the same black as Theo's blood, but still dark nonetheless, and combined with the lighting back in the suite, I could maybe get away with it. Of course, that didn't mean a vampire wouldn't smell it on me ... but maybe, between the champagne flutes of human blood, I'd get lucky and they'd be distracted.

The job I made of smearing it away wasn't perfect—far from it, in fact. And I could see, too easily, where the ooze lay thickly over the denim. But it was as clean as I was going to get with the tools I had.

And that meant it was time to leave.

But as I pushed up, and caught sight of the increasingly tarry, pulped mass that had once been Theo, a wave of nausea—at what had just happened, at the fear of Byron, of being detected, of slipping past that mass of murderous creatures—swept over me. Legs threatening to buckle, I clutched the balcony's rail, and vomited over the edge, loud, racking spasms that emptied my stomach of every last drop, till I was retching and bringing up nothing at all.

Finally, it petered out.

Forehead pressed against the railing—it was cool in the night, a small blessing—I pondered on the fact that if I lived long enough to ever get to a therapist's office, I was going to make that son of a bitch a rich man trying to reconcile myself to the events of the last few days. Something moved at the corner of my eye, past the congealed mass that had been Theo's body.

Standing at the door, Cro-Magnon brow furrowed more heavily than I'd seen yet, was Mill.

He glanced at me, barely standing, nearly mad with fear, then his eyes traced their way over to what was left of Theo's body. He took it in quickly, calculation rolling through those eyes …

… And then he looked back at me.

His body was rigid, and his face was unreadable when his gaze finally found mine again, but it wouldn't have taken a brilliant mind—just a barely functional one, like mine right at that moment—to read the dark thoughts that were written all over his face.

Chapter 20

I held the stake out in front of me like a dagger. "Don't come any closer!"

Mill took a step toward me.

My hands began to tremble in earnest, but I kept the stake pointed in his direction.

"I'm serious!" I said.

Mill lifted his hands in the air. "Listen, Elizabeth ... if that's your real name ..." He nodded his head in the direction of Theo's body. "We aren't all like him."

"Oh yeah?" I said. My brain felt like it was thundering along on a freight train, a hundred miles an hour in any direction. Part of me hoped with everything that I had in me that he was telling me the truth. It was too dangerous to hope for that, though. All I could believe in that moment was the power of the stake in my hands.

"Aren't all like him? So that means that what, ninety-nine percent of you are?"

"No," he said. "More like ninety percent. "

I rolled my eyes dramatically. "And what, you fall into that ten percent?"

He nodded.

"What makes you think I would trust you?"

Mill lowered his hands slightly, and then shrugged his shoulders. "There is nothing I could say now that is going to convince you. But I know something that might."

I grimaced. "I'm not in the mood to play mind games. "

"No games, just the truth," he responded. He took another step toward me.

"There is an entire room of vampires between you and your way out of here. If they catch you having done this … what do you think is going to happen to you?"

I adjusted the stake in my hands, still pointed at him. "So you aren't going to curse me or swear vengeance for your friend?"

Mill spared the body a short glance. "He was no friend of mine."

"Really?" I asked. "You looked pretty chummy to me. "

"Do you have any idea what it's like to live in a world of heartless indifference? To live among a people who kill without conscience, without care? Who feed like locusts on human beings? Whose loyalty is so fickle, so transitory that the alliances change every month or so?" Mill's gaze burned with intensity. "There can be no friends in this society; only allies of convenience." He gave the black puddle that was Theo one last look.

Glancing back at the doors, he said, "I'll guide you back through the room before anyone can come out here and find this. We should hurry, though."

Right. The fact that so much had gone on, that there had been so much noise, and no one had heard and come investigating— was fortunate. My luck couldn't hold forever though.

Mill was offering me an exit—

But then, just ten minutes ago he'd been running like Theo's wingman.

"You don't have much time to make a decision," Mill said. "So you'd better come to it quick."

I glanced back toward the balcony, out over the city sprawled out before me. It was so beautiful.

If Mill was lying, it was likely I was going to die this night, whether by my own hand or by someone else's.

Which meant I didn't really have a choice.

"How are you going to get me through there?" I flicked the stake toward the door.

"The same way you came in—casually."

"So we just walk right out. Like nothing happened?"

"Yes," he said, "it's that simple. Act like you belong, like nothing has happened."

I glared at him. "You know I can't believe a word you are saying, right?"

Mill sighed. "If you want to get out of here alive, I'd suggest you try."

A sound from instead made me turn. Talking, drifting out as someone or someones passed close by the doors—then a tinkle of laughter.

It faded.

Still safe.

Mill said, "You better make up your mind soon."

I really didn't have a choice. I had to trust him. He was quickly becoming the only chance I had of possibly getting out of here alive.

And I hated it.

I harbored a dark suspicion that he was going to turn on me as soon as we were inside and I was surrounded by the blood sucking freaks. He was going to lull me into an even more false sense of security than Theo had by trying to be my friend, and then abandon me, or bite me right then and there. It would be certain death.

But it was my only way out. So: "Okay," I said reluctantly. "What do we do?"

"First, you have to put that stake away."

I laughed hoarsely. "Yeah, right."

"I don't mean out of reach," Mill said. "Just out of sight. Do you want to walk into a room full of vampires carrying a stake? Because it's a little like walking into a human party carrying a knife."

I stared at the stake, then back at him.

I slid it into my messy bun up on top of my head, so it would be easy to reach.

Mill nodded, then gestured at the door. "Come on."

Hesitantly, I approached. My legs felt like they'd gone to jelly—but they took me.

When I was within Mill's reach, I stopped.

He didn't try to grab me—and so, with bated breath, I moved closer still.

He pulled the door open, and immediately he snaked his arm around my waist.

I nearly back-handed him, but he pushed me gently inside.

The music was louder than I remembered, and I could hardly hear Mill when he leaned closer to me and murmured in my ear.

"Pretend we were just having a drink and a laugh outside. Now, laugh quietly, like I just said something funny. "

I surprised myself when I obeyed. It sounded way more nervous than flirtatious, but I think I made my point. Another lie, and they were coming easier all the time.

I had half-expected everyone to look at us when we walked back in, but no one noticed. It didn't make sense. I'd just murdered a vampire outside, wore the murder weapon in my hair, and had his blood smeared all over my jeans, with traces on my face and under my fingernails. How could any of them not see this?

Maybe they weren't as cunning as I thought they were.

Mill took the long way around the room, away from most of the other vampires, and toward the glass stairs. My knees trembled. I hoped they wouldn't give me away.

"Nice idea on the stake, by the way," he murmured, "putting it in your hair like that."

"Not too obvious?" I said, the venom loud and clear in my tone.

Mill laughed quietly, and put his hand on my shoulder, drawing me closer to him.

"Acting like you have something to hide is the surest way to be found out. Putting it in plain sight and walking confidently? It practically guarantees that no one will challenge you."

Another couple was walking up the stairs as we descended. The woman was devastatingly beautiful, with dark eyes and platinum blond hair, long, flowing and perfect. The man she walked in front of was just as gorgeous, with dark eyes and ebony hair.

Xandra was right. Everything about them was meant to draw humans in.

But I could clearly see them all for what they were when they smiled, baring their pointed teeth—monsters.

"I suppose it's a good thing," Mill said when we were on the bottom floor. The lights from the dance floor washed over his face one second, and then plunged him into darkness the next. "That the way you kill vampires is common knowledge, I mean."

"What do you mean?" I asked.

I could see the elevator. It was right there, on the other side of the rounded room. It was so close I was almost in tears. Just a few more seconds.

"You knew exactly where to stake Theo," Mill said, even more quietly. He was walking behind me, bending closer to speak in my ear.

"Like you said, it's well known," I said, pretending like it hadn't been a lucky guess informed by over a century of pop culture. "Like sunlight … right?"

Mill nodded, a fake smile on his face. He was trying to keep up appearances. So I smiled too. To anyone else, we were having a perfectly pleasantly conversation.

"Fire?"

He nodded again.

I grinned, for real this time, in spite of myself. This was helping. "Garlic?"

"Speaking for myself, yes, I am repulsed by garlic. But not because it can hurt me," he added when he saw the smirk on my face. "I just think it reeks. Most vamps would still bite you anyway."

Now I understood why Byron thought it was so funny that I had strewn garlic all over my kitchen.

We made our way through a particularly dense group, who parted relatively easily. They were too immersed in the music to really pay us much mind.

And then we were at the elevator. Freedom—or the confined, steel room when Mill would finish me off, alone, in a space so small I'd never even have a hope of yanking the stake from my hair in time. I would be dead before we reached the first floor.

Mill reached out and pressed the button for the lobby, and I watched with desperation as it bloomed into bright life.

So close …!

Maybe I could distract Mill somehow and get in the elevator and close the door before he could get inside.

"Now, now, are you truly leaving without introducing yourself first?"

The voice flooded my veins with ice cold horror. I swallowed hard and forced myself to remember that I was pretending to be one of them. I couldn't let my guard down.

Maybe the blood draining from my face would work in my favor.

I turned around to face none other than Lord Draven himself, smiling at the both of us, his fangs evident and menacing.

Chapter 21

"Lord Draven," Mill said, inclining his head. There was a small smile on his face, and I was incredibly surprised to see that he was calm.

I, however, was anything but. So I bowed my head a little too to hide my freaking out.

"My apologies," Mill continued. "I was unaware that you had not yet been introduced."

His tone was even, and I was amazed. Was he being serious? No, he couldn't be. If he was trying to help me, then why would he even pretend to want to introduce me to the oldest and probably most powerful vampire here?

This was it, then. The betrayal I had known was coming all along.

I forced a tight-lipped smile onto my stubborn face as I looked at the old vampire.

Somehow, it came surprisingly naturally.

Distinctly more gothic than his cohorts—or minions, or whatever the partygoers were—Lord Draven looked even less human up close. Dark, black veins snaked across his temples and forehead like marble. A chill seemed to emanate from his very being.

Mill gestured to me formally. "This is Elizabeth. She's from New York, but not from the city," he added, just as I had, with a smirk on his face.

Lord Draven, whose fingertips were together, nodded his head, his eyes fixed on my face.

They looked like a snake's, cold and dead. Black and beady and calculating. Little black veins even crossed the white of his eyes.

I suppressed a shudder.

"I had a cousin from there once, before there even was a place called *The City*. Human, of course." His expression did not change. "I assume he died like the rest of them."

I swallowed hard.

"So, Elizabeth, are you here to mount a takeover of the territory?"

I blanched. Mill seemed to be caught off guard as well.

I shook my head, stayed frigidly cool, and said, "Not yet."

Why did I say that? Was I a complete moron?

No, I was trying to play the field. If I was going to pretend to be a vampire, then I would need to act the part—and that meant I had to flex.

Lord Draven's face split into a wide grin, and then he threw back his head, and laughed, a draconic, unnatural sound that hurt my ears. But I kept my smile plastered on—even laughed with him, at a glance from Mill, chuckling politely.

Lord Draven grinned at me. "I like you, Miss Elizabeth. Not everyone would have had the sheer nerve to say that to me." He seemed to take me in with a long, appraising look, before he nodded his head once in satisfaction. "You are welcome here in our community any time you like."

"Thank you, Lord Draven," I answered, and bowed my head again. I had never been so formal with anyone in my life, but when the stakes for being informal involved being potentially found and devoured by bloodsucking vampires, I got really polite, really fast.

"Have a good evening, you two. Oh, and Mill?"

Mill perked up at his name.

"Do make sure you tell Theo that I heard about that girl on Thirteenth Street, and that I do not approve of his reckless attacks. If he proceeds to act like a wild animal running the streets, I will see he ends his days like one."

"Understood, sir," Mill said, expression giving away nothing of what had occurred on the balcony—that Theo was no more.

"Very good." And with that, Lord Draven turned and walked away and faded back into the crowd.

If I hadn't had the elevator right behind me—and been surrounded by vampires who could probably smell weakness—I would have slumped against the wall in sheer relief.

I had dodged death's cold embrace far too many times to be considered lucky tonight.

No, I was past that.

I was a walking miracle by now.

I restrained myself as much as I could from diving into the elevator. I pressed myself as flat as I could against the back wall. Mill lumbered in behind me and pressed the button for the lobby. The doors remained open, waiting for any last-moment passengers … then they glided closed.

I could have shouted with joy when we started to move.

We were halfway to the bottom when Mill cleared his throat.

"Need a cough drop?" I asked.

He barely glanced over his shoulder and snorted with laughter. "I'll pass."

Down, down … then the elevator stopped, there was a genial *ding*, and the doors slid open.

Mill extended his elbow to me.

I looked at it, and then back up at him. Really?

He looked meaningfully at his arm, and then raised his eyebrows.

Ever so slowly, my eyes never leaving his, I slid my arm up through his elbow and allowed him to lead me out of the elevator.

Thirty plus stories—and he hadn't attacked me. Hadn't touched me. Hell, he'd barely even *looked* at me, except for my remark about the cough drop. It floored me.

I almost started to believe his line about that ten percent he counted himself among.

The lobby was full of vampires as we stepped out, mingling and laughing quietly. It was a totally different feel down here, much more subdued and relaxed. Many still held crystal flutes in their hands, the red blood inside of them far more evident in the light of the gold and glass chandeliers overhead than it had been upstairs in the dark.

Only a few spared us a look, and we were able to cross to the tall glass doors with ease.

"What time is it?" I asked as we drew closer to the windows.

"Just after two," Mill replied quietly. He stepped ahead of me and pushed the door open, standing aside to let me pass.

It was almost flattering to be treated like a lady. But I knew better. This was an act on both our parts.

The air outside was still cool, and I was grateful for the breeze on my hot cheeks, in a way I had never been, even after Byron's attempted assault on the bunker Xandra and I had locked ourselves inside.

I was alive.

Alive, damn it.

A number of limos were parked along the curb, most of them with their engines running.

The same tall, green-eyed chauffeur who had brought me to the party stood waiting by the third limo from the door. He smiled when he saw me and lifted a hand to signal me over.

"That yours?" Mill asked, and I nodded. With me still hanging off of his arm, he started over to the green-eyed chauffeur.

I wondered again whether the driver was a human or a vampire. If he was a vampire, it was impossible to tell. He opened the door to the back of the limo and motioned with his hand for me to climb inside.

Mill lowered his arm, and I withdrew my hand from the crook of his elbow. I didn't wait for a further invitation to get inside the car.

As soon as I was inside, the chauffeur closed the door. Mill was standing there, his hands now in his pockets, and I got my first proper look at him in the light.

Out of the dark and dank room upstairs, I could see that he must have been pretty good-looking when he was a human. The strong, silent type. He had broad shoulders, was very tall, and dressed smartly in a black button-up and dark jeans. He wore shoes that were probably more expensive than my parents' car, but he didn't look any older than nineteen or twenty.

His hair, which was closely cut to his head, like he'd been in the military in life. His jaw was wide and prominent.

I had a thing for men with strong jaws.

I rolled down the window, but he didn't move.

I didn't really either, because I didn't know what exactly to say.

"I'm sorry this all happened to you," Mill said quietly.

I could only stare up at him. He was sorry? I'd put a stake in his wingman's heart.

"I had no idea that Theo would do that. I leave him for two minutes …" He trailed off, his eyes on the cracked pavement beneath his feet.

Still I didn't know how to reply. I was still terrified about everything, yet Mill had done as he had said he would, and gotten me out of that party alive.

And he was apologizing after I was the one who had killed his friend.

Killed. *Murdered*. Normally, I'd be looking at a life sentence in prison for what I had done, but I knew that society would thank me from removing even one of those vile creatures from the face of the Earth.

Even so, even knowing that he wasn't really a man, I felt the bubbling in my stomach, heralding extreme revulsion and guilt for my actions. I had seen the remains of his body for myself, felt the hot, sticky muck with my own hands. But that image would be forever seared onto my brain, a memory that would likely haunt me for the rest of my living days.

And all of this pointed back to Byron. The party, the stake, meeting Lord Draven … I'd done it all to rid myself of vampires. But in doing so, I felt like I was only getting deeper into it all.

Mill was looking at me again, with those same intense eyes as when I had first been introduced to him. But the gaze wasn't threatening, I realized. Just … thoughtful.

And he had showed me kindness, when he could have just as easily been just like Theo.

"Thank you," I managed to say. I hoped he knew that I was thanking him for a lot more than just getting me to the limo.

He pulled something from the pocket of his jeans and thrust it in the window at me.

I held out my hand, and a small, cylindrical glass vial, capped with a cork and tied with a red ribbon, fell into my hands. It was no bigger than my palm. A clear liquid that moved just like water splashed against the glass sides, not even enough for a swallow.

"What is it?" I asked, but when I looked up, Mill was already at the glass doors, heading back into the lobby. Only for a moment did he pause, looking back at my limo, at *me* … and then he was gone.

Frowning lightly at the glass vial, I closed my hand around it and leaned back in my seat as the limo began to move. Subconsciously, I reached up and checked to make sure that the wooden stake was still there, and I couldn't decide whether it was because I was worried that I might get attacked again … or because it had changed me, made me different, somehow, than when I'd gotten in this limo the first time.

Chapter 22

If I could have melted into the seat itself, I would have. The level of exhaustion was unlike anything I had ever felt in my entire life, and I wasn't sure I would ever recover.

I pulled my cell phone from my pocket, having nearly forgotten about it the entire night. My eyes nearly bulged out of my head.

Fifteen notifications? More surprising—every single one was from Xandra.

At first, she was returning my text messages and phone calls, apologizing for not getting back to me sooner. Next, she asked what was happening, wondering if Byron had showed up again. When I didn't reply, she started to freak out, and it gradually got worse and worse, with threats to call my parents, as well as to call the police and report a missing person.

That last one was from fifteen minutes before I got in the limo.

I hastily sent her a reply, assuring her that I was fine, and that no, Byron had not sucked me dry like a little kid with a straw and a glass of chocolate milk. I told her that I had a whole crap ton to tell her, though, and that tomorrow, if she was free, we needed to get together somehow.

Xandra was typing a reply when another message blipped up on my screen.

Sorry I didn't get to meet you. You caused quite a stir.

My mystery texter.

I debated sending a reply. Probably not worthwhile—whoever was on the other end of the phone hadn't exactly been forthcoming during our last exchange. The night flashed through my mind again. It didn't seem real to me, any of it.

Yet it had happened—and somehow, the mystery texter knew—or at least knew that I was now en route away from the party, alive and neck intact.

Fear pulsed through me at the thought of someone having discovered Theo's body. They must've by now, surely?

A worse thought sidelined me. Had I left too early? Should I have stayed until they found the body so that I didn't look suspicious?

How could they find me, though? They didn't even know my name.

I put that thought away and sent another reply to Xandra, telling her that I was almost home, and that she didn't need to come to my house.

How do I know it is really you and not Byron? How do I know he didn't steal your phone?

Good point.

Your mom owns a ramen shop, and you snore when you sleep in Spanish class.

The text that came in reply was a grumpy emoji face, followed quickly by, *I'm glad you're okay. I'm going to bed—finally. Thanks for keeping me up half the night making me worry.*

I smiled. I guess that meant that she cared about me. Which felt sort of nice. But she didn't know what it felt like to be sleep deprived. What was I going on now, three nights in a row of little to no sleep?

The idea of sliding in between my cool sheets and laying my head down on my pillow was almost like a drug, and I sighed heavily. I needed to get home, to sleep.

I looked out the window, still considering texting my mysterious benefactor back. What did they know? And if they knew too much, then how much did others back at the party know?

And the better question was … what was going to happen next?

I'd killed a vampire. The idea was both exhilarating and horrifying. I was sure that I would never forget the feeling of the small piece of wood sliding into his chest, the give of his skin, and the weight of his body on mine as he died.

And yet—I now knew that it was possible to kill them. They could die. I wasn't entirely without power. Byron, though he might be persistent, had lost some of his edge over me—not just to the stake, but to sunlight, and fire. I had weapons now—and this one, I would not let out of my sight again. Maybe I would even give it a name, like how some people named their cars. *Slayer* sounded like a good one. Or *Night Killer*.

I was just starting to get excited about the idea when I realized the limo had stopped, and the chauffeur appeared at the door, opening it and offering me his gloved hand.

We'd stopped near my house, although not close enough that the engine would wake my parents. The lights were off inside, so they were back, and asleep—which meant that my best bet was to come in through the garage, where the door inside was as far from the stairs that led up to my parents' room as it could be.

The garage door was operated by a keycode. Luckily, I hadn't forgotten the number, infrequent that my use of this entryway was, and I punched it in. The lock released, and I slowly pulled the door open, now just as afraid of getting caught by my parents as I had been walking through a room full of vampires.

That appointment with a shrink was sounding more and more sensible by the second.

Getting inside was easy enough, although every noise—the garage door, the locking mechanism when I was in, my own damned footsteps—was awfully loud.

The inside of the kitchen was dark when I got in the house, the only light in the room coming through the windows from the street lights outside.

Boots discarded so I could sneak more easily in my socks, I thought, *Sneaking in after two in the morning—this is the normal life of a high school girl.* I might be creeping back after a date, or a visit to the movies—or hell, a club with Xandra, thanks to a fake ID. Any of those things would be better than the actual reason I was sneaking in.

I pulled my phone out of my back pocket and turned on the screen. I dimmed it, as low as it would go—

A lamp clicked on in the living room, practically blinding in the darkness.

I sucked in a gasp. There were my parents: my dad, leaning over the lamp, and my mom, seated on the couch with her arms folded.

Busted.

Chapter 23

Tonight I killed a vampire. And yet still, somehow, my parents manage to make getting busted for sneaking out seem strangely intimidating.

For a few seconds, we all just sort of stared at each other. Me, kind of hunched over, standing on my toes in mid-sneak, and them, having caught me in the act.

Dad spoke first.

"Well?" His tone was quieter than I would have expected. It sounded almost like he had given up on me a long time ago, and that he was less than surprised about this.

"Well … what?" I replied.

Mom laughed, but it was hollow and bitter. She was wrapped in her luxury white bath robe and was wearing her slippers. Exhaustion lined her face—she hadn't slept yet tonight.

"You're joking, right?" she said. "You're out all night now for the second time this week, and that's your answer?"

I couldn't help it, I looked down at my feet. She was right, she was totally right, but she didn't understand. If she knew what had happened to me in these last few nights, if she knew the danger I was in, maybe she would wipe that disgusted look off of her face and care about me for a minute.

For the first time, anger filled me, pushing all of the fear completely out of my head. It wasn't fair, any of it. And I couldn't stand it anymore.

"Whatever," I said, and I started for the stairs.

"You get back here right now, young lady."

I stopped with one foot on the bottom stair.

"You don't understand anything," I said.

"What?" Mom asked.

"I said that you don't understand anything!" I shouted.

I glared at them as I turned back around to face them. "If you knew what my life was really like—"

"Oh yes, your life is just terrible," Mom shot back, dripping with sarcasm. "You live in a beautiful home, you're clothed and fed, healthy, you get almost everything that you have ever asked for—" Her voice caught in her throat. "And parents who love you more than anything."

I closed my eyes, forcing myself to not lash out again. My chest heaved. I focused on tempering the cadence of my breaths to calm myself.

I didn't have the energy to try to explain any of this to them.

I was vaguely aware that they were speaking, mostly to each other. Mom's voice was sharp, and Dad was trying to calm her down. But it didn't matter. Nothing they could say would change what had happened tonight.

What would they think if they found out that I had killed someone? Would they see it as murder? I mean, would it even matter if I told them he was trying to kill me?

Self-defense. It was all in self-defense.

I wrapped my arms around myself, feeling myself starting to shiver, almost uncontrollably. I was definitely in shock. There was no way a rational person would be so okay with killing someone the way that I had.

"You're such a typical teenager," Mom said. "You think that you're unique. Everything is hard. You think that no one has ever gone through what you have gone through."

"You have no idea."

Mom rolled her eyes, and Dad just opened his arms in exasperation.

"Look, sweetheart, we're trying to understand here, but we

can't help if you don't tell us," he said. His tone was steady, but I could tell he was frustrated.

"I …" I started.

"Is it a boy?" Mom asked. "Are you sneaking out to meet a boy, and …" Her voice trailed off as if she couldn't bear to say what she was thinking.

"No, Mom, it's nothing like that!" I grimaced.

Mom must have reached her limit, because she swatted at the air like she wished she could push me away like an annoying fly. "I don't have the energy for this right now. I have a mountain of paperwork and have to be at the office at seven tomorrow. Now, thanks to you, I will probably be late."

I clamped my mouth shut. I did feel guilty for making them worry, for always ruining their lives. That was never my intention.

Damn it. Why couldn't they have just gone to bed without checking on me?

I wished more than anything that I could have just stayed home tonight. I could have slept, and I wouldn't be a killer. Because, whether I could defend myself against the vampire threat now or not, I knew that after tonight, my life was forever changed.

No. That wasn't true. My life changed when Byron appeared next to me on that sidewalk.

This was all on him. He'd forced me to do this, to totally mess up my entire life. He backed me into this corner. Tears filled my eyes.

"Oh please," Mom spat. "I'm not buying this contrition act."

I bit down on my lip until I could taste blood, hoping the pain would quell the tears. It didn't help.

"Go to your room," Mom said. "We'll deal with you tomorrow. And I expect you to tell me exactly where you have been going, otherwise you're getting lojacked the first chance I get."

"Okay," I said. I didn't wait for an answer as I marched up the stairs to my room. I thought that I would feel safer here, away from the party. But climbing the stairs, their disappointed gazes following me, I just felt like a stranger, like this house was no longer my home, no longer a sanctuary.

Honestly, though, after attending the vampire party, seeing just how many there were roaming the streets … I didn't think I would ever feel safe anywhere ever again. I had nowhere to turn. Not my parents. And I had no friends really apart from Xandra, who hadn't got sucked as deep into this rabbit hole as I had, and who could retreat at a moment's notice to the safety of her own life when things got too heavy.

My room, the safest space I had known since moving here, felt just like a room now. It didn't matter that all of my belongings filled it, all of my clothes, my books, my school backpack. It might as well have been occupied by some random girl at my school.

I closed the door without switching the light on and threw my shoes into my closet; no point trying for silence anymore.

The dark and quiet were a small comfort. But my head still throbbed with the beat of the music from the club, and then the confrontation with my parents … it was all just too much.

How was anyone supposed to deal with any of this? None of it made any sense to me whatsoever.

I slumped against the door, locking it as my hands found the doorknob. It was cold against my flesh, and I shied away from it.

I didn't want anything in my life that reminded me of—

A calm voice pierced the quiet, sending a sick jolt through my stomach.

"I've been waiting for you all night. Did you miss me?"

Chapter 24

I wished that I was still holding my boots, because if I had been, I could have chucked them in his face.

My eyes had adjusted to the darkness enough that I could see Byron's silhouette sitting on my bed. I wasn't sure how I had missed it in the first place.

I ran my hand over the wall, my fingers making contact with a switch, and the lights flared to life overhead.

I felt a grim sense of satisfaction when he recoiled slightly, squinting, and leaning away from the brightness.

Handsome as always, like he had stepped right out of Hollywood. His hair had the fashionably messy just-rolled-out-of-bed look that actually takes half and hour and a jar of gel to achieve. His heavy-lidded eyes searched my face, but some of his usual snake-like demeanor was gone. It was like he was tired too.

Good. Let him suffer a little.

"I am not in the mood to deal with you right now," I hissed through gritted teeth.

Byron folded his arms across his chest, his face smooth and unreadable.

I was so done with everything right then. I had just left a party full of vampires, murdered one, and then had to return home to one. It just wasn't fair. Was I ever going to have time by myself ever again?

It didn't seem likely.

"You look really nice," he murmured.

I brushed it away, and moved to my closet, throwing clothes around, trying to find the biggest, bulkiest t-shirt I owned to sleep in. I didn't want to make any sudden, surprising moves for the stake. Having already been in one fight with a vampire tonight, I knew that Byron's speed and strength were overwhelming. Threatening him with the stake would have been similarly foolish; warning him of the danger I posed.

No. If I was going to stake my second vampire of the night … it had to be by surprise. Which meant another lie––acting like a teenage girl who's just *irritated* by a stalker showing up on her. Very unlike how I actually felt.

I could feel Byron's eyes on my back, and turned around, my hands snapping to my sides in exasperation. "What do you want?"

Byron, who was sitting as casually on my bed as if it were his own, shrugged his shoulders. "I just wanted to see you."

I rolled my eyes. "Yeah … okay," I replied in a harsh, sarcastic whisper, and returned to my digging.

It was probably unwise to turn my back to a vampire who was desperate for my blood, but I was so done caring about anything that I probably would have welcomed it. I was done being a scared kitty, cowering before him.

I gently touched my pocket where I had slid the small vial of liquid that Mill had given me. Something about the way he had passed it to me so discreetly told me that I should not let Byron see it, no matter what. Somehow, it was a tool of some sort, something that would help me. Better than the stake, I hoped. I gently nudged it farther down into the pocket while my back was turned to him.

"Listen—" Byron started off, his voice quiet and steady.

I wheeled around, pointing a finger at him. "I don't want to hear anything you have to say to me. Do you understand that?"

He cocked an eyebrow at me, but he didn't react. All he said, in a whisper, was:

"So, where were you tonight?"

I stared at him. He was joking with me, he had to be. He had known my entire life and schedule in the last three days, known where I was and what I was doing. Surely that extended to this too.

I clenched my jaw. Resisting the urge to reach up and touch the wooden stake in my hair, I answered, "None of your business," keeping my voice low.

"I—" he began, but I held up a hand to stop him.

My parents were walking up the stairs, and there was a sharp rap of knuckles on the door.

"Yeah?" I asked, masking my anger as exhaustion. It wasn't hard to make convincing.

"Go to bed," came the voice of my father. "I don't want you to get sick on top of everything else."

On top of everything else. If he only knew.

"I'm just changing," I called back. "I'll go to bed right after."

"Well, goodnight then," he said.

"Goodnight," I said, glaring at Byron, who had suddenly conjured a smirk onto his face.

"Love you," Dad said after a moment of silence. It seemed forced.

My heart sank.

"Love you too."

I waited with my breath held for his footsteps to disappear down the hall.

Between my parents and Byron, I was going to have a heart attack any minute. I decided I should start writing up my will as soon as I had the chance.

"Trouble in paradise?" Byron asked.

I shot him a nasty look again. "Again, none of your business."

"Oh come on," he said. He patted the bed beside him. "I've been waiting so patiently for you."

"You have no shame, do you?"

He shook his head. "If you're wondering if I worried I might be caught, you have to remember: I have better hearing than all three of you put together and would have easily slipped out of the window before they ever saw me. So no, no worries." He smirked. "And no shame."

He cocked his head at me.

"You got all dressed up to go somewhere. After you hopped in that Uber, though …"

"Lose track of me?" I shot back.

He nodded, looking perturbed.

I smirked. "Good."

He shook his head. "Seriously, where did you go?"

I ignored the question. "Why do you keep showing up here if you aren't just going to kill me?"

He seemed confused, his brow knitting together. "You and I have gotten off on the wrong foot."

"Wrong foot?" I retorted. "There was never a right foot with us."

"Hm." He held up his hands placidly. "Well. I hope you'll accept my apology."

Where on earth was this coming from? It didn't fit at all with his character that I had seen up until this point. He was resigned, almost like he was on a leash.

Who was holding that leash?

"I could have been a lot different when we first met. I could have sold this whole thing differently to you. I mean … I really like you—have since the moment I laid eyes on you."

Liked me for me? Or liked me for my blood?

"But … you really don't know what you're missing."

His voice had become silky, almost lilting.

"And you're going to try and sell it to me now? You gotta be joking."

"Hear me out," he said, and he smiled a low, smoldering smile at me.

Despite the adrenaline pumping through my brain, I felt my heart skip a beat too. I had never had a boy look at me like that before. It was almost like he actually found me attractive.

Maybe he actually did.

He stood, and crossed slowly, cautiously to me. "What I can give you is something that no other man in the world could give you."

"An early burial?"

Byron laughed softly, his gaze drawing me in. "No. We could live together … forever."

"The idea of spending forever with you is pretty much at the bottom of my bucket list," I said. He flinched and the familiar flare of anger rose up in his eyes.

But he gained control of himself quickly, steadying himself with a deep breath.

"Just think of all you could do with that," he tried again. "You would never age; you would always be as beautiful as you are right now. Though, I find it hard to believe it would be possible for you to *not* be beautiful at any point in your life."

"Oh, gag me," I said.

His teeth ground against each other. "Don't believe me? Then how about this? Immortality would allow you to go anywhere, become anything, be anyone you wanted to be … as many times as you would want.

Vampires do everything better, you see," he said quietly, leaning closer. His lips almost grazed my cheeks—and I stood, frozen, caught in conflict with my fear, my desire to stake him through the heart and be done with it—and the silky way he spoke, the way he looked at me, worshipping, so good-looking …

"We see better, hear better …" He smiled. "And we love better, because we can love forever."

Goosebumps rippled up the skin on my arms.

He's a monster, I reminded myself—and saw, again, the room full of vampires, lifting champagne flutes filled with blood, *human* blood, high and draining them.

Byron was one of them—another Theo.

That snapped me into action. I shoved him away from me as hard as I could, catching him off guard, and he stumbled backward.

He looked at me with a wounded expression, as if that push

had been an act of ultimate betrayal.

"I would give you the entire world … and this is how you repay me?" Malice glinted in his eyes, welling up and over his hurt. He stepped toward me again.

I was aware of the vial digging into my side as I bent over, ready to fight back.

As Byron approached, his eyes on mine, I slipped it from my pocket, and flicked the stopper off with my fingernail.

"I've given you nothing but my affections, and you still resist me."

"Death threats are classified as 'affections' now, are they?"

He growled, deep in his throat, like a threatened dog—and at the same time, I tossed the opened vial into his face.

His hands flew to his face, and an anguished sob escaped him. He sounded as if he was being strangled. He doubled over, bumping into the dresser, my bedside table.

"You … will be mine!" he snarled through his hands. "You can't resist me in the end. You will be mine!" That was my chance. I reached up into my hair and pulled the stake free.

But as soon as I positioned myself to strike, he leapt across the short distance to the window and slipped outside into the black of the night.

Chapter 25

It took me a few minutes to gather my thoughts and energy to assess what had just happened.

Byron had been the polar opposite of how he had been before—almost civil, rather than total creeper jerk. If not for the fact I knew I had Xandra to confirm it for me, plus the dent he'd made in the bunker door, I would seriously be doubting my sanity right now.

He was gaslighting me. Now, in addition to all the worries on already my mind, he was playing psychological games, too.

I collapsed onto my bed, and stared at the vial on my hands, now empty. I lifted it to my face and sniffed. I couldn't smell anything.

Was it holy water?

It was the only thing that I had read about online that would be remotely effective. But where had Mill gotten it? And why in the world did he give it to me? My first thought was that it was to fend off Byron—but he'd only know about him if the mystery texter passed the information on, and I was dubious about how everything connected. To deal with more Theos?

My head swam, and I had to close my eyes. Not that it helped much. The glow from my light bulb shone through my eyelids, too bright. Sulkily, I threw myself up to switch it off. Then I threw myself back down, eyes closed, trying to calm myself …

And then snatched up my phone to send a text.

Xandra, Byron was just here. No reply; and scrolling through Twitter didn't summon one. Probably had gone to bed after all. But if she hadn't …

He was super weird, like calm and restrained. Then I threw holy water in his face. Yeah, I'll explain that later. That should get her attention. Facebook next … and ten minutes of newsfeed scrolling, which started mundane and grew increasingly dull, I still had no response.

I groaned into my pillow.

There was one other person that I could trust with all of this stuff going on: my mystery texter.

He just tried to get me again, I sent.

I was shocked when a message came back in less than a minute.

We need to meet. Not likely. Grounded until hell froze over, there was no way I was going to be able go anywhere to meet anyone for probably the rest of my life. *I can't,* I typed, then bit my lip. *Call me?*

As a safety precaution, I switched it to vibrate mode, and turned the volume down.

The blanket thrown over my head was an extra precaution.

Finally, a reply: *Some things have to be done in person. I'll be on your roof in a few minutes.*

Excuse me? This person was joking, right?

Panic started to set in now—and with my mystery texter apparently on the way, I turned back to my original shoulder-to-cry-on.

XANDRA PLEASE WAKE UP

I leaned up on my bed and peered out of the window. Empty yard, so at least Byron had run off to whatever crypt he slept in.

The seconds ticked, piling into minutes.

My mind raced. My mystery texter, a weird kind of savior, about to be unmasked … yet in this quiet before the storm, so to speak, I reeled at the possibilities. Another vampire, surely—I was destined to run with them, apparently, the way the past few days had gone—but who? Again, I wondered how to trust them—because how had they known so much about me? My predicament?

Three minutes passed. Then five.

At ten, my grip on the window sill was so tight I was practically an inch from ripping it from the wall.

When fifteen minutes had gone by, I sat rocking, the stake gripped tight in sweat-oiled palms. I had only one question by then, a very familiar one: *Why was all of this happening to me?*

None of it made any sense. There was nothing special about me.

Whenever Mystery Texter arrived, like some kind of occult Santa, it would wake my parents, I just knew it. If, that was, Dad wasn't lying awake right this moment, just waiting for me to try sneaking out again.

"Calm yourself, Cassie," I murmured.

Easier said than done.

Smearing sweat off against the bedcovers, I peered out the window again. Still the yard was empty.

Didn't mean the roof was, though.

I got up from my bed to pull the shade down back over the window when I thought I saw a shadow pass over the glass of the window.

I blinked and looked out. Nothing.

That you can see, I told myself. And if I had learned anything these past few days, it was that you can't underestimate how sneaky vampires can me.

I sagged back against the mattress—

There was a thud, and I jumped, clapping my hand over my mouth.

My entire window was blocked by the shadowed outline of someone crouching on the windowsill.

And then came a small tap of a fingernail on glass.

Chapter 26

Looking back in at me was—I couldn't fathom it for a moment, but yes, it was—a young woman.

She was devastatingly beautiful, with a thin face, pale skin and straight, shining hair as blonde as platinum. It was long, easily to her waist, and in the moonlight, lifted slightly by the wind, it flowed like liquid silver. Wait...hadn't I seen her at the party? Her hair, I think, at least.

She was petite and crouched on the sill like a cat. She wore a black leather jacket over a white tank, and grey skinny jeans that were torn at the knees. She had a pair of black Converse on her feet.

The part of her that was most jarring was her eyes. I could not stop staring. They were like pools of amber, wide, and most of all, sad. The sorrow that exuded from her was almost overwhelming, as if looking at her was like looking into despair itself. A wave of sympathy overflowed me, unbidden. I moved to unlock the window—

The girl smacked her fist against the glass, freezing me in place. I hoped that my parents hadn't heard.

"I won't ask you if I can come in," she said, muted by the glass. Her voice was throatier than I would have expected. Alluring, sure, but where I expected elf, I heard more siren. "You should be more careful. Even opening a window for one of my kind can be perceived as an invitation, which can then ruin the sanctity of your home."

She gave me a pointed look. "As I'm sure that you've already learned with Byron."

I swallowed hard.

"Who are you?" I asked, tightening my grip around the wooden stake.

A perfectly penciled eyebrow rose on a youthful face, no older than mine, snapshotted for eternity.

"I'm you," she said, "if Byron gets what he wants."

Another lump in my throat, not dislodged by my swallow.

I had to remember that this was the same person who had been texting me, trying to help me. She obviously knew all about Byron, and something had obviously caused her to reach out to me and offer a hand.

The girl tossed some hair over her shoulder. "I saw you at the party tonight."

I racked my brains. "I saw...maybe your hair. But you said you wouldn't be there."

"I lied." She shook her head. "I never had the chance to approach you because you were with Mill and Theo."

"You know them?"

She nodded.

I glared. "You seem to know everything about me. Who are you?"

"Iona. I used to be in your shoes." She looked at me sadly. "Byron … found me, too."

My heart fluttered. *Answers*. "Explain," I said.

Iona closed her eyes.

"I was a seventeen-year-old in high school. Byron … latched onto a weakness in my heart. He could see it, even when others around me couldn't. He'd been watching me for some time and picked up on the tension between my parents and me at home. He … understood me in a way … no one else did at the time."

The hair on my arms stood up straight. That sounded awfully familiar.

"Byron is the definition of a romantic," she continued, her

tone taking on a darker edge. "He longs for someone to *rescue*," she made air quotes with her fingers, "from the struggles in her life. He looks for girls who have issues with their parents. He takes his time, slowly chipping away at them. It gives him control."

"He likes the control for sure," I murmured.

"You don't even know the half of it," Iona spat, and I recoiled from her.

She suddenly flinched and went rigid and looked over her shoulder down at the lawn. I couldn't see past her, but I tried to.

Satisfied, she returned her gaze to me a moment later. "It's not him, if that is what you were thinking. He shouldn't bother us at all tonight. Not after the drink you gave him." A smirk lifted the corners of her lips at that, a respectful sidelong look at me. She went on, "You and I are not the first that have gone through this with him. He's left a long, bloody trail in his wake. An endless string of Juliets he's tried to woo."

"Juliets?" I asked, feeling a sense of dread creep into my bones.

She nodded. "He thinks he's Romeo, of course. Looking for that star-crossed lover deal."

I bit my lip. "So he does have feelings for me …"

Iona rapped a finger against the glass.

"This is *exactly* how he pulls you in. It always starts this way. And trust me, I've traced them back quite a ways. He drives all of them crazy, eventually, and one of two things happens." She held up two fingers, then counted them off: "They either completely lose their grip on reality, or they come to see 'reason' and become his next 'object of affection,' as he would call it."

My mouth was dry. So this was what was ahead of me. I could see it. I had already started trying to rationalize things, even when I could feel my own grip on the world starting to slip—had already started to see some twisted *sweetness* in the way he behaved, falling into the trap of his good looks …

"Some have actually gone insane," Iona continued. "The whole nine yards; hospitalized, on meds. One girl took her own life."

"So he just, what?" I asked, "Pries girls loose from their reality, from their sanity, and they either lose their minds or fall in love with him?"

Iona nodded her head solemnly.

"What happened to you?" I asked. I had to know—had to find out—because it was coming for me too if I couldn't stop him.

"I joined him," she said, and then laughed bitterly. "Too strong-willed to go nuts, I guess. We were together for a few years—and honestly, even though I hate myself for it—they were the best years of my life."

I recoiled from the window. "How can you say that?"

Iona shrugged. "He knows how to treat a woman. I traveled all over the world with him, saw things I would never have thought possible. He made me promise after promise, many of which he kept. But those things never last …"

So she was a bitter ex … whatever Byron had in mind for me. "Does he do it on purpose?" I asked. "Charm a girl, knowing he's going to eventually leave her?"

Iona shook her head. "No. He truly believes that every new one he drives mad is the one he's supposed to spend the rest of his life with. *Romeo and Juliet*, remember?"

"Except the story ends in a double suicide," I said. "Not exactly love-life goals … for most of us, anyway."

"It is if you can't die, and are always as young as he is," she replied.

"Byron was violent and pretty dominating the last time he was here," I said. "And the time before that was when I met him, when he chased my friend and me until we were cornered." I shuddered. "What would have happened if he had caught us?"

Iona shrugged her shoulders, and casually replied, "Probably bled you both dry, without a care."

"But then why—"

"You got away," Iona finished for me. "Instantly, you turned yourself into a challenge. You got his attention."

"So this is my fault?" I asked. "What should I have done, let him kill me?"

"Of course not," Iona said. "He's fickle, but like many other idiot, immature men, he tends to fixate. He's perpetually a teenage boy. Don't forget that."

"But tonight he was different," I said, much more quietly. "He tried to persuade me—make me think he was the good guy, like he understood me or something."

"Not surprised. That's how he works," she replied. "Mind games, he enjoys them. It's all psychological to him. He may be a teen, but he is clever. You ever hear of the Joker?"

I snorted. "Who hasn't?"

"Harley Quinn. She started off as a nice girl, right? And we all wonder why she fell in love with the Joker."

"Stockholm syndrome," I said. "Yeah, I've read about that."

"He basically makes it so that whoever he chooses feels like it's him or nothing in the end."

This was exactly what was happening to me. It didn't matter how I looked at it. Byron's appearance in my life had done more to drive a wedge between my parents and me than anything I had ever done in New York. That simple truth was shocking, but also enlightening.

This is what Byron has done to me. I am sneaking out at night to find answers, and then getting caught, stuck in a cycle because I can't tell them.

Distance, more lying, anger, desperation.

"There will be other things," Iona said. "He'll show up at places where you are with your parents. He'll make it obvious that if you don't come with him for a little while, he will kill them in front of you."

The strength threatened to run out of my legs. "What?"

"Or he'll send one of his minions to collect you from school. Push you. Pull you."

This was way worse than I had thought.

"Until," she continues, "he breaks you. One way or another."

Sweat chilled my skin. This girl was telling me the truth. I could see it in her eyes.

"How do I stop it?" I asked, voice quavering—and I slammed my hands on the cool glass of the window. "What can I do? How long do I have?"

Iona stared at me for a long moment. "If you hadn't thrown the holy water in his face, this might have gone on for years. But now …" She shook her head sadly. "You don't have very long at all."

Chapter 27

"Listen, I have to go," Iona said. "I've probably been here too long."

"What do you mean?" I asked. "You can't leave now! I've got so many questions."

"When was the last time you slept?"

The question surprised me. I blinked up at her. "I don't really know …"

"Get some rest," she said. "There isn't much left to this night, and Byron won't be down for very long." She looked at me intently. "Watch your back, Cassie. I'll do what I can on my end."

And without giving me a chance to even thank her, she was gone. I didn't even see her as she silently dropped down from the sill onto the lawn and disappeared.

Shivering, I slipped under my bedcovers. But they held no warmth, and I wrapped my arms around myself.

I had locked the window, not that it helped when it came to Byron. Nevertheless, if what Iona said was true—and I trusted her implicitly now we had spoken face to face, now I had seen the depths of despair in her eyes—I was safe to sleep—tonight, and maybe all of tomorrow too.

I glanced at my phone. Still no reply from Xandra. My last text to her had been a little panicked and would probably set her alarm bells ringing when she read it in the morning. So I texted her, and told her that I was okay, and that I'd fill her in soon. I also told her not to call me before noon.

I hesitated, then scrolled down to Iona's number.

Thank you, I texted her.

Don't thank me yet, she replied. *I don't know if I did you any favors by telling you what I did.*

You saved my life tonight. At the very least, thanks for the stake.

You're welcome.

With that, I rolled over, tucking my phone under my pillow, content that I had an ally to watch over me.

What felt like only a moment later, someone knocked on the door. I rolled over so fast that I nearly toppled off of the bed and onto the floor.

Mom walked in.

"Mom … " I groaned, and pulled my pillow over my head to block out the light.

"No sleeping in today, young lady," she said, and she came across the room and pulled the blankets off of me.

No sleeping in today?

And then I realized: that wasn't the light on—it was sunlight, streaming through the window. Morning had come already, what little remained of the night passing in the blink of an eye.

Instantly my legs shot up toward my body, putting me in the fetal position.

I moaned again.

"Last I checked, you were grounded. And your chores do won't do themselves."

I was glad that the pillow was covering my head, because my face went through the gambit of emotions. First, I was furious at being woken. Then I remembered last night before and getting caught. And then, after that, I remembered Iona's story, and I felt guilty.

Slowly I sat up and pulled the pillow away. "All right."

"Good," Mom said, seemingly pleased that she wasn't going to have to enact World War III today. "I need you to mow the lawn, clean the pool, trim the bushes—"

"All outside stuff?" I asked.

She glared at me. "Yes. You can wear some sunscreen and a hat if you're worried about it."

Definitely not worried about it. *Elated* was the better word. Groggily, I lumbered to my closet, and began sifting through for clothes. In the background, Mom listed off jobs. I nodded my head without really taking them in. I *tried*—but without meaning to my thoughts went back to Iona, and her plight. Sad though it was, she had given me a new perspective on life. Chores, I was perfectly happy to do, because it meant I still had a family to do them for.

"Are you listening to me?"

"Hmm?" I asked, looking over at Mom.

She pursed her lips. "I swear, you are going to give me an aneurism."

"I'm sorry," I said. "I'll make sure it all gets done. "

She stared at me for a minute, her back rigid. But then she sighed and shook her head.

"Cassandra, I just don't know what to do with you."

She had every right to say that. But there was so much more to it.

Iona's words about Byron driving a wedge between a girl and her parents were still fresh in my mind. I had to stop it from happening as best as I could.

I started, "I know that I've been making some bad choices lately—"

She scoffed, and I tried to reign in my temper.

"But I am going to try and be better. I'm just …"

She stared at me, crossing her arms over her chest. "You're what?" she said, when I faltered.

"I'm just … trying to figure out some stuff in my life." I wasn't sure what I was expecting—sympathy was perhaps a pipe dream, while a flare of her temper seemed more likely the way this had started to go—but I didn't foresee Mom's exhale—or what she said, voice tempered again.

"I get it," she said. "You're a teenager. You're trying to figure out what it means to be an adult. There are a lot of changes going on—"

"Mom!" I rolled my eyes at her.

She laughed lightly. "Okay. No, I do get it. And I appreciate the apology."

She crossed over to the door and looked back over her shoulder at me. "But don't think you're off the hook."

"I wasn't expecting a miracle." Though I sure could use one right now. A vampire-killing miracle.

I made my way downstairs after brushing my teeth and putting my hair up and found that Mom had already left. Dad had left a note for me reminding me to behave today, and that we would talk when he got home.

I didn't really look forward to that conversation, but it was inevitable, I guessed.

I made my way outside, slathering sunscreen on as I went. From the garage I withdrew the mower, checked it was filled with gas, and then, mulling over how much my life had changed in the past three days—and the sudden influx of people into it (and then promptly out again, in Theo's case), I set it into motion and began to push it around the yard. It belched fumes, their smell intermingling with the scent of freshly cut grass in a heady, addictive sort of way. It was tough work, but the labor felt good. With every foot of trimmed grass I put behind me, my stress oozed out and left me.

It was still hard to believe that it had only been a few hours before that my stake had gone through Theo's chest, causing him to almost liquefy in front of my eyes.

I had the stake tucked into the back of my shorts, easily accessible if Byron were to appear again—though, now that I knew for certain of his aversion to sunlight, I was much more confident today.

And then there was Lord Draven. I had killed Theo right under his nose, at his big shindig—and then I had lied straight to him. What was even weirder was that Mill had lied right along with me.

It was thrilling, in a way, to have bested the vampires like that. But I knew that it was also foolish. What I'd done was incredibly dangerous. Yes, I'd gotten away with it … but that was so fortunate, a skin-of-my-teeth escape I'd never be able to pull off again.

Again, I felt a wave of gratitude to Mill—and confusion over his motives. Had Iona meant for me to meet him?

So many questions.

Maybe I'd text Iona, ask if she'd meet again, and see if I couldn't wrangle some answers out of her.

It took me a little over an hour to finish mowing. I was making my last round on the yard when I walked by the wall of our neighbor's house. It backed up right to our side yard. It was smaller than ours, and the shades were always closed. Today, though, something in one of those windows flickered.

The blinds. Again.

Someone had been watching me.

Chapter 28

That was *it*. I stared at the window, a vein pulsing in my neck. If this was Byron again, I wasn't going to let him see me afraid.

The nerve he had, gawking at me like some disgusting peeping Tom. Iona was right; it was easy to see how all of those girls before me had gone nuts from his stalking. How was anyone supposed to feel like they had any privacy when he was around?

I chewed on my lip as I pushed the mower out from under the window, but I kept glancing over my shoulder at it. The blinds didn't move again.

I leaned against the mower as I stared at the house.

How would have Byron gotten in? Was the family never at home? Was it a vacation home, only used for a few weeks out of the year? Or were they all away on a Sunday morning? Church? Shopping? Brunch? Damn it, why hadn't I paid some more attention to the goings-on of my neighbors since moving here?

I seethed, first at myself, and then, snapping that chain of thought, at Byron. I wasn't to blame here, and I wouldn't allow my sanity to be eroded to the point that I thought anything else. He was a damned stalker, and I was through with it. Grabbing my flip-flops, I stormed toward the neighbor's house, hands balled into tight fists. Last night, I killed a vampire—one that had taken me off guard, no less.

I wouldn't be so stupid again.

I considered moving the wooden stake out of the back of my

shorts and into my hair, but I didn't want Byron to know that I even had it. I couldn't be sure he hadn't seen it the night before, but it was the best chance I had.

The front of the neighbor's house was a lot like ours, but only a single story. The stucco was painted a sandy tan color, with red shutters, and the red door was bright apple red. There was a nice bench on the front porch with a few cute pillows thrown on it, and a basket full of seashells beside it. It was a cross between cutesy and tacky, but the overall effect was somehow homey.

I approached the front door—and stopped short.

What was I doing here?

Apparently, last night's victory against Theo, eluding Draven from right under his nose, and the information Iona had given me, had me convinced I could take on the world.

Maybe all of this miraculous success was going to my head?

Would it be smart to follow through? What would Byron do if he saw me? Would he freak out? Try to kill me right then and there? Would he try to be cool like he was the night before?

There was only one way to find out.

I reached out and knocked on the door, then quickly stepped out from beneath the overhang and back into the sunlight. Behind my back, I clasped my hands—loose, in easy reach of the stake.

It was getting warm, probably in the low seventies. It felt like early summer weather for me. Crazy to think it was still only the end of January.

Time dragged … and no one came.

I listened, ears pricked. He might not have the balls to open the door to me, but surely he'd come down to investigate.

But I heard nothing from inside the house. Only soft noises from outside came to me: birdsong, the low hum of intermittent traffic, another mower being pushed around a garden a block over.

Was Byron hiding like a child? Did he not expect me to come over and confront him like this?

I smirked. Maybe I had, for once, surprised him. Still, my satisfaction about that aside, I was getting exactly nowhere here. And though I could start hammering away on the door, shouting—making the sort of scene psycho ex-girlfriends were famous for—it was no more likely to bring Byron out here. So, with a huff and a last glare at the door, as if it was the guilty party, I turned around—and the door opened.

I wheeled around, expecting to see Byron's heavy-lidded eyes and tousled hair, hands moving to my stake in case he tried to get the drop on me—but instead I saw a tall, thin high school kid with sandy blond hair, bright blue eyes, and glasses.

"Hey, I know you!" I cried, pointing accusingly at him. All of the anger toward Byron took a sharp turn, redirecting itself straight at him. "You're in like … half of my classes."

The boy nodded his head and leaned against the door frame. "Can I help you?"

He was one of the smart kids, always knowing the answers, always paying attention in class. I had never spoken to him before. I was pretty sure that he didn't even know I existed.

He wasn't bad-looking, really. Kind, gentle eyes; well built, if maybe a little lean, but he carried himself well, and he definitely didn't hang out with any of the losers I was aware of.

"You've been watching me from the windows, haven't you?"

He stood up straight, unfolding his arms. Yet though my words would've made anyone else blush or go on the defensive, his expression remained fairly passive. Most of it was his gaze drifting away, for a moment, and a casual, small shrug of the shoulders.

"Who are you?" I pressed. "I forgot your name."

The boy rolled his eyes with obvious disdain but sighed. "My name is Gregory Holt. And yes. We have Spanish, English, Pre-calc and History together."

Wow. He knew exactly which classes. So much for not paying attention to me.

I squinted at him. "Okay then, Greg—"

"It's Gregory."

"Okay," I repeated, more slowly. "*Gregory.*" Jeez, did I sound like such a loser when I corrected people like that? "Do you want to tell me why you were watching me out of your window? I saw you close the blinds today, and yesterday."

Gregory stared flatly at me, unflinching.

"Dude, I caught you. You might as well fess up."

Still he said nothing.

I held my hands out, palms up, totally at a loss. "Come on, man. I wasn't born yesterday. It was definitely you—or are you going to tell me it was your dad being a creeper? Or your dog?"

"Don't have a dog," he replied.

I put my palms to the side of my head in exasperation. This guy. Why was he avoiding the obvious?

Could be embarrassment. I mean, how do you reply to getting called out like that?

I exhaled. "You know what? Whatever," I said. "I don't even care right now. Just don't do it again."

I made to turn around and walk right back down the path and around the back of the house when he spoke and made me stop.

"I've seen some weird stuff from your house. And I think all of it has something to do with you."

I froze and turned back to face him.

He was still casually leaning against the door frame, but his eyes were scrutinizing me.

Now *I* was embarrassed.

I glared right back at him. It was hard to not notice just how blue his eyes were. The glasses didn't even look all that dweebish on him.

"What do you mean?" I asked, a lot more acid in my voice than I had intended. He shrugged his shoulders and moved his gaze to something behind me.

"There have been these people hanging out at the window up there," he said, pointing over his shoulder with his thumb back toward my house.

I bit down on the inside of my bottom lip.

Here I was, coming over here to make a scene, when he,

apparently, had a bone to pick with me.

I tried to smooth my expression into a smile.

"Oh?" I asked. He wasn't buying it, going by the look he gave me: flat, but close to bordering on irritation. Like a cat getting pissed off with its owner for touching its tail. Might be enduring it for now, but much longer and the claws were coming out.

"One was a boy," Gregory said. "He's showed up several times. And last night there was a girl who sat on the sill for at least ten minutes."

Oh, you have got to be *kidding me*. I knew I wouldn't be able to conceal all of the shock on my face.

I was right, because his gaze became even more curious.

"That, and I saw you getting into an Uber last night. Dressed to the nines for clubbing or something."

I wanted to smack this guy. Maybe it would make him forget.

In all of this time, I had wanted so badly to tell someone what was going on with me. I wanted someone to be able to believe me.

And here that someone was! Standing literally in front of me, and I immediately wanted to cover it all up. I wanted to lie and hide it.

But why?

Then it hit me. Maybe this was a trap. Iona made it very clear that Byron was manipulative to a fault and would do all he could to ensure that I was cut off from everyone and everything.

Why would he allow someone who lived so close to go unnoticed?

I glanced over his shoulder, almost expecting Byron to slip back into the shadows, grinning.

I shook my head. This was all just too much.

"Yeah, well," I retorted, my hands on my hips, "it's none of your business."

Gregory's curious eyes changed, and it took me a second to realize that he was looking at me with—*sympathy*. He was *concerned*.

Something in my heart stirred. Someone had a suspicion that

something was wrong and cared enough to say something. And it gave me … *hope*.

I decided then and there that Gregory, though kind of weird and annoying, but also kind of cute, was not a threat to me. And somehow, Byron had missed this little possibility.

Byron wasn't perfect at what he did, after all. Like Iona said: he was perpetually trapped as a teenage boy, with all their janky-ass thought processes. For the first time in all this, I gave mental thanks to his total fixation on me.

"I just …" Gregory started, and his tone had completely softened. "There was something weird with that guy when I saw him out on the lawn. I know that we hardly know each other, and maybe this is totally out of line …"

"What?" I asked.

"Cassie … do you need help?"

The question that I never thought would come but had longed for. But how was I supposed to respond?

The truth, the ugly bitter truth, was that he had no idea exactly what was going on. He saw weird stuff, stuff that hinted at stalkers and night visitors … but that wasn't even a fraction of it. And if I spilled any details—that I'd fallen into a dark world filled with vampires—Gregory's concern for my safety would transmute itself into a concern for a very different sort: concern for my safety at my own hands, off the back of some very serious worries regarding my sanity.

So despite this offer of assistance, this life preserver thrown to me as I struggled against the current of a rapid river, I had only one choice.

"Thanks anyways," I said heavily. "But no."

And without another look over my shoulder, I made my way back to my house, feeling Gregory's eyes follow me until I was out of sight.

Chapter 29

When I got back to the yard, I grabbed the clippers as I passed them.

Sighing heavily, I slumped down onto the grass in front of the bushes. I was just so tired. Four hours of sleep were just not enough to make up for the sheer amount I'd missed since Byron stepped into my life.

Insane to think that it had only been days ago. It felt like weeks, or months. Already I'd become a totally different person … one who I was still figuring out.

I dug the end of the clippers into the ground.

How much had Gregory actually seen?

I picked at some of the thick grass beneath me, and then shrieked as I saw almost a dozen fire ants start to race up my legs.

I tried to brush them off of my legs, but I couldn't get tear them loose. I could feel the bites, sharp, intense, tearing into my flesh. I screamed and kicked and danced as I slapped my thighs and shins, trying to smash them, knock them loose—

A hand landed heavily, grasping my shoulder, and I almost tipped over as I dropped another stinging blow on an ant sitting mid-calf. They were endless, swarming, crawling all over me—

"Cassie, what's the matter?"

I glanced over, sluggishly, and saw my dad, staring into my face. His hand was the one on my shoulder.

I breathed heavily, my chest burning, sinking into his grip, and I pointed at my legs. "The ants … they … they're …" I couldn't finish my thought. My legs were burning, itching.

Dad looked down at my legs and brushed his palm over my knees and my ankles.

"I think you got them all," he said gently, looking at me with concern behind his glasses.

I tried to get my breathing under control and forced myself to look at my legs.

He was right. They were gone, all of them. I held onto him as I steadied my footing.

"There's an ant hill," he said, pointing to a small, grey pile of what looked like sand not far from where I had been sitting. "You must have stepped in it."

"They … they were everywhere," I said weakly. How many had there been? It had seemed like thousands when I was in them.

"Did they bite you?" he asked. I nodded: tiny stinging, throbbing spots itched all down my legs.

"Okay, let's get you inside and irrigate them as much as we can."

Dad turned me around and started ushering me back toward the lanai's back door back inside.

There was a shadow beneath one of the trees along the outside of the yard, near Gregory's house, that seemed to stutter like an old home movie tape I'd once seen. I blinked, trying to clear my eyes. Someone stepped into the light.

I jumped back, my mouth opening wide in horror.

It was Theo.

He was grinning, but half of his jaw was unhinged. One leg dragged behind him like a dead weight. Dark, black wetness oozed down one side of his face.

The leg he dragged was too much: he stumbled to his knees—but still he kept coming, crawling toward me.

"No … no, no, no, no …" I said, trying to move away from him. Why had Dad not seen him?

"Are those bites bothering you?" Dad asked. "It's all right—we are almost inside. We'll get some calamine lotion on them or something."

I barely heard his words. All I could do was stare in absolute horror at Theo's shambling crawl toward me.

But … he was dead! I had killed him!

"I killed you!" I gasp.

"Yes, you got the ants, sweetheart," Dad said. "But we need to get you cleaned up before those bites get infected." He continued to push me along. "I hope you aren't allergic …"

Theo's body crumpled, as if it were deflating, and it shriveled up into a pile of ash, only to be blown away by the breeze that rushed through the yard.

My heart hammered. Cold sweat had broken out on my skin.

Breaths quick, my eyes darted, taking in every shadow, every shape that might be the vampire I had killed.

Something was seriously, seriously wrong.

I let Dad lead me up the stairs and into the bathroom. He sat me down on the toilet and went to their bathroom to retrieve some things to clean the bites with.

I scrubbed my eyes with my palms.

When I opened them, Lord Draven was standing in my bathtub, head brushing the ceiling.

I shrieked again and tumbled off of the toilet onto the floor.

When I looked at the tub again, he was gone.

I was breathing heavily, almost hyperventilating, when Mom walked in.

"Cassie? Are you all right?"

I was back up onto the toilet seat, Mom's hand on my arm. Had she just helped me up?

What the hell was happening to me? Hallucinations?

Was this some form of PTSD from what had happened last night?

Were Byron's predations finally taking its toll? Was he actually driving me mad, in real time?

Or was I just utterly exhausted and bereft of sleep?

I lost a few more moments, snapping out of a short interval of silence to hear my parents discussing whether or not to take me to the emergency room. I was slumped over on the toilet with my head in my hands.

Tell them, I thought wildly, the words echoing and rebounding in my mind in a mad cacophony. *Tell them what's been happening.*

I couldn't. They wouldn't understand—and nothing I could ever say would make them.

"I'm fine," I said faintly, speaking into the ball of my hand. I pressed my fist to my clammy temples, willing myself to calm, to shake loose this fear. "I just need a shower or something."

"I'll run to the drugstore," I heard Dad say, "and get some Epsom salts and anti-inflammatory lotion."

"Good idea," Mom said. "I guess we were bound to run into fire ants sooner or later. This is Florida, after all. I hear they're everywhere down here."

Mom came into the bathroom and moved to start drawing a bath. The sound of the rushing water was surprisingly soothing, like a peaceful waterfall beside me.

"Don't get in all the way," she said. "Just soak your legs where the bites are."

I obliged, but my mind was not totally with it. It was starting to come back to me though, piece by piece. Some of the nauseated feeling that had overtaken me was dissipating too, running out of my body along with the adrenaline, like someone had opened a hatch in my feet and let gravity do the work.

It wasn't real. Theo was dead. I killed him.

My mind was just playing tricks on me. The ant bites, my fatigue … maybe Byron's influence too, I thought, remembering what Iona had said: that some of his victims ended up being hospitalized.

I couldn't let that happen to me. Wouldn't.

"Seriously, I'm fine," I said at last. "I'm just going to go lie down for a bit."

"All right," Mom said. "At least put some coconut oil on those bites."

"I will," I promised. And she let me go back to my room.

The bites were itching madly, so I did as she asked and grabbed the small jar of organic coconut oil from my dresser that I used as a hair mask. I slathered it all over my legs and then went to lie on top of my blankets.

I couldn't keep doing this. I had to rest. I had to get away from my parents' scrutiny. I had to do it as much for me as I did for them. But with being grounded, I didn't think I would ever get that chance.

"This sucks …" I murmured to my ceiling. My phone lay on the side table. With nothing to do but mull over the way my life had taken a dive off a cliff into actual Hell, I picked it up and lit the screen. Xandra had texted. A few times, actually. Just checking in though—no real panic about last night. Which was totally annoying, because if it had been me and I woke to terrified texts from her, even if she later messaged to say it was all cool, I'd be a bit more concerned than she was right now.

Still, I owed her an answer.

Everything sucks, I typed. *I haven't had a decent night of sleep in three nights. Some random girl who apparently used to be Byron's ex swung by last night. And now I'm seeing dead vampires.*

I closed my eyes, enjoying the cool flow of the air conditioner, and the low hum of the fan overhead.

You can stay with me tonight, Xandra texted back three minutes later. *My parents said it's totally cool.* Ulterior motive: I imagined that she wanted to know what had happened. When had I actually seen her last? Friday? What day was it today?

Ulterior motive of my own: if school was tomorrow, I definitely needed the rest.

Problem was, I was grounded, and if I asked my parents to let me stay at Xandra's, they were liable to blow a gasket and lock me in my room.

On the flipside, I was going literally crazy here. I'd accidentally invited Byron into my house, which meant it wasn't a safe haven for me anymore … whereas Xandra's at least offered me respite—respite I sorely, sorely needed, if I hoped to ever have a normal life again.

That settled it. If I left, then at least my parents would be out of danger. He wanted me, not them. And the prospect of rest was *seriously* enticing. Yes, Byron knew that Xandra knew about him—but I had a stake now.

A stake. Sleep. Protection, for myself and my parents—and the truth from Iona.

There was a light at the end of the tunnel.

I was going to get through this.

I just had to hope my parents did not discover me sneaking out—and accept that, if they did, I would sacrifice their opinion of me one more time.

I could only hope it would be the last time.

I had to move fast. Dad was leaving, or gone already, to go get some lotion for me. Mom was hopefully downstairs, or in her room. I would plan my exit based on where she was. I texted back asking for Xandra's address.

Then, hurrying, I threw a change of clothes into my school bag, in case I didn't come back before nightfall. I had no idea how long I might sleep for.

"Mom, I'm hopping in the shower!" I shouted down the stairs, my bag slung over my shoulder.

"Okay. I'm just getting dinner ready."

"I'm not hungry. I was reading that ant bites can make you sick to your stomach …" I said, hopefully making it sound like the truth.

She was silent for a moment. "Okay. But you're going to school tomorrow, young lady. I'll come check on you in a bit."

"That's okay, Mom," I said. "I'd rather get some rest. I'll text you if I need anything."

I knew that she hated that, but she also liked when I relied on her.

"All right. If you need me, I'll be out back with the grill. You sure you don't want some steak?"

My mouth watered, but I called back, "No, thanks. It doesn't sound good right now."

I waited until I heard the sound of the sliding door open, then close, before I hurried downstairs and out of the front door, stepping out into the warm afternoon sun.

This was just for the night, I told myself. Or the afternoon. A short respite, and I'd be back, refreshed. Maybe then I could think straight, without hallucinating about dead vampires or endless swarms of fire ants.

Just a short break.

I pulled open my map app and started walking down the sidewalk in the direction of Xandra's house, in search of rest.

Chapter 30

Xandra lived in a small cul-de-sac about two miles away from me in the same development, surprisingly enough. All of the houses nearby all looked the same, and I felt it in me that much of what I had seen looked exactly alike. Was that the lack of sleep?

The idea that I might be hallucinating even normal, ordinary things was pretty terrifying.

I walked up to the door, numbered 4961, and knocked.

I didn't have to wait long, as a tall, thin Vietnamese woman opened the door. She had short black hair cut close around her ears and wore a pair of pretty blue eye glasses.

"Oh, you must be Cassie," she said, and her dark, onyx eyes crinkled when she smiled. "I'm Mai, Xandra's mother."

Instantly, I liked her.

"Come in, come in," she said, standing aside.

I smiled and thanked her, stepping inside the foyer.

The scent of ginger and cilantro hit me. Something was cooking, sizzling softly from a kitchen where a television played the local news, volume down low.

"Xandra was just finishing some of her homework, I believe," Mai said, leading me in. "Xandra," she called. "Cassie is here." Xandra's house, I discovered, was totally different to my own. Clutter covered near every surface. My mother would have freaked to have seen stacks of mail on the table near the door, or the jackets hung over the backs of the chairs around the table in the kitchen, or the basket of laundry outside of a closed door, waiting to be folded.

The kitchen was smaller than ours, and the cabinets had been painted by hand, but the bright blue color on the walls was eye-catching, and the mismatched chairs circled around the wooden table were charming.

The living room was pretty normal, with a big overstuffed couch, a cluttered coffee table, and a large flat screen situated between two large, totally full bookshelves.

But it felt so real, so lived in.

It felt like a home.

A deep, unexpected pain blossomed deep within me.

My home always felt so empty, so sterile. Is this what a normal household was supposed to feel like?

I reprimanded myself. Everyone's home was different. Mine was just … meticulously clean and organized.

"Xandra said that the two of you met recently. She says you are new?" Mai asked as we waited for Xandra.

"Oh," I replied, trying to smile at her. "Yes. I started just after the Christmas break."

Xandra appeared out of one of the doors down the hall, and she smiled at me.

"Hey," she said, padding down the hall in a mismatched pair of socks. She looked super comfy, with baggy pants that cinched at the ankle, an oversized sweatshirt that hung off one shoulder, and her wildly vibrant hair tied in a knot at the very top of her head.

She reminded me of a pixie, with her hands in the pockets of her pants, and her toes pointed in slightly.

"Ah, our guest has arrived."

Another voice appeared in the room, and I glanced over across the wide living room to the sliding doors to the backyard.

A tall man with large shoulders and a balding head stepped inside, carrying a plate of shrimp skewers. They sizzled away on the platter, and the smell was almost intoxicating.

"That's my dad," Xandra said.

He came across to where we stood and passed the shrimp to his wife.

"Thank you, sweetheart," she said as she accepted the platter and walked into the well-lived-in kitchen.

He looked at me, and offered one of his large, strong hands.

"Mr. Stewart," he said, and I took his proffered hand.

I smiled up at him. He looked intimidating, but his eyes were gentle.

"I'm gonna go help Mom with something real quick. You okay?" Xandra asked, gesturing over her shoulder into the kitchen.

I waved her away. "Yeah, sure, that's fine."

Mr. Stewart slid onto the couch, and exhaled with relief, putting his feet up on the coffee table in front of him. "Go ahead, take a seat," he said, gesturing to the large leather armchair in front of the glass doors.

I hesitated. Not wanting to appear rude—plus the facts that I was totally whacked and that chair looked ridiculously comfortable right now—I lowered myself carefully into it, a wave of pleasure I'd rarely known sweeping over me as I sank into it.

Ooh, I needed one of these. It totally enveloped me, cool on my flushed skin.

"So, Cassie, right?" Xandra's dad asked.

"Yes, sir," I said, straightening against my desire to curl into a ball right here.

He smiled and nodded his head. "Where you from, Cassie? Originally, I mean?"

"New York, sir," I answered. "But not the city. Closer to Rochester."

"I had to go to Syracuse for a business trip once," he commented. "Middle of the winter, though. The snow was pretty amazing." He laughed heartily. "What about you? Do you miss the snow yet?"

"No," I laughed, but it felt hollow. "No, I don't. I think the snow was what I hated most about living in New York. The heat suits me better."

Aside from the vampires that seem to be crawling out of the woodwork, it did suit me better. Nevertheless, not for the first time, I felt homesick for New York. I hated the snow, but damn, did I miss those cool nights, when the sky was so clear that you could see every star overhead and the air was so cold that your eyelashes could freeze. I missed my friends.

And I missed a time in my life when I was not stalked by vampires.

The television flickered, and there was a low rumble of thunder outside.

"Guess those storms are coming in a little early tonight," Mr. Stewart said. "Not usual for this time of year."

I winced. I hate thunderstorms.

He picked up the remote control and changed the channel to the weather channel.

"Hey, honey," he said, calling over his shoulder. "Looks like the weather will be fine to go fishing this weekend."

Huh, a fishing trip. A family thing? I could see it with him and Mai, but Xandra … try as I might, I couldn't imagine her holding a fishing rod, or even having the patience to try and wait out a fish on her line. The image of her in a wide-brimmed fishing hat and wading overalls amused me, but not enough to show on my face.

"So how long you been here?" Mr. Stewart asked, returning his attention to me.

"We moved into our house a few days after Christmas."

His brow furrowed. "Seems like an odd time of year to move a family, especially with someone your age. Mind if I ask why?"

I felt my face flush, so I focused my eyes on the television. Apparently it was unseasonably warm for this time of year, and beachgoers could expect a clear, mild weekend.

"My dad's a doctor, and took a job transfer," I answered. It was true, but I definitely did not feel like explaining to a complete stranger that he'd taken the transfer because of me.

"I see," Mr. Stewart replied. "But you and your family are enjoying living here?" He chortled. "The thing about Florida is that you either love it or you hate it."

I forced a smile. "I like it so far," I answered. "Maybe ask me again once the summer arrives."

"You're right about that."

Something about Xandra's dad just exuded *dork* for me. I didn't really mind, but he seemed awfully chummy with someone he had just met.

Then again, I guessed that was just normal friendliness—something I wasn't used to a great deal of—from my peers, or my parents.

"How about school?" he asked, easing over on the couch to face me more fully now the weather channel had sated his curiosity. "How's that going for you?"

For a few seconds, I was taken aback. This was the first time what felt like a long time that someone had asked me about my life, a question that had nothing to do with vampires or why I was sneaking out and defying my parents. No, instead I got a completely normal question, one that any person would ask a seventeen-year-old girl—and that simple question had temporarily frozen me.

"Great," I lied, and oh, how I wanted that lie to be the truth. I wanted to leave all of this ridiculous vampire stuff behind and live a normal teenage girl's life. "I've got tons of friends," I continued, heaping on the lies, "my grades are awesome, and I think I'm finally starting to fit in."

Just saying it felt like I had taken a sharp knife and stabbed myself repeatedly in the chest—because that was what I really wanted.

More than anything.

I couldn't remember the last time I wanted something so much that it hurt like that. A painful lump rose up in my throat. I could never have it. Even if Byron went away, and vampires were gone from my life forever—there was no denying how I'd changed; what I'd done.

Theo's putrefying body jumped sharply into my mind—flashes leading up to it, of him trying to bite me, holding me—then my thrusting out with the stake, the resistance as it sunk into his chest …

I tried to swallow the lump away, knowing that it meant that tears were not very far behind.

"Dinner will be ready in five minutes!" called Xandra's mom.

"Your parents must be really proud of you," Mr. Stewart said with an easy smile. I stared at him blankly until he added, "That you're adjusting so well."

"Yeah …" I murmured, my chipper façade wavering, bottom lip threatening to tremble—and the sheer weight of everything fell upon me all at once. Exhaustion hit me like a tidal wave, and the comfort of the chair seemed to pull me in.

I leaned my head back, hoping to just clear my head for a second, not wanting Mr. Stewart or anyone else see just how close I was to the brink.

But as soon as my eyes closed, my body betrayed me, and the last thing I heard was, "A cold front is headed …" and I sagged into blissful, easy sleep for what felt like the first time in ages.

Chapter 31

My neck ached. My back too.

Faint light poured in through the windows, bathing everything in the room in a pale, cool blue light. Night—but dawn was approaching. Noise came to me that I struggled to place what I was hearing, then I caught a whiff of meat cooking, and my stomach gave an appreciative gurgle, and I realized it was the sound of something frying in oil. What, I wasn't sure exactly—a blend of spices, ginger and garlic its highest notes, masked it—but I didn't care. I'd eat squid right now, if that's what was offered to me.

It took me a minute to register where I was and what had happened. The last thing I could remember was that I had totally fallen asleep in a chair at Xandra's house. From what I could see, that was where I still was.

I must have slept for the entire night. That meant that it was Monday morning, and I had school. I groaned.

It also meant I'd been out the whole night when I left early yesterday afternoon—and I had very low hopes that my sneaking out remained undetected at this point. I was just wondering where my cell phone was, and whether I really wanted to check it for a tirade from either or both of my parents, when Mai's gentle face appeared over me.

"Good morning," she said, looking closely into my face. "You must have been exhausted."

I nodded, still trying to clear my head. Everything felt foggy, like I had slept for days, and not in a good way. And somehow I *still* felt sleep-deprived.

"Are you feeling all right?" she asked. "Would you care for a cup of coffee? Or some tea?"

"Tea sounds wonderful," I said hoarsely. I cleared my throat. "Thank you. And thank you for letting me stay here last night. You don't know how much I appreciate it."

"You are welcome," she said. She smiled again, and then disappeared into the quiet darkness of the morning.

I decided against getting my phone. There'd be an onslaught of calls and messages awaiting me, and I was so not ready to deal with that right now. Plus, what was a couple hours' more radio silence? I'd text them when I left for school. I'd tell them that I honestly never meant to fall asleep there, I just wanted to get out of the house for a little bit. Or maybe tell them that Xandra was having some kind of existential crisis and needed my help.

Neither of those excuses would fly, I knew, but I had to come up with something to soften the blow. Besides, I was doing it for my safety and sanity as well as theirs. Why couldn't they see that?

Oh, right. Because I'd buried the truth about vampire stalkers and parties under a mountain of lies to cover up my endless rule breaking.

Xandra's mother reappeared a few minutes later, with Xandra in tow. She plopped down onto the couch, the farthest end away from me.

Her hair was all disheveled, part of it sticking up out of her messy bun that was lopsided. There were dark circles under her eyes where her makeup had smudged. She hung her head as if she were still asleep.

And if I wasn't mistaken, I was pretty certain that those were the same clothes she had been wearing last night.

"So you totally just fell asleep before dinner," Xandra said while trying to stifle a yawn. "Missed a good one, too. Mom makes a mean phở."

As if talking about her had summoned her, Xandra's mother appeared with a bright green steaming mug, and handed it to me.

"Thank you," I said.

"Are you hungry?" she asked. "I could make you some eggs, or bacon, or toast, or heat up some of the noodles from last night—"

"The noodles sound amazing," I replied, mouth watering.

She smiled at me and returned to the kitchen.

Xandra moved closer to me, to the other side of the couch. She glanced over her shoulder toward the kitchen, and leaned a little closer to talk to me.

"Seriously, you slept for like sixteen hours. You weren't kidding when you said stuff was insane."

"You literally have zero idea," I whispered, stretching my legs. Everything ached. I made a mental note to myself to never sleep upright again.

But at least I had slept.

Xandra watched me closely. "What happened this weekend?"

I watched Xandra's mom, who was humming to herself in the kitchen. I leaned in a little closer too. "A lot." It was a little overwhelming, how much I had to tell her. It didn't make much sense to start here, in her living room. I probably would have been able to talk for an hour or two, easily. "Literally so much that I'm having trouble keeping up."

I reached up, and felt the thin, long wooden stake that I had stashed in my hair before leaving the house. "Can we go talk in your room?"

"Here we are," Xandra's mom said at the same time I spoke, appearing behind the couch, bringing a wonderful, heady aroma with her. "Eat. You both have at least an hour before you need to leave for school."

She passed me a large bowl with a pair of chopsticks that was totally full and warm. She handed Xandra a bowl as well. Then she reached over to a tall standing lamp behind the chair I sat in, and turned it on, filling the room with much needed light.

"I hope you like shrimp," Xandra said, as she pulled her chopsticks apart and dug in.

The noodles smelled spicy and sweet. They were warm, and the shrimp were coated in a spicy, rich sauce. I mimicked Xandra, pulling the chopsticks apart, though a little less gracefully.

Even less gracefully, I attempted to hold them properly between my thumb and fingers. They didn't want to hold still and kept slipping. When I did manage to keep a shaky hold, I failed to pick anything up.

"Do you want a fork?" Xandra asked, laughing.

I shook my head, determined to get them to obey me. Failing that, I speared a shrimp instead, and quickly brought it to my mouth before it fell off.

It was divine. The sauce was spicy, but not so much that it burned. The vegetables were crisp, and the noodles were springy and perfectly cooked.

"This is the best breakfast I've ever had," I said through another mouthful, mostly green onions and peanuts I scooped up. It didn't hurt that my stomach felt like I hadn't eaten in weeks.

Xandra smirked.

I swallowed another bite. "But I haven't ever had noodles for breakfast before," I added.

"Not a common thing, I know," she said. "But a lot of Asian cultures have noodles or rice for breakfast."

I had finished the bowl before I had even realized—and my stomach sunk sadly. Was it bad of me to hope for an offer of seconds?

Xandra took my bowl from me and motioned with a nod of her head for me to follow her.

"Thanks for breakfast, Mom," she said. "We're going to get ready for school."

Xandra's room was not quite what I expected. A diffuser on a shelf breathed the subtle tang of vanilla and cedarwood into the air. Stacks of books cluttered the floor. Gauzy, bright pink drapes hung over the window, parted to reveal the first light of sunrise, a band of peach that caressed the horizon. Her dresser looked like it was hand-painted, with small square mirrors glues onto the front of the drawers. Her bed, unmade, was covered in throw pillows and the fluffiest-looking down comforter I had ever seen. Considering how much black she wore, her room was surprisingly girly.

"Sorry it's a mess," she said, stepping over a laundry basket near her door and slumping down onto her bed.

I sort of hovered near the door, unsure if I should join her.

"So … this weekend?"

I sighed heavily. "I really don't even know where to start," I said.

"Did something happen with your parents?"

"Sort of," I answered. "I was grounded."

"Why?"

"I got caught sneaking back in the other night." I bit down on my lip. "At two in the morning."

"And you snuck out to come here last night?" Xandra asked. "My mom is going to freak if she finds that out. Don't tell her, please."

"Definitely not." I looked at her earnestly. "Look, thank you for letting me come over here. I desperately needed to sleep … I hadn't had a full night of sleep since the night before Byron chased us."

"So … summation of events since then?" Xandra said. She picked up her phone. "That text you sent me last night was really weird."

I furrowed my brow, trying to think back. "I'm sorry. All my recent days and nights are kinda blurring into one …" I searched my memories until I remembered. "Oh, right. Iona."

"Iona?" Xandra asked.

There was a knock at Xandra's door. Xandra and I looked at each other. "Yeah?" she said.

It was Xandra's dad. "I'm leaving in a few. Do you girls want a ride to school?"

Xandra gave me a searching look.

"I need to get my school stuff," I said, quietly. "You go ahead. I'll just walk to school." Not that I didn't appreciate the offer. I just didn't think it would be wise to show up at home with Xandra's dad. My parents might have a heart attack on the spot.

"No, Dad, but thanks," Xandra answered, voice raised to carry through the door. "We have to go back to Cassie's house to get her school stuff. She forgot her backpack."

"All right," he replied. "Love you, sweetheart."

"Love you too," she answered, and then lay back on her bed, her arms splayed out beside her.

I looked at her curiously. "You don't have to go with me."

She shrugged her shoulders. "I'm interested enough in what happened to you. And who this Iona is."

I smiled. "All right. Wait until I tell you about Theo."

Xandra's face lit up. "Theo?"

"Another vampire. He tried to kill me ..." And she listened, spellbound, as I went on, laying out the tale of all the unbelievable stuff that had happened to me just since the last time we'd seen each other.

Chapter 32

"I just can't believe you actually *killed* one of them …" Xandra said as we stepped into her garage.

I had not truly realized the burden of the knowledge I was carrying around until I shared it with her. The relief was blissful. I felt almost happy. I had never imagined that keeping all of this inside hurt as much as it had.

It was easy to see how some of the girls Iona talked about had gone completely insane.

But I knew better than they had, and I was determined not to let Byron cut me off from everyone in my life. I would keep making connections, keep building bridges, even if it was purely for my own sanity. I would not let him do that to me.

"It's not like it was easy," I said, for probably the seventh time. "It was terrifying. All of it has been terrifying."

"He really just jumped you? And you beat him?"

I shuddered despite the warmth of the day. "It was weird. Everything just kind of … slowed down. Like in the movies? But it happened in, like, less than a minute. The entire fight. He was …" I gritted my teeth. "He was toying with me, and then when I cracked him in the eye, he got mad, and that was when I fell on the floor …"

I touched the stake again. "If I hadn't had this, I wouldn't be here."

We turned onto the sidewalk in the direction of my house.

Birds sang. Squirrels darted, racing each other up to the trees and up their trunks. The smell of the saltwater from the bay was strong on the breeze.

Xandra asked, "So who was the guy who was with him? You said that he helped you?"

"Mill," I said, feeling a wave of the same uncertainty about him that I'd felt when I was with him. "He got me out of the club. I kinda expected him to turn on me every second he was with me. But he had a million and one chances, and he never took any of them. Even when we were in the elevator alone together."

"Maybe he's just biding his time," Xandra said hesitantly.

"I thought about that too. But then ... he gave me a gift, and it ended up being really useful at scaring Byron away. Or at least annoying him by hurting him."

Xandra looked at me questioningly.

"Holy water, I think," I answered. "It burned him when I threw it in his face."

She laughed. "You threw it in his face? Nice."

I shrugged. "I don't know. Iona told me that it just bought me a little time, but he was probably going to be angry."

"You've mentioned her name a couple of times," Xandra said. "She's the one who invited you to the party, and gave you the stake?"

I nodded as we crossed the street.

"Who is she?"

"One of Byron's exes."

If Xandra's eyes could have popped out of her head, they would have.

"Is she a vamp, too?"

"Yeah, but she's different," I replied. I told her about Iona texting me, and then appearing the night before I stayed over at her house—and what she had told me about her past, and Byron's. By the time I'd recounted it all, we were meandering down my street, the last leg of our journey to my home.

"That's crazy ..." Xandra said. "So why are these two helping you?"

"I have no idea," I said. "But they haven't given me a reason to not trust them yet. If anything, they have kept me alive."

"You think they're *good* vampires?"

"I don't know." I was saying that a lot lately.

"Because there is no such thing," Xandra added, pouring on the heat. "There can't be. Vampires need humans to survive, but we're no more than cattle to them."

The words of Lord Draven's toast pressed against my mind with unrelenting force. Cattle. She was right. That's all humans were to the vampires. Even Mill and Iona might have felt that way. The worst part was that I had no way of knowing their true intentions. But there was no point in freaking Xandra out more than I probably already was.

"I mean, even Byron wants you for your blood, regardless of what that Iona says," Xandra went on. "All that talk of wanting romance and a soulmate?" She made a dismissive click with her tongue. "It's ridiculous. Vampires have no hearts, no souls. They can't possibly love like you and I can. Lust, maybe. But even that's superficial and empty."

"I am not saying that I don't agree with you," I said slowly, "but Mill and Iona *are* different in some way. Why would they care about keeping me out of Byron's grasp? Why would they risk keeping me alive at the expense of their own safety?"

"As far as you know, only Iona cares about your fate with Byron, and I'm not entirely convinced it isn't some form of revenge disguised as help."

I chewed the inside of my lip. I hadn't thought of that.

"Mill just helped get you out of a sticky spot when you murdered his friend."

"Does it count as murder when the person is already dead?"

"Are you trying to be funny?"

"No, seriously," I said. "I've been asking myself this for the last three days."

"I … don't know. But I bet the vampire underlords or whatever would hold you accountable for your actions."

That pit in my stomach was back. "I just hope they never find out."

"So we still have the question of why Mill really helped you," Xandra said.

"I seriously have no idea," I said. "He barely said anything to me. He just seemed …"

"Different," Xandra finished. "Because you are such an expert when it comes to vamps now."

Despite my intention to build as many bridges as I could instead of continuing to burn the damn things down, I was tempted to bite off something scathing. But I couldn't. My house was a few dozen yards away now, no more, which brought its own sense of panic to focus on.

Slightly more pressing, though, was the issue of the person stood on the stoop of the neighbor's house.

Gregory.

"Oh, please, no …" I murmured. I did not want to deal with him right now. I had too much else going on, and I didn't feel like having to explain all of that to Xandra as well.

"What?" she asked, and she followed the direction my gaze had taken. "Is that Gregory Holt?"

"You know him? I asked. "Come on, if we walk fast enough, maybe he won't notice us. "

"Why, what's the matter with him?" Xandra asked. "He's just a nerd who sits behind you in Spanish. What's the big deal?"

I didn't say anything—and Xandra took the silence in the worst possible way. "Oh, I get it!" she said, a bright grin blooming. "You have a crush on him, don't you?"

"That is the absolute last thing on my—"

"Hey, Cassie!" I heard, and then the sound of footsteps hurrying across the grass met my ears.

Damn it.

"Oh, hey Xandra," Gregory said, his tone light and pleasant as he fell in beside us.

"Hey, Gregory," she said, overly bright.

Between looking at him and looking at Xandra, I was in a bit of a Catch-22. He was annoying if only for being somewhat good-looking, even in those dweeb glasses, his sandy hair tangled with sunlight like spun gold. Xandra, on the other hand, bore a big grin, looking between us like this was some kind of Ross and Rachel thing.

She was worse by far.

"Oh, well if it isn't the creeper," I said in a sickly, sweet tone to Gregory. "Taken to sitting outside waiting for me now?"

"What?" Xandra asked, peering back and forth from me to him.

"It's nothing," Gregory said, adjusting his glasses and looking at me pointedly.

"He's been staring at me from his windows for the last few days," I said sourly. Maybe making his actions known to others would make him stop. "I caught him red-handed and came over to his house yesterday to confront him."

I swelled with satisfaction as his cheeks burned.

"Wait, what?" Xandra said. "Ew, Gregory!"

Gregory turned to her, his hands held up defensively. "It's not like that," he said. "There's been some weird stuff happening at her house, and I just wanted to know what it was."

Xandra looked back at me, the question obvious on her face. *Does he know?*

I shook my head. Of course he didn't know. But he definitely seemed to know too much or had at least seen too much.

"Apparently, it's too hard for you to keep your big nose out of my business," I retorted, and started down the sidewalk toward my house.

Xandra followed, and to my great annoyance, Gregory fell into step right beside me. He hitched his backpack over his shoulder.

"Is everything okay?" he pressed me.

I kept my face forward so I didn't have to look at him. "Yep."

"It's just … were you not home last night?"

There was a chill to his words that set my stomach churning.

"No, I stayed over at Xandra's house. Not like it should

matter at all to you. Why are you so nosy?"
"Um … it's just …"
I looked back at him.
His face was pale—frightened.
A chill ran up my spine. Gooseflesh broke out on my arms.
"What is it?" I asked.
"That guy … the scary one? He came back last night."
And my heart sunk right down to the sidewalk.

Chapter 33

I was running before I even realized I had made the decision. I only had one thought in my mind, and that was to get back before it was too late.

If it wasn't already. Gregory and Xandra hollered at me, but I didn't care. It didn't matter.

They didn't understand what was at stake.

The front of the house appeared peaceful. The sunlight glinted off of the windows, and the mourning doves sitting in the tree in the front yard were singing happily. The pink hibiscus flowers were in full bloom and subtly sweet-smelling, turned up toward the sun. I could smell the sulfur in the water from the sprinklers, and the grass was still wet. They must have just turned off. A dog down the road barked excitedly, most likely at the mail truck making its rounds.

The bucket and sponges Dad had used to wash his car the day before were still outside of the garage door beside the hose. The door was locked. I grappled with it, my hands trembling. The damned key wouldn't get in the hole …!

Just as I was about to scream a shrill curse word, it found purchase. I twisted it, clicked it open—pushed through—

Dad's car was in the garage, pristine and waxed. Mom's car was there too, also freshly washed. It smelled like leather seats, and the dust that was suspended in the streaks of light filtering through the cobwebbed windows.

Xandra and Gregory had caught up to me, cautiously stepping into the garage behind me. The sound of their quick, heavy breathing filled the otherwise silent air.

"Why did you stop?" Xandra asked, just above a whisper.

I didn't answer. I was staring at the door into the house. It was open, and I could see a portion of the hallway into the kitchen through the opening. A key, my dad's key, was still in the lock, hanging there, as still as death—

As if something had prevented him from coming back out to get it.

Maybe he had run inside to get his briefcase. Or his phone charger. Or his coffee. There were a million reasons why it could have been there, apparently forgotten, and not one of them gave me any peace.

There was a low throbbing in my ears as I stepped toward it and pulled the key from the lock. I slid it in my pocket, trying not to think about the fact that it may have been the last thing that my dad touched at the house.

Please be home, Mom and Dad. Please be here, waiting inside, pacing around the kitchen, on the phone with the police, ready and willing to scream at me until you are blue in the face. Please be here, ready to ground me and lock me in a closet so that I can't ever escape again. Please still be in the dark about the truth of what is going on in my life.

But they weren't.

They weren't there.

The kitchen lights were on over the island. The smell of Mom's favorite magnolia lavender candle hung in the air, but it was strangely stale this morning. Her purse was on the edge of the counter, her favorite lotion sitting right beside it, as if she had just used it, or was getting ready to pack it for work. Dad's coffee cup was right next to the coffee pot, with his two packets of stevia right beside it, ready to go.

There was a throw blanket, one of mine, tossed across the back of the couch.

Had Mom slept there, waiting for me to come home?

Everything was still, eerily quiet. It frightened me more than if the house had been torn to pieces. Farther in—I caught a whiff of cologne. It wasn't my Dad's.

Byron's shadowed face flashed across my memory.

There was a pot in the sink that was only partially full of water. Mom was such a completionist that she never would have let only half of it soak away the grime and caked-on food. One of the blinds behind Dad's armchair was not pulled closed. Dad hated anyone being able to see into the house once it got dark out. One of Mom's favorite trinkets, a parrot that she had gotten on our vacation to Cozumel, had been turned to face the east, where it had always been facing the west.

"No one's here …" Xandra said, looking all around. "It's totally quiet in here."

I walked over to the shelf where the little bird sat and expected to see the ring of dust where the statuette had once sat, now having been obviously moved. But the shelf was totally clean, utterly free of dust.

I turned and looked back around the room, paying attention to every detail.

The books that normally sat on the coffee table were perfectly aligned, stacked by size, biggest to smallest. Mom usually organized them by subject, with her favorites on top. The title of the one on top was *Fresh Fun Food.*

Was that some kind of sick joke?

"Everything is wrong," I said to no one in particular. "Everything is normal, but it's not." I pointed over at my Dad's chair. "See that book? He was reading it last week. He just finished it two nights ago."

I wheeled around and pointed at the stairs going up. "Those stacks of clothes were not put away. My mother never leaves laundry unfinished, no matter how late it gets."

And then I pointed back at the door. "And my dad's keys," I pulled them out of my pocket, "were here in the door. Something is wrong."

And that last truth …

I hesitated, before breathing, "They aren't here."

"Your parents?" Xandra asked.

I nodded shakily.

Gregory watched me closely. "How do you know?" he asked, a quiver of fear in his voice—because, the truth about vampires totally removed from the situation, he still knew of strange comings and goings—and it wasn't difficult to draw grisly conclusions from them. "How do you know they haven't just gone to work, or—"

"I just know," I said. "Everything is untouched, like they were …"

I couldn't finish the thought—but it screamed inside my brain.

Abducted. Killed.

Turned.

"My Mom would never leave her purse," I said, "not in a million years. And my dad had work today. Both cars are in the garage." I looked back over my shoulder at the parrot.

"Look at this," I said. "This bird always looks out toward the bay, toward the west. But now it is pointing east—toward the door outside."

Gregory licked his lips.

"You do know that you sound a little crazy, right?"

Xandra shook her head. "No, I believe her," she said. She looked back over at me. "This is all Byron, isn't it? He's trying to leave you a message or something."

I nodded. "I smelled his cologne when we walked in."

Gregory looked between the two of us. "Is Byron the creepy guy I saw coming over here last night?"

Xandra nodded. "So the vamp strikes again."

Gregory said, "… Whut?" at the same time that I said, "Xandra!"

We all just stared at each other, Gregory's mouth open, his brow furrowed.

"I …" she started. "Yeah."

I swallowed. "Well, the cat's out of the bag." There was no point in hiding it. Gregory had already seen too much. He looked at me through wide eyes, as if from a great distance.

"So … that's what you didn't want to tell me yesterday … this guy is a … vampire?" The disbelief hung pretty thick as he spoke.

I knew what would follow: an accusation that I, that *we*, were both nutjobs who needed locking up—and he'd burst out of here, run to the nearest phone he could find, and call for a crazy van to come pick us both up, carting us off never to be seen again.

"I don't really care if you believe it or not," I said. "I have to find my parents."

But what Gregory said next was—

"This makes so much sense."

Okay. The whole world was going crazy—or crazy according to my worldview just a week ago, anyway. That someone else believed in vampires—someone right next door to me!—would've been kind of sad last Monday, confusing on Wednesday, incredibly unlikely on Friday, and damned appreciated this weekend. Gregory's eyes were glued to the hardwood floor. "But why would vampires set up shop in freakin' Florida?"

I should've been thanking the heavens for someone believing me. I would have yesterday. But now, with my parents gone, perhaps in danger—danger that grew every passing second I didn't move—I didn't care if the whole world was on my side or not. I needed to find them. Up the stairs I ran, looking for more clues, ignoring the slew of questions Gregory began to fire off at Xandra, who was now the vampire expert once again. My parents' room was perfectly made up, but that was not anything out of the ordinary. Mom always made sure that it looked like it was right out of a magazine. Only, the window looking out over the front lawn was open behind the blinds, and they rattled in the wind. That gave me no answers, so I made sure to cross across to the window and slam it shut. No sense in leaving the air conditioning on when the windows were open.

I froze as I slid the lock home on the window. Was this how

Byron smuggled my parents out of the house? Or did he use the door?

I forced myself not to think about how he had taken them. I didn't think I could stomach the idea of them being hurt or knocked unconscious or …

I tried to force my knees to stop shaking as I made my way across the hall to my room.

My room was an awful, terrible sight. My bed was made, with my pillows fluffed and arranged nicely on top of my tucked-in comforter and sheets. My clothes had all been scooped up off of the floor and dumped into the laundry basket, and my closet was shut. My perfumes were arranged by color on a shelf, and my makeup was laid out on the silver tray on the dresser as if it were a salon display.

Gregory appeared behind me, Xandra in tow. "Wow, your room is immaculate," he said, looking in. "I always assumed that girls' rooms are total messes, with clothes everywhere and bras all over the place …"

Xandra elbowed him in the ribs.

"Ew, did Byron touch all of your stuff?"

I looked around and shuddered. "Yuck …"

"Hey, what's this?" Gregory asked.

There was a bright pink sticky note stuck to the mirror above my dresser. It was so bright I was amazed that I had missed it before.

I stepped closer to read—and my heart slammed against my ribs at full force.

We will be together, it said.
Or else.

Chapter 34

The mixture of emotions swirling within me, each vying for attention, was odd. Not because of the fear of the vampires—and in particular one vampire—out for my blood. Nor was it because of the anger at this situation having spiraled so wildly out of control, and the fact that my parents, who so often infuriated me and were infuriated by me, had been taken, drawn into something they would never understand.

What was strange was the apathy clouding it all. Because after everything that had happened, and after all that was at stake now, I just wanted to leave, to just get on a bus and never look back. I had nowhere to go, but I was going to be eighteen in six months. Maybe I could get help from the state, if my parents were declared dead.

I just wanted to stop fighting. I wanted it all to just go away.

But I couldn't leave my parents there in Byron's hands. Their blood would be on my hands. And I was the only one who could actually help them. They would die if I didn't find them.

I crumpled the sticky note up in my hands and tossed it across the room.

I pulled my phone out and combed through my texts. I tapped on Iona's name.

He took my parents. I don't know what to do next.

And then I waited. Xandra watched me with wide eyes, like she'd seen a ghost. Gregory, at her side, was wary, pale.

"What … what do we do now?" Xandra asked. Her voice was choked.

"I don't know," I replied.

Gregory nodded to the bright pink note near my trash can. "What did that mean?"

"It means that he won't give up until he gets what he wants."

"Which is … ?"

"Me," I answered flatly. My phone vibrated. I snatched it up to see—an email. My heart sank. Why couldn't she be timely when I needed her to be?

Damn it, why hadn't I gotten contact details for Mill? Iona might be MIA, but she wasn't the only vampire around to have been willing to stand by my side and help me.

And in the fight against Byron, I needed all the hands I could get.

And that was what I had on my hands. I'd known it was coming, I supposed, since this started, even more so when Iona first got in touch with me. Now it had come to a head … and only I could finish it.

"I'm going to have to go after them," I said quietly.

"Do you know where they are?" Xandra asked. Her features were tight, pale.

I shook my head.

"Do you know where he is?" Gregory asked.

I shook my head again.

They looked at each other. Compassion and pity passed between them.

"I just can't sit here and do nothing," I said. "My parents are in this situation because of me."

Gregory looked at his feet, and then back up at me.

"I dunno, this is sounding a little like a Rickon Stark situation to me. Spoilers, by the way. But … I don't think this guy—assuming he is a for-real vampire—is going to give them back no matter what." He shook his head, watching me sadly. "Look, Cassie, I'm sorry about your parents. But I just …"

I held up my hand. "I get it. I'm not expecting your help or anything."

He opened his mouth, his brow furrowing, and then closed it again. "All right," he said finally. "I guess I'll see you around."

And with that, he turned and left.

"Well, he took that rather well," Xandra muttered.

"That's if he actually believes any of it."

"He said he saw Byron jump up to your window," Xandra pointed out.

I pinched the bridge of my nose. "Whatever."

"So …" Xandra continued.

I looked up at her, and her large blue eyes were staring at me expectantly.

"What?" I asked.

"What should I do … ?"

I sat down on my bed, my forehead in my hands. "I don't even know what *I* should do."

What I did know, what I did have, was some sense of what was right—a code of honor that I knew, even if being a perpetual liar put me as far away from honor as a person could be without committing hate crimes. And so Xandra … I couldn't make her go through this with me. This was not her fight.

"You should go home," I said.

A hesitation. "I wouldn't feel right leaving you here like this," she said.

No denying that hope in her tone—or the way her eyes lit. She wanted to leave.

How could I blame her?

"You need to go home and be with your family. Better yet, go to school like everything's normal. If we're lucky, Byron won't know that you and Gregory followed me here."

Xandra pulled at the end of her shirt nervously.

"I can't put you in harm's way too," I continued. I tried to smile. "I appreciate all that you've done for me. You stuck your neck out for me by letting me stay over last night."

"But your parents got kidnapped because of it …"

I choked on the words that I was about to say. She was right. If I hadn't gone to her house, Byron wouldn't have needed to exact revenge on my parents. If I had just stayed, my parents wouldn't have had to be involved at all.

"You should go," I repeated.

She turned toward the door but stopped short. "You sure?" she asked hesitantly.

I nodded, hoped she wouldn't ask again, that I wouldn't cave and beg her to stay.

The corner of her lip turned up in a sad smile. "I'm sorry about … all of this."

And she, like Gregory before her, left me.

I had never imagined what it would feel like to be in such a big house all alone, not knowing if anyone apart from me would fill it again. It was cold, silent, like I was in a prison cell. I could hear the birds, see the sunshine, and I could smell the freshly cut grass. But it was all out of reach.

Real life seemed fake now.

Even if it were real, I had one focus and one focus only: getting my parents back. Question was, how? I had no idea where Byron was, or where he took them. Was I just supposed to wait here for him to come back for me? If that was the case, it wouldn't be until nightfall.

That was much too long to wait.

Think, Cassie, I cajoled myself.

If I knew anything about the situation, about Byron, it was that he was totally obsessed with me. Like, entirely. There was probably nothing in his actions that didn't revolve around me in some way now. Iona had made that pretty clear. He would follow me to the ends of the earth. If I ran, he would follow.

I pulled the stake out of my hair and twirled it between my fingers.

Byron now had a bargaining chip. Before, it was only his infatuation with me that protected me. Even without Iona saying so, it was obvious that he enjoyed the chase. But he did not take it well when the control was taken from him, like when

I tossed the holy water in his eyes.

I pressed my palms into my eyelids, trying to block everything around me out.

He had my parents. And he would think nothing of turning them to spite me, and then still coming after me.

I couldn't bear the thought of my parents being vampires. Who knew what would happen? They would be no better off than dead.

My mind swam with the idea of them being tortured for my sake. Blood everywhere, Byron's teeth flashing, Mom screaming …

I got to my feet and ran down the stairs.

I couldn't stay in the house anymore, not with the reminders screaming at me from every angle that this was all my fault.

I tried to control my breathing, but it started coming fast, and hard. It hurt.

I fell to my knees on the cold tile floor, my hands flat on the floor beneath me.

If I had been honest with them from the very beginning about all of this, then maybe, just maybe, it wouldn't have come down to this. Maybe things could have turned out differently. It wouldn't have stopped Byron from coming around … but maybe, if I had told them the truth, they might have believed me.

And then everything could have happened differently.

My phone vibrated, and I anxiously pulled it from my pocket with sweat-slicked hands.

With a blow to the chest, I saw it was from Mom.

Sweetheart, it's fine. We're just fine. Your daddy and I are safe, for now. Be brave, baby girl. We love you to the moon and back.

I could have chucked my phone in disgust. Instead, I quickly replied:

Byron, cut the crap. Where are they?

I didn't have to wait long for the answer.

He sent me an address, and when I pulled it up on the GPS on my phone, I realized it was about five miles from the Tampa International Airport, on a tiny, one-road-wide inlet along the bay. All the houses in that area were mansions. I didn't surprise me that Byron would like to live large.

I swallowed hard, and I quickly ordered an Uber. I knew it would only take me a few minutes to get there.

While I waited for it to arrive, I replaced the stake in my boot, knowing it was the only thing standing between saving my parents—and losing them forever.

Chapter 35

Byron's street was quiet, stretching all the way to a dead end that looked out onto the bay. Palm trees lined it, along with southern oaks and tall, flowering bushes.

The house Byron had led me to was enormous. It stood before the water, its massive yard extending all the way to its glimmering edge. The building was three stories of pale blue stucco, with windows everywhere, a huge wooden front door, and a three-car garage. Every floor had a balcony that overlooked to the bay. This close to the sea, the salt in the air was pungent, overpowering the sweet scent of gardenias. The landscaping itself was immaculate, with hibiscus flowers, aloe plants, and countless other brightly colored flowers and plants that I didn't recognize.

There was a large pool behind the house, enclosed in a two-story lanai.

A wrought iron gate, twisted in a complicated, elegant pattern, stood slightly ajar on the driveway.

I stepped up to the gate and pushed it open.

There were no cars visible. All of the garage doors were closed tight.

I walked toward the front doors. As I got closer, I noticed that all of the windows had their blinds pulled shut, preventing any sunlight from getting in.

No question that this was the right place—as if there was any possibility Byron would have sent me elsewhere.

The front door stood ajar.

I had seen enough horror movies to know that I should not enter.

But I also knew that if I didn't, I'd never see my parents alive again. So, with a last look at the outside—perhaps my last ever—I drank in the feeling of life, of peace, that touched me but could not penetrate the black fear that hung over me … and then I stepped inside.

The foyer opened up into a huge space, with long, wide, dark wooden floors. A huge staircase wound its way up along the circular wall, and I could just barely see up into the second floor. Up above that was another staircase, winding up to the third floor. A huge gold and crystal chandelier hung from the ceiling, stretching from the top of the third floor all the way to the first floor, flooding the house with dancing rainbows of light.

The air was cold. My skin pimpled, rising into bumps. The scent of roses filled the air, breathing from vases on every surface; on side tables, on windowsills, on tall, free-standing pedestals.

Roses … and blood.

Each footstep I took echoed. A living room loomed, larger than the entire first floor footprint of my house. All of the furnishings had to have come from high end designers, with a huge gray L-shaped couch, a curved television, and a solid, marble-topped coffee table. The view out of the windows must have been breathtaking, but the blinds permitted only the faintest light to peek through the edges. The stairs were carpeted with white shag.

I stepped onto the first one and froze.

Crimson spatters.

Had he already hurt them? Turned them?

He had to have known that I was here. He didn't miss much, if anything.

I eased away from the steps. He was probably trying to lure

me up there. I didn't want to give him the satisfaction of following his little trail just yet.

I tried to push the nausea down as I headed down a hall toward a kitchen.

This far inside, it was pretty obvious that I was not going to be able to use sunlight to my advantage. He wouldn't follow me outside in the middle of the day, and if I kept creeping through these rooms that were away from all of the windows, then I wouldn't be able to utilize it at all. Upon further inspection, the blinds were not actually blinds at all, but some kind of metal welded to the window frames, with just enough light coming through to be able to see the time of day. Unless I had a soldering tool or a powered screwdriver, they weren't coming off. And if I left the house now that I had come inside, who knew what he would do to punish me for that?

The kitchen smelled like fresh coffee and chocolate. Still no sign of anything, or anyone, aside from the small flecks of blood on the stairs. Frigid air seemed to emanate from the tiles.

For a place so large, so open, it was hard not to feel claustrophobic. The lack of sunlight helped with that.

The fact that I didn't know where Byron was, but knew he could lunge at me from around a corner at any moment, dialed the tension up to its maximum.

I found a large den, a luxurious dining room that could seat at least twelve, and a four-seasons room that dumped out into the lanai and the pool.

All of the other external doors were locked, funneling my way in and out to one door.

Like a lab rat.

First floor exhausted, I found myself again at the base of the stairs … and those claret drips, leaching into the shag. There was not enough here to account for the metallic tang in the air, not even half a percent of enough—which meant there was more of it somewhere.

Above me … with him.

My heart thudded sickeningly. No place else to go, though.

Steeling myself with the deepest breath I could manage, I put my foot on the bottom stair, careful to avoid the droplets of dark blood. Up and around the spiral, slowly. More flecks passed me by—a breadcrumb trail, almost methodical.

Or a result of more damage than I wanted to think about.

I reached the landing and peered over the banister down into the large foyer. Closer to Byron now, wherever he was, the tension was ratcheting up. The stake in my boot was no longer enough—especially considering how difficult it had been to free it when Theo lurched at me. So I took stock of my surroundings, then, deciding I was safe enough for the moment and that Byron couldn't spring at me, I removed my boot, took the stake out, and slipped it into my hair.

He'd see it—but he knew I was coming. He knew I was here. And he'd know exactly what I aimed to do to him. Because between my evasion, and the holy water I'd singed his face with … Cassie was not coming easy, no, sir.

I couldn't just bank on finding him and getting close enough straight away to stab him through the heart—not least because my parents were pawns now, and he'd certainly have them close by to threaten if I made so much as one wrong move. So I had to buy myself some time.

The only way that I could have any hope of stalling him log enough to figure out my next steps was to make him think that he had won. I hated the idea of it, but if I got him to believe, even for a moment, that somehow I had given into him, succumbed to some rapid case of Stockholm syndrome— which would not be what he expected, given my behavior up to now— he might drop his guard.

I would have to lie.

How ironic it was that the very thing that had gotten me into this situation – the lies that caused me to be dragged down to Florida – was the same thing I was going to have to use to get out of it.

At least I was good at it. It was the only thing I was good at, it seemed. Lying to him meant proffering myself as his Juliet.

It meant loving him—

or at least making him believe that I loved him.

I closed my eyes, taking another deep, steadying breath.

I could do this.

"Hello, my darling," a cold, smooth voice whispered in my ear.

My eyes shot open to see Byron standing inches away from me.

Chapter 36

I amazed even myself when I remained still, given how close he was to me.

I looked up into his eyes, hoping that all he could see of me was what he wanted to see, not what was actually there, which was boiling, raging hatred.

As quick as I blinked, Byron was no longer standing in front of me, but lounging on a plush blue settee beneath another row of windows that, if open, would have provided a beautiful view of Tampa Bay. Relaxed as he was, he might've been sprawled there all afternoon. He held a crystal champagne flute almost lazily.

I fought not to look at it—at what it held inside—and to tamp down the burning fear that the crimson fluid might have been, until recently, flowing through Mom's or Dad's veins.

Byron smiled. He seemed incredibly pleased with himself, with one of his eyebrows slightly arched, and a smirk tugging at one corner of his mouth.

"So you came willingly," he cooed, leaning his chin in his hand, his elbow perched on the arm of the seat.

I wanted to vomit at his tone, but instead, I made myself bow my head as if humble.

"I did," I replied. I didn't have a choice, really. He and I both knew that.

It was my motivation that mattered in that moment, and I

needed to convince him that it wasn't just for my parents, but for our relationship as well.

A relationship that would be over before the sun went down if I had any control over it.

He rocked the glass in his hand back and forth slowly, studying me closely, that playful grin still etched on his face.

He looked like he wanted to eat me—literally. Nevertheless, there was more than that in it, a hormonal teenage boy's fantasies, his twisted, sick view of—love? Lust? It made my skin crawl. To hide my disgust, I wrapped my arms around myself and shied away. Shyness—that would sucker him in; my face hidden modestly, fingers fiddling with my hair, like the virginal waif he hungered after. I knew that it was a stretch, seeing as how I could have spit in his face any other time he was around, but I had to try.

It was the only advantage I had.

Glancing carefully around, I assessed my surroundings.

My parents were not here, on the landing looking down over the foyer, that much was certain. A hall wound away from me out of the corner of my right eye, and a few doors were shut tight along the wall to my left. The large crystal chandelier that the staircase wrapped around cast a multitude of shimmering lights on the large mirror on the wall to Byron's right, filling the room with brilliant colors.

I realized, with a small shiver down my neck, that Byron did not have a reflection. Confirmation that none of the other signs had misled me.

"I just …" I started, looking down at my worn sneakers, noticing the tear on the toe of the right foot. "I just realized that I didn't want to fight you anymore."

Ugh, gag me. That was so much harder to say out loud than I would have ever thought it could be.

Byron chuckled, and took a draw from his glass. "Did you?" he asked. "Good. All I've ever wanted was for you to realize that we should be together. That we belong together." He leaned forward. "Fighting that, fighting … *destiny* is futile."

"Yes," I replied. "Destiny." Hold off the gagging.

I had to be careful not to let my true thoughts show. Some truth was always ideal. It allowed me to control the situation. I had the ability to choose the lies that I told.

And some truth in every lie made them that much harder to detect and untangle.

I was the master of weaving truth into my lies.

"You're quite lovely, did you know that?"

It was a mix of condescension and flattery, and it was maddening.

Byron definitely had the advantage. Even if I were to go and sit on the couch opposite him, it would still be easy for him to intercept me if I decided to run.

Funny. Try to run from a vampire. Good one, Cassie.

"Not as handsome as you are," I said, and then giggled.

Giggled.

"Byron …" I said, almost amused by the stunned look that had crept onto his face. "My Romeo …" Again, I had to bite the tip of my tongue not to give away that I wanted to laugh—or vomit my freakin' guts up. "Please … I'm here now. Could we just … let my parents be on their way?"

Byron's one-sided smirk quirked higher, and then stood, casually walking back over to me—the picture of a cocky teenage boy.

A manipulative, long-lived, evil teenage boy.

"I suppose that you've been a good girl," he said. "It's natural to be concerned for your parents." He smirked. "I'm surprised it took you this long to get around to them. You're always so … forward. So … direct with me."

Opposite me now—near enough that I could stab him through the heart—he brushed a stray strand of hair from my face.

It took every ounce of my strength not to cringe back from him.

Softly, he lamented, "I remember how I cried over my parents' bodies the night I was bitten …"

The surprise that showed on my face was genuine.

I lifted my hand gingerly, and laid two fingers, as light as a feather's touch, against his chest. I stared up into his eyes.

It was almost like I was talking to Theo again.

"You know, Byron," I said, putting extra silk into my tone when I spoke his name, "you know everything about me, and yet … I know so little about you." I blinked slow blinks up at him, lashes waving. Every pathetic damsel there had ever been breathed through me as I lured him in, softened his guard.

Byron caught my fingers. The lack of warmth on his skin still frightened me, but I allowed the touch. I had come too far to back down now.

Maybe he was actually buying my ruse. If I could just get him to believe me …

He laced his fingers in mine and led me over to the settee. Still gazing into my eyes, maybe trying to catch me losing my ground, he sat down, pulling me with him to his side.

A glazed look passed over his face, and he took another sip from his glass, then set it down on an ornately carved side table.

"So, you want to know about me?"

Definitely. The longer he talked, the more he got wrapped up in his memories, in feeling that he was opening up to a lover who had finally fallen for his charms, the easier it would be for me to find a break in his defenses—then whip the stake out of my messy bun, where it blended in, looking more like a chopstick than anything else, and plunge it into his chest.

"I don't even know how old you are," I said quietly. "I don't know where you come from, or if you have any friends …" I looked back up at him and smiled knowingly. "I know you don't go to my school. You just wanted to be near to me, didn't you?"

His heavy lidded eyes gazed down at me, through his eyelashes. "I did."

It was really hard not to focus on the fact that I was sitting next to my stalker like some sort of enraptured (read: groomed) schoolgirl. I shifted back against the seat, moving my hand onto my leg. Slowly, I could work that around to my hip, out of sight … then, when the time was right, perhaps pretend to fiddle with my hair …

Then Byron's arm snaked around my shoulder. I tensed—at how cold it was, how strong, the way he pulled me into his chest, like we were on a date at a movie.

Relax, I willed myself.

Somehow, my tension uncoiled, just a fraction.

Still, it was impossible to avoid being aware of the fact that my stake was now effectively out of reach—which meant I needed a new plan of action. "Tell me," I breathed. "Tell me all about … *you*."

"Where to start …" Byron said, sighing heavily. "I'm seventeen, of course, but I know that isn't what you want to know." He squeezed my shoulder so tightly that it hurt. I wondered if he'd done it on purpose, or if his excitement made him forget that his strength outstripped mine. "I was turned in 1945. I know, that doesn't seem right, does it? But it's true."

Being so close, it was hard to crane my neck up at him, so I contented myself with laying my head on his shoulder. He would like that, I knew—like it a lot.

Hard to forget too, though, that it put my neck well within striking distance of his fangs. I was like a mouse snuggled up against a hungry cat. He would be able to smell my hair, feel my heartbeat, hear me drawing in each and every breath. I hoped that it would drive him crazy enough that it would allow me to figure out what I needed to do.

"My dad was a war vet, Mom was a typical housewife. She always wore this powder blue apron with yellow flowers. Told me that my father got it for her in France. I never actually found out if that was true."

"I'm sorry," I said hesitantly, catching him in the subtle probing for sympathy, a small, tentative manipulation.

"It was early October. I lived in Michigan as a child. Middle of nowhere. There were trees all the way around my house. My father always believed in having ample space for my mother and us children to live. I had five siblings, by the way."

He sighed, though I knew he probably didn't actually need to breathe, and his tone became more somber. I listened.

"I was a senior in high school. I was the oldest and had a part-time job at the grocery store in town. I'd gotten a car as a birthday present just a few weeks before. My girlfriend at the time, Melody, was the cheerleading captain, and I planned to ask her to marry me that summer.

"After dropping off some fresh sunflowers off at Melody's house, I drove home. My mother always insisted that we all make it home for dinner during the week, even if that made the rest of the family wait." His eyes flashed. "Family was very important to her. No one would eat until we all were home. That night, they were all waiting for me …

"When I pulled in the driveway, I saw Father's car, and all of the lights on inside. Without a care, I stepped up to the front of the house. I remember that I was whistling some sort of happy tune. I realized that the front door was slightly open. I thought it was odd, not because we had any fear of theft, but because none of my siblings were outside."

I chanced a look up at him as I ran a hand through my hair—fiddling, idly, enraptured … and inches away from the stake pushed through my bun.

"The first thing I remembered was the squelch that my boot made as I stepped inside the house. I was screaming before I realized why. Red was everywhere. It coated the flowered wallpaper as if someone had thrown buckets of it against the walls. Rivers of it snaked through the entry, into the kitchen, from the living room. There was even a slow trickle from the stairs, a steady drip, drip, drip."

I clenched my teeth, picturing it—picturing it having happened to *my* family. It was not impossible that I could have walked into the house this morning to discover this very scene Byron described to me now, transposed from 1945 Michigan to 2018 Tampa Bay.

"And their bodies …" Byron's voice was grave, thick.

I almost believed him. It would have been easy to. How could anyone talk about this without getting choked up?

"My little sisters were sprawled across the floor in the room the three of them shared. My brother, who was only two years younger than me, was lying awkwardly on my father's armchair, his neck exposed, blood coating the front of his shirt. And my parents …

"I found them in the kitchen. Mother was bent over the sink, her head in the basin. My father was on the floor, one of his legs tangled in the legs of the chairs around the table. But they weren't the only ones there. There were two men, tall, ghostly pale, red dripping down their cheeks to their chins, the fronts of their shirts drenched.

"'Oh, look,' one of them said. 'I guess I could go for another drink.' The last thing I remember is the sharp pain at my neck, hands as strong as iron around my body, and this pulling, as if the very life of me was being sucked out.

"They left me alive, though. I don't think they knew that they had," Byron said. "Maybe they had gorged too much on the rest of my family. But three days later, I was a vampire. And I fled."

He pulled his arm back from around my shoulders—just as my fingers grazed the stake in my hair.

"That must have been awful," I said, hoping that he would continue. I was almost ready. He just needed to get lost one more time.

I could do this.

"The fear and the rage that I felt that vampires had intruded on my life was unlike any hatred I had ever felt, you know? Well, I know you understand. It is just like the hatred that you feel toward me."

I blinked. Hatred? I thought he was buying all of this lovey-dovey nonsense.

He looked at me with a twisted, monstrous sympathy. "It is impossible for a human to ever truly love a vampire. I have come to that realization. Which is why I have turned all of the women I have fallen in love with. No, none of you can understand. You won't understand until you too have been turned ... your destiny.

"You understand what I mean, don't you?" he asked suddenly. "That fear that I felt. The hatred. I have never made you that afraid. Angry, of course, I know. I like your fierceness. But Theo ... he frightened you to your core, didn't he?"

I froze, my fingers tightening. How ... how did he ...

He knew. If he knew about Theo, then he knew about Mill, and Iona, and the holy water, and—

"Oh, yes," Byron said, his dark, piercing gaze fixing me to my seat. "I know everything, Cassie. Just like ... I know about that stake your fingers rest on this very moment."

Chapter 37

He was suddenly across the sitting room, standing beside the staircase, blocking my way back downstairs. He was twirling my stake between his fingers like a bored student in a boring lecture class, having pulled it easily from my hair and dismantling the messy bun barely before my mind had registered what he was doing.

The smirk on his face was poisonous. Sickeningly sweet, and expectant.

I just gaped at him, my jaw slack, my eyes wide.

He snickered. "Cassie, Cassie, Cassie. Well done, truly, a riveting performance. Absolutely captivating." There was a flicker in his eyes as his lips straightened, leaving amusement behind for regret. "You have no idea how much I wish I could have believed you."

He leaned casually against the banister, the lights from the chandelier creating a halo around his tousled hair, bright and golden.

"It would have made all of this that much simpler if you had just given in, instead of fighting me."

He stopped twirling the stake, and then his face turned sour, his smile melting into a grimace—and then he snapped it in half, and then those halves into halves, each no longer than my pinkie finger.

"Iona is behind this, isn't she?" he growled. "Hell hath no fury and all that … I should have seen it earlier."

"She was scorned," I said. I couldn't think of anything else.

"That's her interpretation." He rolled his eyes and tossed the remains of the wooden stake over the side of the banister. He locked eyes with me. "There was nothing between her and me—nothing of consequence at least. It wasn't like what you and I have."

"She disagrees," I said.

"Well … I'll have to deal with her later," he spat, but he leaned unperturbed against the banister once more, crossing his arms over his chest. "You remind me of her, you know. Just a little. You both have a certain spunk about you. The resistance makes the chase all that much sweeter. But it'll be different between you and I—you're not as finicky as she is. You're more … true. Dedicated. I can see it in the way you conduct yourself."

My stomach turned over.

"You and I—it'll be forever," he continued. "It was never going to work out between Iona and me. I should have seen the signs; they were all there early. She hated me all the way through. Not like you. There was a grain of truth in your performance just now. I saw it. You're different than the rest. Special."

"What's so special about me?" I asked, my voice almost at a shout. "Why did you pick me out of … everyone else, the world over?"

Byron's brow furrowed, and he tilted his head, looking at me like I was an idiot. "I thought it was obvious," he said. "I came to save you from the life that you hate."

Iona's words reverberated in my mind. She was right. He had been watching me for longer than I had originally thought.

"I first saw you at that little coffee shop near the school just after you moved here," Byron continued. "I thought you were pretty enough." A melancholy note suffused his voice as he added, "You had the same hair color as my Melody did."

I grimaced. It was almost enough to make me feel sorry for him. Almost.

"Let me guess," I said. "Iona had her eyes?"

Byron shook his head. "No. She had Melody's wistfulness."

"So you pick all of your victims because we remind you of your long lost love?" How ... sad.

"*Victims*? Please, Cassandra." Byron pursed his lips. "I figure if I loved like that once, I should be able to find it again, right? But it's different this time, you see—you are my forever. You are the end of the line."

I bit the inside of my lip. My only weapon gone, and Mill's gifted weapon already used, I didn't see a way out of this. I had to buy time, though, to at least think ...

"How'd you find me?" I demanded.

Ego got the better of him.

"I overheard you talking with your Mom on the phone that day in the coffee shop. I could smell the tension between you— the deep-rooted problems there. And so I started following you.

"You lived inside your own head, and it made me long to get inside of it. Your own world in there ... so deep, so fertile. Look at how easily you spin lies. Yours is a brilliant imagination. So ... I waited ... until that night when you walked home from school. "

My stomach twisted sickly, remembering the phone call.

He grinned again and took a few steps toward me.

"Oh, Cassie. If you had just been like every other girl your age, and swooned at my attention, then things would be so different right now. You would be in love with me and unharmed, you wouldn't be a murderer ... and your parents wouldn't be locked in the wine cellar. "

Bingo. He let it slip. I felt my eyes widen momentarily, but I quickly hardened my gaze.

"I'm not a murderer," I said."

"Is that so?" Byron asked with a trace of amusement.

"Theo was already dead. And I killed him in self-defense, anyway."

Byron flashed his fangs at me in a wide grin. He reminded me of Lord Draven with that smile. "You aren't fooling me. You feel it, don't you? I can tell. You're sweet—you have a conscience . It prickles, like the thorns of a rose."

I licked my lips, my eyes darting around. I had to get away. But how was I going to? I was out of options. He'd figured me out, knew that I wasn't there to be wooed by him after all. And my only weapon lay in pieces on the floor of the foyer.

"I enjoyed learning about Theo, to be honest," Byron said. "News spread like wildfire that a vampire was killed at a peace gathering." He laughed heartily. "I never liked him, either. Too egotistical, too reckless. He lacked the patience that most vampires learn with time. Not his fault, of course. He was only turned a few years back.

"But don't worry. I kept your secret from Lord Draven. Your ferocity just made me crave you that much more."

His last words came out in a low growl.

"I'm going to give you one more chance, Cassie," Byron said, his voice even, coated in honey as he advanced again. "To start our relationship off on the right foot. Let me give you the gift, let me turn you, willingly … or I will go downstairs right now, and kill your parents." His eyes flicked toward the stairs. "I want us to be together … for you to feel my love … and if that means I have to bring you low, to make you feel as I did on that day in Michigan so long ago … I will do it." He smiled tightly. "But … I'd rather you give of yourself, freely." His smile turned somehow warmer … and yet still left me cold. "It will make everything … sweeter, if you just … give in."

Almost out of time, damn it.

I had to make a choice—make a break for it—now. *You beat Theo,* I told myself—or a disembodied voice that sounded like my own, but came unbidden, alien to my mind. *You had no idea what you were doing, went completely on instinct. You can do it again.*

Could I?

You don't have a choice.

No. It was win or lose—kill or be killed.

Slowly rising from the settee, I wiped my face clear of every emotion, every tell.

A sense of calm passed over me. My breathing steadied. And I accepted my fate. Gaze locked on his, I hoped, prayed, that this time he bought it. Hoped that he would see the defeat that I actually did feel deep in my bones, the inevitable fate that had finally caught up with me, after having been staved off since that first night he fell into step beside me.

I crossed the distance between us.

Tears drew hot tracks down my cheeks.

Was this it? Were these the last moments that my heart would beat against my rib cage, trying desperately to remind me that I was very much alive? Was the blood that was flowing through my veins about to satisfy one of the most wicked creatures to walk the earth? Would I wake, cold and dead, but conscious of my life shattering into brittle, insignificant pieces around me, forever doomed to walk the earth?

I reached him. A grin hitched up on his face.

I laid my hands on his chest. His cologne was strong and musky, like old wood and leather. His flesh was cold and hard beneath his shirt.

He stared down into my face.

Slowly, I leaned up toward him, stretching my neck out. Gently, I pulled my hair aside so that the pale, soft skin of my neck showed under the refracted light bouncing from the chandelier's many hanging crystals. Byron's eyes lit.

"There we are," he whispered, fangs extended. "That wasn't so hard, was it?"

I took a deep breath, my hands returning to rest on his chest.

He put his hands on my hips, and his gaze broke from mine as he slowly lowered his lips down toward my neck—

I shoved with all my might, pushing him back—

And over the railing overlooking the foyer.

He shrieked, a surprisingly heartrending sound, as his body tumbled over the banister, knocked against the chandelier—and fell through the open air to the ground below.

I was running before I heard the resounding thud of his body slamming against the wide wooden planks.

Chapter 38

I tore around the corner of the nearest hallway and hurtled down it as fast as I possibly could. My palms were sweating, and my chest heaving. It had worked. Somehow, I'd suckered him in.

It would only buy me a few seconds' lead, though. It was imperative I put it to good use.

I picked a room and threw myself inside, slamming the door behind me. Byron screamed in rage from the stairs.

My fingers fumbled with the lock on the door. Crouched low, I listened, breath held. He thundered up the stairs.

I hoped, prayed, that if he did have extra-strength hearing, he was too enraged to hone in on me quickly. With luck, he'd check every room leading up to this one, buying me just a little longer. The one I found myself in was an elaborately decorated bedroom. A king-sized bed with a canopy bed frame reached almost all the way to the ceiling. There were large windows against the far wall, also bolted up with metal sheets. Dust clogged the air. No one had been in here in a long time.

There was a loud crash against the wall in the hall, and I nearly leapt out of my skin. The door would not hold him.

I lunged into the en suite bathroom.

Another door led out from it—into, I hoped, another hall. A splintering explosion went off behind me.

He was through to the bedroom.

"Come out, come out, wherever you are … my princess!" Byron hollered.

I shoved through the next door, trying to make as little sound on the carpeted floor as I could. I cried out in pain when my elbow caught the doorknob, and then bit down on my hand until I drew blood, furious with myself as I ran farther down the hall. The lanai had been two-story, which meant that there had to be an entrance upstairs somewhere. It would either be attached to the master bedroom, or to some sort of living room.

As I ran, I grabbed a door or two and pulled them shut, hoping and praying that the sound would throw Byron off of the trail.

Then I dove into a room on the eastern side of the house, closest to the pool and the lanai.

I also made sure to keep the door open that time. Double doors beckoned on the back wall. Desperately as I ran across to them, I hoped with everything in me that they were unlocked—or that I could force my way through before Byron caught up.

I threw myself against the doors and pulled against the handle. They didn't budge—but my knuckles grazed the lock, a simple twist mechanism without a key.

I didn't think I had ever felt terror and then elation back to back like that.

I hoped never to again. The doors opened easily. I slipped out, closing them as quietly as I could behind myself. No lock on this side, unfortunately—but if Byron caught up, it wouldn't matter anyway; he'd pull a Jack Torrance and be through the door without a pause.

I was out in the lanai, but I was trapped up on what looked like was a balcony. The pool and concrete surround were far below me. It would be suicide to try and jump from here. I'd easily shatter my legs if I even landed in the pool; the water couldn't have been more than four or five feet deep.

I ran to the door on the other side of the balcony, grabbing at a stitch in my chest.

I tried the handle. It was locked.

I screamed in frustration and ran to the next closest door.

It flew open as I threw my weight against it.

I knew that there had been a chance that Byron could have been waiting for me on the other side of the door, but he wasn't, and so I didn't stop to count my blessings.

I ran out into the hall and heard Byron's voice back near the room I had just left.

"My bounty is as boundless as the sea!"

I ran back toward the stairs, as quickly as I could.

"My love as deep. The more I give to thee—"

He laughed, and I wanted to hurl on the carpet.

He was *enjoying* this.

"The more I have, for both are infinite!"

And here I'd thought that the only way to die listening to Shakespeare was from boredom. Down the stairs, past the shattered remnants of my stake, toward the front door … It was locked.

"Love is a smoke raised with the fume of sighs."

I whipped around, and there stood Byron at the top of the stairs, looking down at me with an utterly deranged expression. His chest heaved, yet he looked exhilarated. His ruffled hair was askew, his eyes wide with rage and longing.

He took one step down the steps.

I was frozen in place.

"Love is a smoke raised with the fume of sighs; Being purged, a fire sparkling in lovers' eyes; Being vexed, a sea nourished with loving tears. What is it else? A madness most discreet, A choking gall, and a preserving sweet."

I threw myself against the door.

Still it didn't budge.

Byron threw his head back, belting a high, wild laugh.

No way out—I was trapped with him. And again, that meant I had to find some way to defend myself.

His laughter followed me as I hurried back down the hall on the first floor, heading for the dining room. He didn't run down after me, though. He could have been by my side instantly.

Instead, he just laughed from high up—savoring the chase.

If I could get inside, close the French doors, I might, *might*, be able to bar myself inside.

The doors were already ajar, and when I leapt inside, I slammed them shut.

Without hesitating, I grabbed the dining chair closest to me, and I swung the arm of it over one of the handles, preventing it from being opened. Another chair secured the other door.

Then I overturned the table—it was a heavy thing, took almost all my strength to do it—and shoved that against the chairs to lock them in place. Even so, it still might not be enough to hold him back.

I yanked the rest of the chairs over to the doors and intertwined them on top of one another, the arms and legs all tangled together, creating a sort of shield between myself and the doors.

Byron started to beat against the door, a whirlwind of explosive thuds louder than any punch delivered by a human had any right to be. The first made me jerk in terror, even though I knew they'd be coming.

"Cassie, really, your determination is admirable," he shouted over his furious pounding. "But you're destroying our house. I understand that the style may not be to your liking, but we could have discussed it before you started the demolition." Again and again, he pounded—and with each echoing *THUD* there came a splintering sound as the wood began to give way to his fists.

I whirled around, looking for something, anything, that I could use to help me.

My eyes fell onto a picture on the wall of a quiet harbor with a flock of seagulls circling above. With a leap of my heart, I realized that the frame itself was made of wood.

I yanked it off of the wall as the doors into the dining room broke apart.

I slammed the frame against the floor, ripping the canvas, and snapping the frame into two splintered pieces.

Over my knee I broke one of the corners—and whirled round just as Byron shoved my tangle of tables and chairs aside, leaping over what remained of the barricade.

I thrust the improvised stake out in front of me like a child's toy sword—

And Byron laughed at it.

"Cassandra," he purred, pacing before me, out of reach, "you can't try the same trick on me twice. Besides, I'm not Theo. I'm not going to leap at you like some wild, feral animal you can skewer."

"How do you know that's how I killed him?" I said, keeping him in front of me, the broken frame between us.

"Well, you wasted the water on me," he said, a darkness passing over his face. "So it wasn't that. And you already made it obvious that Iona helped you …"

He stopped pacing and took me off guard when he launched himself across the distance between us, knocking the frame out of my hands, and then knocking me back into the stacks of chairs.

I cried out—

"You just don't get it, do you, Cassie?" he asked, in my face.

The chair I had landed on had snapped under me. Blood, hot and wet, ran down from somewhere near my shoulder. A shooting pain radiated from my hipbone, and I worried that I might have broken a rib.

I winced, trying to sit up—but Byron's body was strong against mine, holding me down. My hands couldn't find purchase, anything to lever myself up with. Whatever I did find shifted as I leaned against it.

Face inches from mine, Byron inhaled deeply. His eyes rolled into the back of his head.

"We are fated. Destined to be together."

I shoved him, desperately—

He stumbled back, the headiness of the coppery scent of my blood having overpowered him. But it was only a moment's respite—and as he righted himself, he twitched, neck and shoulders jerking in horrific spasms—

He staggered closer, his eyes jerking frenetically between a euphoric glaze and the determined fire of a man whose lust absolutely had to be sated, this instant. I gripped for the nearest thing I could find—and found smooth wood.

The leg of a chair.

The leg of a *broken* chair—and the one last shot I had at staving him off.

He came closer, closer …

My heart thudded madly against my throat. I could smell it too, my senses heightened, my nose picking up the awful iron tang of blood spilling down my arm, making it slick …

My blood-soaked grip tightened, praying that the broken chair leg was sharp enough to do this, praying that it would come free when I bid it.

"Cassie …" Byron whispered—

His feet tangled over a broken chair back. A spasm gripped him at the same moment—

He went down.

And I sprang. Lunging forward, I yanked the shattered chair leg up, free—and then slammed it right into Byron's back. It tore right through him with a grisly sound, bones and whatever lay between it and his heart giving way—then slammed the floor.

The stake ripping through his body unleashed everything he had held back. Neck snapping up, eyes ferocious and dark, he roared a screeching snarl, like a trapped bear. His arms and legs whipped out in a mad frenzy, clawed, grabbing for anything he could find—

But it was no use.

As I backed up toward the wall, panting, the wound where the chair leg had pierced him had started to turn black and collapse in around itself. Realization passed over his face, cold and hard. The fight leaving him, he gasped, horrorstruck, the way I suppose I must have looked when I realized the true extent of the vampire plague.

He choked a cough. Dark, thick blood sprayed from his mouth.

"Cassie," he whispered hoarsely.

My back hit the wall behind me. I slid down to the floor, keeping Byron in my sight.

More of the black, tarry liquid had spread from the wound. His body was starting to cave in on itself.

"We could have been …" he gasped. "Happy … together." He coughed, more blood spewing. "I …"

His head fell against the floor.

"Melody …" And he said no more.

I leaned back against the wall, and cried and cried, until my throat was raw, and the tears had all dried.

Chapter 39

Cassie, pull yourself together. Byron is dead. Dead. *And you need to find your parents.*

I kept repeating this over and over to myself until I was able to stand up on my shaking knees. What remained of Byron was now the same large, black, acrid puddle that Theo had decayed into. The last that remained of him in his putrefaction was his face, which I watched disintegrate into the stinking mess of rotten gore with a mixture of disgust, terror, and spine-tingling relief.

It was over.

He was gone.

I was free.

When I finally could bring myself to, I rose, then carefully clambered over what was left of my pile of chairs. I pulled as many as I could away from the door and made my way out into the hall. Broken wood littered the floor like a tornado had blown through. One hand on the now softly oozing wound at the top of my arm, I crossed shakily to the wine cellar. The door was unlocked,and opened into cold darkness.

At least a dozen rows of shelves stretched all the way to the dark ceiling. The shelves themselves were curved, and in the slope of each curve sat a wine bottle.

The distinct, metallic scent of blood filled the air.

Anger bloomed in me, hate.

If Byron had killed them, had given me false hope …

I made my way around the shelves, slowly, hesitantly.

The rows and rows of wine bottles seemed to never end, all stacked neatly, most covered in a thin layer of dust. And then—a cry, muffled.

I turned, heart thrown into my mouth and beating so, so wildly—and there were Mom and Dad, up against the back wall of the cellar, their hands tied behind their back, their ankles bound, blindfolded and gagged.

"Mom! Dad!" I cried, and I threw myself onto them, pulling the ties around their eyes away, and untying the gags from behind their head.

I gave them a quick once over, and with an immense relief, I realized that they were unharmed.

"Cassandra!" Mom cried, her eyes red and swollen from crying under the blindfold. "Oh, Cassie!"

My dad just gaped, his eyes glued to my face, as if I had come back from the dead.

"Sweetie, you're bleeding!" Mom exclaimed, immediately grabbing at my arm as soon as I had helped untie her.

I pulled my arm from her grasp. "I'm fine, Mom, I'm fine," I insisted.

"Sweetheart," Mom said, taking my hands in hers. "There is a crazy man here. He is the one who kidnapped us!"

"We have to find a way out of here," Dad said.

I studied their faces for a moment.

They didn't know that Byron had been a vampire, did they?

I grimaced. He had stashed them here before they discovered the truth, still keeping that wedge between them and myself.

He was still trying to ruin my life, even though he was gone now.

I had to decide what to do.

I didn't want to lie anymore. But how was I supposed to tell the truth now?

I shook my head. "It's okay. He's gone. But we should go."

"We need to call the police!" Dad said. "We can't let a

psychopath like him go free!"

I knew that was the absolute last thing we should do. All they would find would be the black goo in the dining room. It would be obvious that a fight happened, and there was blood on the stairs.

But they would never find the culprit.

"Let's get out of here first," I agreed. I had to get them to safety first, out into the afternoon sun.

They agreed, and we all rose and started for the door to the wine cellar.

"How do you know that he's gone?" Dad asked. "For sure?"

"Shh," I said, and peered out into the hallway.

Only when I was certain we were in the clear did I lead them out.

My mother let out a yelp of surprise when we passed the dining room, the wreckage that had once been the doors leading inside, and the tables and chairs I'd used to fashion a crude barricade.

"Cassie, what … ?"

"Later," I said, both to get us out of here and to buy me some time to get my thoughts in order. "Let's just get out of here first."

The front door had been locked with a key. Where it was now, I had no idea. Probably in The Goo Formally Known as Byron. I wasn't much interested in fishing it out.

My dad's approach was a good, old-fashioned show of force. Slamming his shoulder against it, on the fourth impact the lock gave and the door rocketed open.

Sunlight spilled across us, and I was sure that I had never been so happy to see the Florida sunshine.

We stepped outside, and I felt safe. Well and truly safe.

"Cassie, what happened in there?" Mom asked, grabbing my shoulder, and turning me to face her.

My dad had pulled his phone out of his pocket and was dialing. I knew it had to have been the police.

I knew they would find Byron's text messages. I would have to answer questions from the police for a police report.

I didn't think I had the strength to totally keep all of this from them anymore. They had to know.

At least some of it.

"This guy …" I started. "He … he's been stalking me."

My mother gasped, and my father lowered the phone from his ear.

"What did you say?" he asked.

I felt my bottom lip start to quiver. I suddenly felt like a six-year-old with a skinned knee at the playground.

More than that, though: I was tired of running, tired of dealing with it all.

I needed their support.

I couldn't tell them everything. But I could tell them enough.

"Sweetheart …" Mom said gently, pulling me into a tight hug, "… why didn't you tell us?"

"This … certainly explains a lot," Dad said quietly, coming to put his arms around both Mom and me.

"I didn't think you'd believe me," I said, my cheeks hot with tears.

Top tier lie. Because it was damned near the whole truth.

"This guy …" I started. "Byron. He's … he's really bad, Mom. He's … he's a monster."

Mom pulled me away from her and looked into my face.

All she would be able to see was the truth. Because that was all that was there.

Mom, being the attorney, knew what I was trying to say. It was enough to get her brain moving. Not that Dad missed the point. His face had lost all of its color.

"He made me do … things," I said, knowing what they'd make of that. They'd be wrong —but it was easier that than telling them all the things I'd done since first crossing paths with him.

"Those things that you said to us the other night when you snuck back home …" Mom's eyes welled with tears. "If only I'd listened to you. "

I wiped my face. The gash on my arm was throbbing, but the bleeding had stopped, the dried streams of it forming a dark crust all the way to my fingertips.

"Maybe we should just go," Mom said. "Get home. Talk about what to do from there."

I could see the lawsuits and the court time and the immense invasion of my privacy flicker across her mind. Her wheels were spinning. Figuring out the exit. There might have been something else going on there, I couldn't tell. Her face was closed, lacking the anger that had been so prevalent in recent days. She was subdued, as though her guilt for not trusting me, for this whole situation, was blanketing her.

After a long pause, Dad said, "Let's leave. And not talk about this—unless … do you think that this—this Byron … do you think that he is going to come back?"

The tension between all of us was almost suffocating. They were so many questions that we all were just agreeing to circle around—the most prominent being what had actually happened in the house between Byron and me.

I looked back at the house. Hard to think it was still only the afternoon, the sun's rays dazzling as they reflected off the softly rippled surface of the bay. Birds sang cheerily. A white heron walked lazily along the edge of the water.

"No," I said, turning away from the shadowed house, from the sunlit bay, gleaming in the daylight. "I don't think he's going to be a problem anymore."

Chapter 40

I yawned, the tip of my pencil putting some finishing details on a small rose at the top corner of my notebook.

A clock ticked between the scratch of two dozen other pencils.

"All right, next question," the teacher said, adjusting the long, jeweled necklace that she wore over her coral pink cardigan. "Who wants to tell me what the square root of 120 is to two decimal places?"

Night hung, dark, outside the classroom windows. Math League, again. But different, this time.

I raised my hand. "Ten point nine five," I replied when she turned her gaze to me. Her eyebrows raised in surprise.

"Cassie. I'm pleased to see that your indifference has passed. Can we write that off as shyness?" She smiled and turned her back to the board to write down the next problem for us to work out.

A week had passed since the event at the house on the bay. And my life had sort of fallen back into a state of normalcy. Well, as normal as it could be, anyway. First major change: I actually enjoyed homework now. It was totally monotonous, but I relished doing anything that didn't involve talking or thinking about vampires. Considering I'd been so sure I would never achieve or experience "normal" again, I threw myself into each and every moment of it.

With two aced quizzes already under my belt, and improving

homework scores, all of my teachers commented on my sudden increase in studiousness. I had to admit, I kind of liked the flattery. I was proud of myself.

My relationship with my parents had changed drastically as well. No longer was there this underlying tension constantly working at us like fraying rope. Instead, Mom often looked at me with pity, or sympathy. Dad always looked angry, but I knew it wasn't at me, because he would cross the room at random to kiss me on the top of my head.

I still hadn't told them anything more, but nor had they really pressed. I think they assumed I would talk about it when I was ready, and they seemed content to wait.

Neither of them had mentioned Byron since leaving the mansion. I was grateful. They'd probably talked about it together, probably a lot, and I knew, and so did they, that something would have to be done about that situation eventually. Mom had brought up the idea of therapy. I'd been tepid at best. Confession may have been good for the soul, but talking about Byron … about Theo … about all that had happened?

I didn't have the energy to bring it up yet, though.

For now, I was happy with just being on my best behavior.

Willingly, no less.

Mom had promised to pick me up tonight, and it hadn't even crossed my mind to argue. I even joked that we should go get something at Panera together afterward. She had seemed delighted, and asked Dad if he wanted her to bring anything home for him.

I felt a prod in my back as the teacher took another question to the blackboard.

I glanced over my shoulder and saw Xandra, with her pencil hovering near the back of my chair.

"You still up for boba tea this weekend?" she whispered.

I grinned. "That sounds awesome. Yes, for sure."

"Sweet."

I glanced at the clock. Five minutes till it was over. My

stomach growled, and the image of creamy macaroni and cheese danced through my mind for at least the tenth time this past hour. There was a movement at the window in the door—and I froze.

Iona. Fear pricked at the back of my mind. Her eyes met mine. Wordlessly, she slunk out of sight.

I raised my hand. "Miss Patterson?"

"Yes, Cassie?"

"My mom said she might be here early tonight. Is it okay if I split now?"

Miss Patterson checked her watch. "Sure, no problem. See you next Tuesday."

I waved at Xandra, who gave me a quizzical look.

I faked a smile and shook my head. Everything was fine. If anything was going down, she knew I'd tell her—just like I'd told her all about my fated run-in with Byron when I saved my parents.

I caught up with Iona just inside the doors leading out to the parking lot. Headlights shone through; parents were already waiting. Today she wore a black leather jacket, black jeans, and a white band tee. Leaning against the wall, she brushed some of her silvery hair out of her sad eyes as I approached.

"Glad to see you're all right," she said, folding her arms across her slender body.

"It's good to see you too," I replied.

"Sorry I didn't find a chance to meet up with you sooner. Things underground have been … difficult," she said with a sideways glance at me. A pause, and she got right to it. "So … what happened at the mansion?"

"How did you know it was there?"

She shrugged. "It's been his house for as long as·I've known him. We …" Her eyes flashed, hints of anger, "… lived there with him. A long time ago."

I rubbed the back of my head. "I kind of destroyed the dining room. That's where I killed him."

"Good," she replied. "I always hated that room." She looked

at me more pointedly. "How did you do it?"

"I staked the asshole with the leg of one of the dining room chairs." I felt a little smirk bleed through. Was it wrong that I relished his death? It was damned sure hard fought. Him or me, and I squeaked it.

"I'm impressed." Iona's eyebrows rose. "And also happy for you. You get to go back to your family." She brushed some hair back, eyes lingering on the hard-scuffed floor. "Your world." The sadness in her voice was palpable.

"I'm sorry," I said.

She just shook it off, looking back up at me. "Draven is looking for you." The simplicity of her words floored me.

"What?" I breathed, heart rate quickening. "Why?"

"Because of Theo, mostly," Iona replied. "But Byron, too. Deaths at his party, in his territory … it's quite the insult. Lucky for you, he's looking in the vampire world right now, because that's what believes that you are. He can't imagine a human coming into our turf, his home, and doing what you did … much less twice."

Leaning in closer—students were filing in now, passing us—she murmured, "Draven's spies cast a wide net. My advice? Stay out of our world, Cassie. Take your victory … and just … stay in your world from now on."

She turned and started to leave—but then turned, looked over her shoulder at me.

"Because if you don't," she said, "sooner or later, he will find you. And unlike Byron … poor, pitiful lonely Byron … you won't be able to stop Draven."

With a wave of her hand, she disappeared out of the doors and into the dark, the shadows of the night swallowing her.

Cassie Howell will return in

SOMEONE SHOULD SAVE HER
**Liars and Vampires
Book 2**

Coming May 2018!

Author's Note

Thanks for reading! If you want to know immediately when future books become available, take sixty seconds and sign up for my NEW RELEASE EMAIL ALERTS by visiting my website. I don't sell your information and I only send out emails when I have a new book out. The reason you should sign up for this is because I don't always set release dates, and even if you're following me on Facebook (robertJcrane (Author)) or Twitter (@robertJcrane), it's easy to miss my book announcements because...well, because social media is an imprecise thing.

Come join the discussion on my website:
http://www.robertjcrane.com!

Cheers,
Robert J. Crane

ACKNOWLEDGMENTS

First off, many thanks to my co-author, who did a fabulous job bringing Cassie to life. Additional thanks to Nick for polishing things up, Bria Quinlan for helping to tighten up the first 10,000 words, as well as Sarah Barbour for adding her respective contribution to the editing process and Jo Evans for finishing up with proofreading. Any errors are probably still mine.

The cover was once more designed with exceeding skill by Karri Klawiter of artbykarri.com.

The formatting was provided by nickbowman-editing.com.

Once more, thanks to my parents, my in-laws, my kids and my wife, for helping me keep things together.

Other Works by Robert J. Crane

The Girl in the Box
and
Out of the Box
Contemporary Urban Fantasy

Alone: The Girl in the Box, Book 1
Untouched: The Girl in the Box, Book 2
Soulless: The Girl in the Box, Book 3
Family: The Girl in the Box, Book 4
Omega: The Girl in the Box, Book 5
Broken: The Girl in the Box, Book 6
Enemies: The Girl in the Box, Book 7
Legacy: The Girl in the Box, Book 8
Destiny: The Girl in the Box, Book 9
Power: The Girl in the Box, Book 10

Limitless: Out of the Box, Book 1
In the Wind: Out of the Box, Book 2
Ruthless: Out of the Box, Book 3
Grounded: Out of the Box, Book 4
Tormented: Out of the Box, Book 5
Vengeful: Out of the Box, Book 6
Sea Change: Out of the Box, Book 7
Painkiller: Out of the Box, Book 8
Masks: Out of the Box, Book 9
Prisoners: Out of the Box, Book 10
Unyielding: Out of the Box, Book 11
Hollow: Out of the Box, Book 12
Toxicity: Out of the Box, Book 13
Small Things: Out of the Box, Book 14
Hunters: Out of the Box, Book 15
Badder: Out of the Box, Book 16
Apex: Out of the Box, Book 18
Time: Out of the Box, Book 19
Driven: Out of the Box, Book 20+ *(Coming June 1, 2018!)*
Remember: Out of the Box, Book 21+ *(Coming August 2018!)*
Hero: Out of the Box, Book 22+ *(Coming October 2018!)*
Walk Through Fire: Out of the Box, Book 23+ *(Coming December 2018!)*

World of Sanctuary
Epic Fantasy

Defender: The Sanctuary Series, Volume One
Avenger: The Sanctuary Series, Volume Two
Champion: The Sanctuary Series, Volume Three
Crusader: The Sanctuary Series, Volume Four
Sanctuary Tales, Volume One - A Short Story Collection
Thy Father's Shadow: The Sanctuary Series, Volume 4.5
Master: The Sanctuary Series, Volume Five
Fated in Darkness: The Sanctuary Series, Volume 5.5
Warlord: The Sanctuary Series, Volume Six
Heretic: The Sanctuary Series, Volume Seven
Legend: The Sanctuary Series, Volume Eight
Ghosts of Sanctuary: The Sanctuary Series, Volume Nine
Call of the Hero: The Sanctuary Series, Volume Ten* *(Coming Late 2018!)*

A Haven in Ash: Ashes of Luukessia, Volume One *(with Michael Winstone)*
A Respite From Storms: Ashes of Luukessia, Volume Two *(with Michael Winstone)*
A Home in the Hills: Ashes of Luukessia, Volume Three* *(with Michael Winstone—Coming Mid to Late 2018!)*

Southern Watch
Contemporary Urban Fantasy

Called: Southern Watch, Book 1
Depths: Southern Watch, Book 2
Corrupted: Southern Watch, Book 3
Unearthed: Southern Watch, Book 4
Legion: Southern Watch, Book 5
Starling: Southern Watch, Book 6
Forsaken: Southern Watch, Book 7* *(Coming 2018!)*
Hallowed: Southern Watch, Book 8* *(Coming Late 2018/Early 2019!)*

The Shattered Dome Series
(with Nicholas J. Ambrose)
Sci-Fi

Voiceless: The Shattered Dome, Book 1
Unspeakable: The Shattered Dome, Book 2⁺ *(Coming 2018!)*

The Mira Brand Adventures
Contemporary Urban Fantasy

The World Beneath: The Mira Brand Adventures, Book 1
The Tide of Ages: The Mira Brand Adventures, Book 2
The City of Lies: The Mira Brand Adventures, Book 3
The King of the Skies: The Mira Brand Adventures, Book 4
The Best of Us: The Mira Brand Adventures, Book 5⁺ *(Coming 2018!)*
We Aimless Few: The Mira Brand Adventures, Book 6⁺ *(Coming 2018!)*

Liars and Vampires
(with Lauren Harper)
Contemporary Urban Fantasy

No One Will Believe You: Liars and Vampires, Book 1
Someone Should Save Her: Liars and Vampires, Book 2
You Can't Go Home Again: Liars and Vampires, Book 3
In The Dark: Liars and Vampires, Book 4⁺ *(Coming 2018!)*
Her Lying Days Are Done: Liars and Vampires, Book 5⁺ *(Coming 2018!)*
Heir of the Dog: Liars and Vampires, Book 6⁺ *(Coming 2018!)*

⁺ Forthcoming, Subject to Change

Printed in Dunstable, United Kingdom

65076401R00137